CHAPTER ONE

ONE MORNING, a week after New Year's, Maxwell Crane found a surprise on his porch.

He'd been getting ready for work when he heard a pair of resounding thumps from outside before someone rang his bell, then a car drove off. Max had put on his boots and opened the door. He hadn't ordered anything from Amazon—his go-to retailer—and saw no carton with the company's signature logo. Max had never been first in line at some big-box store on Black Friday either, fighting over bargains, and in small-town Barren, Kansas, there wasn't any such place. Besides, he'd been, as he was every season, one of those Christmas Eve shoppers. He was glad to have the holidays behind him.

Puzzled, he stared down at the basket at his feet then scanned the area. On Cattle Track Lane in December many of the houses had sported blow-up snowmen and reindeer on their lawns. Blinking lights had outlined roofs, and even now a few decorated trees still twinkled in windows, but in the steadily falling snow he didn't see a single car on the quiet side street. White had already blanketed the lone set of tire tracks. He didn't see any fresh footprints.

Who had left him a present? A late one, at that.

Max stamped his feet to keep warm. Many area ranchers, being land rich but cash poor, sometimes traded in kind for his veterinary services. A smoked ham, or a dozen eggs. They tended to drop off presents at his office, though.

Was it Miss McGillicuddy, who taught English at Barren High, and often supplied him with home-baked cookies? For his thirty-fifth birthday, she'd gone overboard and baked him a massive cake with sparklers on top. It had taken him days to finish it.

But she'd left town a month ago to spend the holidays with her family. Her elderly Brittany spaniel had been boarded at Max's clinic and she would pick him up tomorrow after she reached home.

The basket, covered with a blanket, made a sudden mewling sound.

Max startled. Kittens?

But again, why be surprised? He was always getting live gifts from people who thought surely, as a veterinarian, he had room in his heart for a pet of his own.

Max had learned the hard way that matters of the heart were not for him, and that included animals living in his home. After sharing the house with his sister and her dog, he was now, blessedly, alone again—or soon would be. From inside, he heard Rembrandt whine. Max had agreed to pet sit today while Sophie and her husband, Gabe—Max's best friend—moved into their new home at last. He hoped the old border collie, a rescue that had spent most of his life outdoors, didn't leave another treat for Max on the living room carpet. Remi was mostly house-trained by now but...

The noise repeated then a third time.

Max shivered. He'd only been outside a minute or two without his coat, but it was freezing. Who else, then, had left him a gift? After her cat had kittens, Mrs. Higley had tried to leave an adorable pair at the clinic, but Max had caught her sneaking back to her car. He'd placed the kittens instead with another of his clients.

This time the noise was more of a snuffle, then a whimper. The basket began to wriggle.

Max spent his days taking care of animals, large and small, and only last night he'd helped to deliver a dozen goldendoodle puppies that would soon need homes. Hadn't he made himself clear that he wasn't looking for a pet? His love for animals stopped at his clinic's door. He'd even resorted to putting up a sign in his waiting room. *No, I do not want a companion. Thanks, the doc.*

Because pets weren't the only thing. Half the women in town were trying to fix him up with someone.

"Not going to happen," he muttered. Before last March any gift might have come from Averill, yet their relationship, after much back-and-forth, had finally ended then. He'd been knitting himself together like an old sweater full of holes ever since. And—the most important part—the rest of his heart. The townspeople were wasting their time. Max would never fall for another—any—woman.

If he'd briefly thought about marriage once, a family of his own…

But his lone New Year's resolution had been to avoid any further entanglement, a promise to himself that he meant to keep.

The basket moved again. Max stuck out a foot to stop it from tipping over and the blanket slipped to expose—

What seemed to be a newborn *baby*! Unable to believe what he was seeing, he reeled back. This was no sweet kitten or puppy from a well-intentioned yet misguided client. Someone had made a serious blunder.

Wearing a tiny snowsuit, he/she blinked up at him with milky-blue eyes. Probably all it could see this soon were light or blurry shapes. Despite his vow not to get involved, even briefly, Max hunkered down to pluck a note from the folds of the pink blanket.

Obviously, this "gift" had been left at the wrong address. *Okay, read the message, genius. Then call…whom?* He could phone Travis Blake, the town's latest sheriff. But who would leave a *baby* on his snowy front porch—anyone's porch—then run? His truck was still in the drive and whoever it was had rung the bell, but he didn't want to think what could have happened if he hadn't been home. What if he'd left early for work?

The callousness on someone's part made his blood boil.

Then suddenly, without reading a word of the note, he knew. The calculations, the months, flipped through his head like the calendar pages in an old movie, and his stomach dropped. This was far more personal, the handwriting all too familiar, and Max's battered heart turned over. He didn't need the missing signature now.

Dear Max. I can't take care of her. Too much going on right now. She's yours.

CHAPTER TWO

"SHE'S MINE," Max told Sophie, who'd answered the door at her new house. He was still shaken, after reading the note, by the undeniable fact that he was suddenly a father.

Sophie gaped at him. "You found her on your porch?"

"Yep."

"Wow. Unbelievable. I need a minute to digest that news."

"Me too," he said.

"Come in—if you dare." She ushered him inside, weaving her way through dozens of boxes that filled the entryway of the sprawling house and spilled into the kitchen where shiny new stainless-steel appliances flashed in the morning sun. A moving van sat in the iced-up driveway, which was, he'd discovered while his truck slipped and slid toward the house, probably half a mile long.

"Moving day," she said with an eye roll. Her blond hair was in its messy trademark bun, and she was wearing her oldest gray sweats with a shapeless top. Only last year Sophie, the town librarian, had worn tailored suits with high-heeled pumps to work like a uniform. Max hid a smile, though he wasn't feeling humorous, more like panicked.

He cradled the baby as he might a football. He was better acquainted with the sport than he was holding a child, but thankfully she'd fallen asleep after he'd given her a bottle. His ex-girlfriend Averill, the baby's mother, had also left a tote bag at his house—the second thump he'd heard—containing a package of diapers, some clothes and half a dozen prepared bottles plus a box of dry formula. Could he figure out how to mix it properly with the right amount of water?

As Sophie often told him—he had to admit this was true—Max was known to be clueless in every aspect of his life except for his work. Sometimes she called him the "absent-minded professor."

He had been trying to become more "present" in the real world, but his job came first. Especially after his disastrous relationship with Averill McCafferty. The clinic had to be his life now. What was he going to do with a baby? Even one that was his. Perhaps temporarily, because from her note, he had no reason to believe Averill wasn't coming back.

Sophie led him through the kitchen, dodging cartons, to the family room that adjoined it. Open floor plan, tons of light, enough space to have as many kids as she wanted. He could easily see, though, that moving, this monumental event in her life and now Gabe's, was a bit overwhelming. Not to mention her pregnancy.

But then, so was the surprise infant Max carried in his arms.

"How do you feel?" he asked his sister, not ready to discuss his own dilemma.

"Queasy. It's my new default mode." Which didn't seem to trouble her. "My doctor—Sawyer—tells me I have a few more weeks before the nausea should subside."

"Remi's doing okay at my house."

"Did you leave him in his crate?"

"After a brief scuffle, yeah. I thought you were getting that dog obedience lessons."

"We are. Remi starts next week." She gestured at the mess around them. "Gabe and I have been kind of busy, Max." Sophie dropped onto a cushioned chair, waving him toward its mate in the center of the room. "We're basically camping out. At least most of the furniture's in, though. The crew is taking a break." Finally, Sophie seemed to come to terms with Max's new situation. "You really have a *baby*? Talk fast before I have to tell them where the rest of the stuff goes."

"You already heard the important part."

Sophie leaned toward him. "You're sure? She's yours and Averill's?" It had to be a rhetorical question. He hadn't dated anyone else, before or after Averill. "All right," Sophie said. "I'm ready. Let me see her."

Max gently pulled the blanket away from the baby's face and Sophie's eyes met his. Hers were like puddles of blue with tears welling in them.

"Oh, Max, I'm an aunt. She's beautiful. So little. How old, do you think?"

He gazed down at the baby. "I'd say a few days, a week maybe. But what do I know?" He touched her downy cheek. She had Averill's blue eyes, at least for now, and his dark hair. "Why would Averill do this, Sophie? The only reason that makes sense to me is that this is about Lucie." Averill's much-younger sister had disappeared from a local mall ten years ago when she was only five and Averill was in college. She'd never been found. "What if Averill got a fresh lead to follow?"

"Isn't that unlikely after so much time has passed? Didn't she tell you beforehand she was expecting?"

"Not a word. She didn't even sign the note she left. But I know her handwriting."

"What if you'd already gone to the clinic?"

"I know."

"Max, it's hard to imagine any mother abandoning her child without a very good reason. Even if you're right about Lucie…" Sophie touched her own still-flat stomach. A single tear rolled down her cheek. "What are you going to do?"

"No clue," he muttered. His days and nights were filled with animal emergencies, essentially keeping him on call all the time. He knew nothing about babies.

"What's going on?" The back door had slammed, and Gabe walked in. He shook his shoulders and snowflakes flew everywhere, some sticking in his mink-dark hair. It always amused Max to see Gabe in his rancher garb, a shearling-lined coat, dark jeans and boots, when he was also a very rich man, heir to an oil fortune in Texas. His dad lived in a mansion there while Gabe had chosen to run cattle near Barren.

"Gabe," Sophie said. "You're wet. Please leave your boots and coat in the mudroom."

"Soph, rules don't apply today. I'll mop up after the movers are gone. They've already tracked through this house. Their break's almost over. They'll be ready to start upstairs soon. You able to direct them?" He glanced at the bundle Max held, his amber gaze amused. "Not another puppy? We're full here, man." Meaning Remi.

"It's not a puppy," Sophie murmured. "Come see."

Gabe hunkered down to inspect the infant in Max's arms. "Whoa."

"Averill left her on my porch," Max said.

Gabe straightened. "You're kidding."

"Nope. And I have no idea why. I tried to call her, but her landline account is inactive. Her cell went straight to voice mail. Half a dozen times."

"You think she left town—that new place outside of Farrier where she's been living?"

"I don't know anything except that this baby's mine. Ours."

Gabe trailed a tentative finger along the baby's cheek, as if he was no more familiar with infants than Max was. "Cute. What's her name?"

"Averill didn't tell me in her note."

Neither Gabe nor Sophie seemed as rattled as Max felt, which gave him a possible solution. Maybe the two of them could... It was on the tip of his tongue to ask, even on moving day and with Sophie pregnant, if they could help him out when she made a sudden strangled sound, then bolted from her chair and ran for the bathroom.

"Morning sickness," Gabe said.

The two men looked at each other, then at the baby.

"Some surprise, huh?"

"The biggest," Max agreed.

RACHEL WHITTAKER HATED SURPRISES. Even more, she hated being the surprise.

Still, there was no other way to do this except to open the door to the Barren library the next morning as she'd done every weekday in this job, then walk right in before she lost her nerve.

The latest overdue-rent notice in her apartment mailbox had motivated her. Bypassing the night depository bin, which she usually emptied first thing, she strode into Sophie's office and said, without giving herself a chance to change her mind, "I quit."

Sophie looked up from her desk. "Rachel. Are you serious? Why?"

She took a breath. "I appreciate the raise you gave me last year, but I'm behind again in my rent. I can't make ends meet. I need something full-time." She hated to leave her job, but if she didn't, she might soon be living in her car. Also, she had her dog to consider. She needed to think seriously about getting a new line of work.

Rachel had lain awake all night, trying to perfect her resignation speech, but what else was necessary except to blurt it out? Her salary as Sophie's assistant didn't work any longer.

Sophie's face fell. "I know part-time isn't enough, and if I could give you more hours I would…"

But Rachel knew as well as Sophie did that the library budget, like most, kept shrinking until it was now bare bones. Rachel felt like a traitor. Sophie had mostly been good to her, and despite the differences they'd once had they generally got along now. Still, it was clear Rachel had nowhere to go within this library. She loved her half-time, if dead-end job, but she'd held on as long as she could. There was no reason to hope that, in such a small library, in such a small town, things would improve.

"I may even have to relocate," she admitted, "to a bigger city with greater opportunities. I could try to get my degree in library science online then, but first I need financial stability. I shouldn't have sprung this on you right now—I wouldn't have if I could put it off." She studied Sophie's pale face. "How's the morning sickness?"

"It's my waiting game," she said. "The stress of moving hasn't helped. I seem to live on saltine crackers and water. I've lost five pounds."

"You'll gain it back," Rachel said, although she was no expert. Her one pregnancy had ended during its first trimester. Losing her husband, too, shortly before that, had also been devastating. She'd ended up trusting the wrong person to comfort her, and the fall-out from that had become her everyday companion. Her nighttime one, too, when Rachel stared at her bedroom ceiling, reliving every bad moment and wrong decision of her life. "I can stay on here for two weeks if that helps while you try to find a replacement."

"Of course that helps. Don't worry about me, Rachel. I'm fine—and very happy to be in my own house. It's official, as of yesterday, although I could do without all the boxes I need to unpack. Living with Gabe, Remi and Max in the house where I grew up had begun to feel a bit crowded. Gabe's pleased to have our privacy again." She paused. "And then there's Max. I can't imagine us being there now. He has plenty to deal with."

"Is his clinic super busy? I know people like to give puppies for Christmas." Then, when the reality of caring for, and training, a dog became real, they looked for alternative solutions. Sophie's brother had had more than one unwanted puppy dropped off at his clinic.

"Not puppies, no." Sophie quickly explained about Averill's note and the baby that had been left on her brother's doorstep.

Rachel blinked. "That's like something out of Charles Dickens."

Sophie shook her head. "Max with a baby?

He's never home. He knows nothing about childcare." She touched her stomach. "Neither do I but I guess we'll learn. Gabe and I might take her, but with so much going on and our own baby coming… I told Max yesterday to call Shadow Wilson. Maybe her agency has someone who could fill in temporarily as a caregiver until we all figure out a better plan. Or Max finds Averill."

"Then I still don't like her," Rachel murmured, which must be obvious to Sophie. They'd had enough words once about Averill when she'd stolen several books from the library. Rachel had urged Sophie to confront her but, because of Averill's relationship then with Max, and as his employee at the clinic, she'd held back until she could no longer avoid seeing the truth. A baby was orders of magnitude more life-altering than stealing some books.

"In any case," Sophie said, probably not wanting to revisit that topic, "it's the baby who matters most. Can you believe? She doesn't even seem to have a name. At least there was none in that note."

Rachel rose from her chair. "Well, this is a

library. We have lots of name books. Let me pull some. You can take them to Max."

"I'm not sure he'll need them if Averill turns up, but thanks, Rachel. Not about quitting your job," she added.

In the doorway, Rachel stood for a moment, then walked from the room toward the nonfiction stacks, her feet dragging with every step. It would be hard to leave. For the first time in a while, Rachel had a friend. *Friends,* she thought, including some of the other women in town. She was beginning to feel like she belonged here, and not only in this job. For the most part Barren was a welcoming place with people who had accepted her almost as one of their own.

"I wish I didn't have to," she called back to Sophie.

Which seemed to be the story of her life.

"Averill, pick up your phone."

Across town at his clinic, Max shoved his cell back into his pocket. After her cryptic note, Averill owed him an explanation. Frustrated, he looked around the waiting room, the most familiar space in his daily life—often nights, too—but it seemed almost unrecognizable, as if he'd never been here before. The chairs, the sofas, the big coffee table stacked with outdated magazines, the far wall of shelves lined with books about pets, which Sophie had helped him choose, and an array of prescription foods in small bags, diets for renal and heart problems. Max kept the larger sacks in the back storeroom.

He yawned. Having no one to stay with the baby yesterday—Sophie had her hands full with her move—he'd gone home rather than to the clinic. He hadn't gotten a wink of sleep while walking the floor last night. The baby he didn't know how to care for lay this morning, quiet for now, on a nearby sofa in her makeshift bed, a padded dresser drawer he'd brought from his guest room. Obviously, he couldn't have left her at the house alone today while he held office hours …but he was out of his depth. He'd never even babysat in his teens as Sophie had.

Max was still trying to stay awake when the clinic door opened. Clara McMann, slim and even a bit thin, bustled out of the cold into the small lobby, then behind the front desk, where she deposited her usual tote bag on the floor. She removed her snowy boots, exchanging them for the shoes she kept here. He'd hired the older woman, who owned a ranch near town, as his receptionist after Averill quit. Clara volunteered for everything.

"Morning, Max." She eyed him as she booted up the computer, her graying brown hair neatly styled, her warm, light brown gaze sharp. "You look wan, dear. A bad night? Or, I hope, a very good one at the Bon Appetit having dinner with a pretty woman. Did you get home late?"

"No pretty woman in sight," he muttered, then realized what he'd said. "Sorry, Clara. You know I adore you." There was no way he would hire another younger woman like Averill and risk getting himself in trouble again. "You're still gorgeous. In fact, I think I'll call you that from now on. Capital G."

Clara waved a hand. "You're getting in deep here. Quit while you're ahead."

Until now Max had been moving toward a regular life, or so he'd thought, until he and Averill broke up—for probably the sixth, and last, time—and he'd decided that cutting his losses was the right thing to do. Considering Averill's tragic past, how sweet yet lost she could seem, she needed more emotional help than he could provide. The search for her missing sister had long ago become her obsession. He suspected he was right, that she'd gone after some lead as to Lucie's whereabouts now...but look what she'd left behind. A blessing certainly, but... "I didn't sleep much last night. I have a baby," he announced.

Another weird aspect of this latest bombshell in his life. He didn't know how to tell anyone. What to say. *She's mine. I have a baby.* Way to go, Max. He'd never been the smoothest guy, kind of nerdy, in fact. In high school he was the kid slinking around the sidelines at social events while everyone else got acquainted and danced. In college he'd commuted between home and school. As Sophie's guardian after their parents were killed when she was just sixteen and Max twenty, he'd been needed at home. He couldn't live on campus. He'd never pledged a fraternity, gone to basketball games, dated anyone. In vet school he'd buried his nose in his books, learning his craft, and at the clinic now he kept a laser focus on his work. Saving animals. Not people.

"A baby," Clara repeated as if she'd never heard the word.

He groaned. "I would never have thought little more than a seven-pound infant could make so much noise. She never stopped crying all night. She was still sobbing when I tried to make a pot of coffee just as the sun peeked over the horizon. I forgot to add water." He paused. "I don't think she likes me. It's a good thing I like her."

The statement surprised Max. It was true, though. Not only was she adorable, so tiny that she fairly cried out for his manly protection, but the very weight of her in his arms turned him to mush inside, the sweet scent that rose from her skin...

Max gestured at the dresser drawer he'd set on the sofa while he opened the clinic this morning. "You remember Averill."

"I do," she said, then the light dawned. "You mean you and she—" Clara was already out from behind the desk, crossing the room, leaning over the makeshift crib. "How precious, Max. A girl you said?"

"Yes," he said, then explained about the note. "As far as I know, she doesn't have a name."

Clara made a tsking sound. "Well, that's just unacceptable."

So was leaving her on his porch. "What am I going to do? I can't keep her, Clara, but I can't very well turn my own flesh and blood over to Child Protective Services, either."

"No, of course not."

He ran a hand over the nape of his neck. "I've tried to reach Averill. She won't answer. I even called her landlord before I got to the clinic this morning. He tells me she's moved out. She must have left the baby on her way out of the county—maybe the state. She could be halfway to Florida by now." The search was like looking for a needle in a haystack. "She's not close to her family in Farrier. I wonder if she's even talked to them."

Clara laid a calming hand on his arm. "Stop obsessing. We'll have to think this through."

"Yes, we will—and fast." Max glanced out the front window. Office hours began in five minutes, and he expected to see cars and pickups pulling in soon. After that, he wouldn't be able to take a breath for the rest of the day. "For now, can you—"

"You need to ask?" Clara bent closer to the padded drawer. "Aw, sweetheart, look at you."

Misty-eyed, she glanced up at Max. "If I were thirty years younger, I'd take her home with me."

And I'd be tempted to let you. But what kind of person would he be then? Even the flash of thought had made Max feel guilty. Clara talked softly to the baby, who was beginning to fuss, and gradually the baby settled down. Clara knew her stuff. Years ago, she'd been a foster parent for kids in the state system. Something Max hoped to avoid.

"She probably needs another bottle," he said, "but I'm running low." Overnight he'd practically force-fed her, hoping to quiet her distress, pacing the bedroom while she wailed loud enough to wake the dead. Thank goodness, Remi was back home again with Sophie and Gabe, or the dog would have joined her, the two of them sounding like a pack of coyotes. His nerves were so shredded this morning his hands were shaking. How would he be able to treat patients today?

And above all, he felt like a heel. Also, shell-shocked. Averill had had nine months to get used to the reality of another tiny human being in her life. Where had she given birth? At Farrier General? At home in that apartment she'd just vacated? Why had she never told him she was expecting?

"Here comes the Higley woman with her cat," Clara said, straightening to look out the window at the sound of an approaching vehicle.

"Not pregnant, I hope." Mrs. Higley had refused to have the cat spayed after its surprise litter of kittens. Since then, she'd come into the office regularly, sure that her Beauty had some terrible disease. A cat parent hypochondriac. Who knew? The woman swept through the door with one minute to spare before the clinic officially opened.

"Mrs. Higley, good morning. Take Beauty into number two. I'll be right there." Max pointed her toward the exam rooms, hoping she hadn't seen Clara standing in front of the drawer, as if trying to block anyone's sight of the baby. He didn't need questions when he had no answers. Still, Mrs. Higley's keen gaze had swept the area and Max was sure he'd seen her mouth tighten.

He turned back to Clara and lowered his voice. "You can handle the baby and the phones until—"

"Five o'clock," she said, smoothing the baby's hair. "At lunchtime you'll go shopping."

"She will need a car seat."

"More formula, too. Diapers. I'll make you a list." She paused. "I'll cancel your appointment with Hadley at our ranch. He can wait until tomorrow for you to see that injured calf. Nothing serious, and he's quite capable of treating it in the meantime." Hadley Smith had been one of her foster kids and now ran the McMann spread for her.

"Clara, you're a gem."

"I know," she said with a grin. "Now scoot. Mrs. Higley is waiting."

Max obeyed. If he could afford to, he'd double Clara's salary—though she'd once offered to work for free. She was worth her weight in gold. Which he didn't happen to have.

She was a lifesaver, for sure.

Max needed one. So did his baby.

CHAPTER THREE

AT NOON TRAVIS BLAKE kicked back in his chair and fought an urge to groan aloud. In the reception area of the local sheriff's department—his turf now—a woman had walked in, full of her usual bluster, then marched up to the front desk, which he could see through his office window. Mrs. Higley was demanding to speak to him. What he had learned thus far about small towns didn't thrill him. Maybe he should have become a security guard in some big city mall instead. Yet, thanks to the election he'd won more than a year ago and courtesy of the brass plaque on his desk, here he was, writing a few tickets on snow-packed Main Street every day, hustling the occasional drunk out of Rowdy's bar on Saturday nights. And listening to complaints from people like Higley.

Travis sighed, as he did half a dozen times each day. No one had forced him to move here, to run for office. Nothing, except the debacle at his former job that he was still running from. He rose from his chair and motioned through the window glass at the deputy on duty out front. *Send her in.* He would gain little by trying to ignore her. If she wasn't pestering him, someone else would. "Mrs. Higley. What can I do for you today?"

She'd bustled into the room to take the same chair she'd sat in a week ago when a neighbor's tomcat had shown a fond interest in the base of her maple tree as its outdoor bathroom and marking territory. "Sheriff, I am deeply concerned."

"I'm sure you are. What seems to be the problem?"

"Are you acquainted with Maxwell Crane?"

"The vet, sure." Although Travis didn't know him well, they could be called casual friends, and he made it his business to at least get to know as many of the town residents as he could. His radar was always spinning, which was part of the job, the good and the bad. As a former federal agent, he should feel satisfied with the lack of actual felonies here, yet he always expected one to crop up. He hoped that wasn't today. "Max runs the clinic down the street."

"I took my cat Beauty there earlier," she said, settling into her seat as if for a long chat Travis didn't want to have. He fussed with a stack of papers on his desk, hoping she'd get the message that he was busy and come straight to her point. In his experience that didn't seem likely. He and Mrs. Higley were spending too much time together. If she wasn't worried about her own cat—Travis wasn't a cat person—or one of her neighbors who hadn't put his trash in the proper place for pickup on a Tuesday morning, she felt obligated to make a citizen's report on some other presumably nefarious activity on Juniper Street, where she'd lived for the past forty years. Now it appeared she had branched out to the center of town.

"Don't tell me," he said. "Beauty is going to be a mother again." And why would that be his or the county's problem?

"I should hope not. Max explained to me that she would be better off as an indoor girl rather than roaming around at night—and I saw his point. However." She patted her corkscrew gray curls. "I feel that, as a resident of this town, I must do my duty."

"And what is that?" Travis couldn't wait to hear. He was tweaking her, couldn't seem to help himself because, really, he snatched any moment of entertainment these days wherever he could. One of his favorite pastimes was to have lunch at Jack Hancock's place or the café, where he liked to invent backstories for anyone who walked in—a conspiracy theory here and there or a major crimes fantasy, once removed. Mrs. Higley herself might be an international jewel thief with diamonds stashed in a flour canister in her pantry, a closet spy with strong ties to the Kremlin, or... He straightened. "I hope nothing serious has come to your attention. Barren's a pretty peaceful place, wouldn't you agree?"

"I saw a *baby*," she announced in a shocked yet haughty tone. "The mistreatment was obvious. In a *drawer*, can you believe?"

"A baby in a drawer," he repeated. Travis quelled a storm of memory that wanted to rush through him. He'd seen worse. Far worse. Now she had his attention.

Mrs. Higley nodded, the fire of a zealot in her eyes. "Something must be done."

"Whose baby?"

"I have no idea. But Max had no other clients at the time. Only he and Clara were there. Obviously, it's not hers. Years ago, she and I went through menopau—"

Travis felt heat creep up his neck. TMI. "So. You think it's *Max's* child?"

"I'm not a prying person. I didn't ask, but—"

Talk about a lack of self-awareness. "Mrs. Higley, I don't see that anything here needs to be done."

"You should go to the clinic, find out what is going on. Deal with the situation. Immediately. I didn't vote for you—I wish Finn Donovan had remained in the job—"

I do too, Travis thought, fighting another sigh. Still. He'd had little choice in that matter except to leave Wichita, courtesy of the federal government and his own need to keep food on his table, gas in his truck and clothes on his back. As strange as this was, Mrs. Higley and others like her who seemed to be legion in Barren made up his days now. The town must have capped the market on gossips. He pushed his chair back, then stood.

"I'll pay Max a call." And hope that satisfied her. Which, of course, it didn't.

"You must contact the authorities," she insisted as if Travis wasn't law enforcement himself, however much lower on the totem pole he might be now. "It's obvious there is abuse. Neglect. That infant, I tell you, is not being well cared for. Who indeed would let a baby sleep in a *drawer*? As if it were a document to be filed away?"

Travis had no reason to believe Max Crane was mistreating an infant that most likely belonged to another client, perhaps one who'd been in an exam room at the time with an ailing pet. Maybe someone who had walked to the clinic. The drawer aspect was mildly interesting, but not sufficient reason to—

Mrs. Higley was still sitting there. "Perhaps I should call a social services agency myself."

"Let me handle this. If that becomes necessary, I'll contact them." He held up one hand. "Trust me."

Finally, she got up from her chair. "Well. I hope that trust will not be broken. In Barren, we take care of our own and I could not, in good conscience, turn a blind eye to what I saw. That poor little tyke." She stopped halfway to the door. "Wait. I haven't filed my formal complaint."

Travis fought back a third sigh. "After I've spoken to Dr. Crane, I'll give you a call and we can go from there. You have my word." Which didn't mean a lot these days in Barren or anywhere else.

ON HER LUNCH HOUR—which she seldom bothered to take—Rachel walked from the library to the Baby Things shop on Main Street. Across from Earl's Hardware and the Bon Appetit, it was the only store in town that carried items for the well-turned-out infant. Rachel's friend Annabelle Donovan was expecting a child in March, and their Girls' Night Out group members were giving her a shower soon.

Sherry, the proprietor, greeted her at the door. She occasionally came to the group's meetings. "Rachel, hi. I can guess what you need."

A baby of my own. The flash thought caused a twinge of sorrow, but it wasn't to be. Instead, she would buy Annabelle something special. Knowing her face must look pale, she returned Sherry's smile. "What do you have in crib comforters or maybe I should look at clothing?"

"Good choices."

And another painful reminder of all Rachel herself had lost. When she'd received her invitation, she'd been half tempted not to attend the shower, but her desire to belong to the group had won out.

She and Sherry were oohing and aahing over a beautiful but impractical lacy shawl when the bell over the door jingled, and Max Crane walked in. He shut the door behind him, then sent them both a rather sheepish smile.

Sherry left Rachel's side to exchange cheek kisses with him like the old friends they probably were. Everyone in town knew everyone else.

It also seemed that every woman in Barren, young or old, felt tempted to flirt with Max, and Sherry was no exception. Earlier Sophie had told Rachel about the baby, which must explain why he was here. Rachel had met him several times at the library when he came to have lunch with his sister, and her gaze as well was always drawn to him.

Max nodded in her direction. "Rachel."

Sherry excused herself then kept her arm tucked through his as she led Max toward the rear of the store where a display of high chairs, changing tables and cribs filled the space. "Clara emailed me your list. You need a car seat? Instead, let me show you our newest all-in-one stroller."

Rachel's gaze followed them. In Barren, someone always seemed to be getting engaged, married or having a baby, which must keep Sherry in business. But having an infant left on the porch was certainly new. Rachel drifted from one table to another, then inspected the racks of hanging clothes. Adorable. The merchandise—not Max, she told herself.

She couldn't deny he was an attractive man. Tall but not too tall, dark-haired with a boyish cowlick, and those amazing brown eyes. Warm, trustworthy, straightforward. Single. Her awareness of Max surprised her. Because of her losses, and the guilt she bore, she still felt mostly frozen inside.

She lowered her gaze and, with her heart aching, picked up a sweet pink dress with eyelet trim and a hefty price tag then put it down again. Was Annabelle having a girl or boy? She should buy something more neutral. She looked at a few comforters after all.

"Actually," she heard Max say, "I just need the car seat."

Sherry clucked her tongue. "Don't be hasty. I sell a lot of these convertible strollers—it's a car seat, a baby carrier, too. Very practical. This one's light, easy to load in your truck. You can even go jogging."

"If I had time," he said, tilting his head to examine its tag. As he straightened, his eyes met Rachel's across the room, as if he were similarly aware of her. "Okay, fine. I'll take the stroller."

Sherry said, "Let me see if I have a carton in the storeroom. If not, I can order."

She disappeared into the back, and he called out, "I need something right away." Max turned to Rachel. "Sorry, I know you were here before me, but I'm in kind of a hurry."

"I know you're busy. I can wait."

Max came over to her. "Sophie tells me you've quit at the library."

"Yes." Rachel didn't explain. Had the news of her resignation spread all over town? She saw no need to mention her overdue-rent notice. Or her dog Sky's welfare. Or the fact that she needed a new job here to avoid having to leave Barren. She barely knew Max, mostly from a distance. Up close he was even better-looking, and she caught a mix of scents: fresh air, some subtle aftershave, and was that a whiff of horse?

"Sophie's going to miss you."

"I hope we can still be friends," she said, although Rachel wondered. Their relationship hadn't always been smooth-going, and now Rachel had kicked up the friction a notch by leaving Sophie with no backup help except the after-school and Saturday morning kids who were paid a small wage to serve as library pages. She repeated her new mantra. "If I didn't need full time, I would have stayed."

He glanced toward the storeroom, where Sherry was making a racket, probably shifting cartons around, looking for the fancy stroller. Max checked his watch. "Wish she'd hurry. I have a twelve-thirty appointment near Farrier."

Rachel didn't think before she spoke. She wouldn't examine her reason to keep him talking, giving Sherry more time to find the convertible stroller. "I, um, heard about the baby."

"So has everyone else in town by now."

His and Averill's baby.

She'd always thought Averill had issues beyond once taking a few library books that
didn't belong to her, but would she abandon
her own child? Still, she did feel a bit shocked
on his behalf. Max, with a baby.

"I've been improvising so far," he said.
"Praying Averill turns up."

"I hope she does, Max. Until then you have
your work cut out for you," she said.

"Yeah. That." Then his classic features softened. "You should see her, though."

"Sweet?"

"Beyond," he said but shook his head. "I
can't figure out why Averill would do this—
even for her sister."

"From what I know of Averill…" Rachel
stopped. She wasn't usually a vindictive person or envious—except about babies. On that
topic, she envied all other women, including
Averill. "Not my place," she finished. "I wish
you well."

"Thanks."

Sherry came out of the back room lugging
a large box. Max hurried to take it from her.

"The package isn't in great shape," she
said. "The delivery guys bashed in the cor-
ners, but the contents should be fine except

for maybe a small scratch or two. Let me know if it's more than that. Right now, I'll give you a fifteen percent discount."

"I'll take it," Max said, looking more grateful than a price reduction warranted. Then Sherry pulled out a portable crib and the other supplies on his list.

They went to the front counter to complete the sale, and Rachel did some more browsing among the displays. Toward the rear of the shop, she also paused to look at the strollers and cribs. In the first days of her own pregnancy, she'd gone to a similar store, dreaming about the future, earmarking items to buy later. She wouldn't have hesitated to purchase the all-in-one stroller. She'd bought a dozen books about becoming a mother, only to return them after her miscarriage. With Jason's death, then their baby's, all her dreams had died, too.

Sherry held the door for Max to wrestle the boxes outside. His truck was parked in an angled space in front. "Thanks, Doc."

"Good luck," Rachel called out.

The door closed, the truck started up and she and Sherry looked at each other.

"That man," Sherry said. "He's a great guy,

handsome—and what did Averill do? Break his heart." She added, "A ready-made family waiting now for some other lucky woman."

Rachel's heart turned over again at Sherry's poignant comment, which reminded her of the family she'd lost. Well, what did she expect, standing in the middle of a baby shop? In Barren, where families were a hot topic?

"I almost feel sorry for him. There are a lot of matchmakers in this town."

"He's hard to resist."

Yes, he was. Even Rachel could appreciate that. She was still holding a colorful comforter she'd picked up with a whimsical design of elephants and lions, neutral enough for either a boy or girl. "I'll take this," she said, hoping to end the conversation about Max.

"You don't agree?" Sherry asked.

"I do, but I'm not interested."

She watched Max back out of his parking space, frowning.

But then, for a different reason, so was Rachel. Which she didn't care to examine.

AFTER WORK, Rachel let herself into the apartment she would soon have to leave. Clearly, no amount of cajoling, even pleading, would soften her landlord's heart. Or rather, the snide woman's tone at the management company. Not that the apartment was paradise. Her noisy neighbors, above and below the second floor, annoyed her and the landscapers always seemed to fire up earsplitting garden equipment at 7:00 a.m.

Still, a chorus of yips and barks, and a warm, wriggling body met Rachel at the door, wiping out with one swish of a tail the less-than-happy events of her day. Including that unwanted attraction to Maxwell Crane, which had left Rachel frowning too. "Hey, Sky. How's my girl?" she crooned, leaning down to pet the dog she'd rescued a few months ago. Rachel had thought only to fill the empty space in these few rooms, but Sky had filled her whole being with the love she'd been missing.

"What's for dinner?" she asked, leading the way into the kitchen. "You didn't cook tonight? I'm disappointed, baby." Sky, a mixed-breed dog with a silky mahogany coat that spoke of some Irish setter genes, whined, not because she hadn't been able to fix a meal for them but because her food and water bowls were empty. She gazed at Rachel with liquid-brown eyes. Rachel supplied the water, then rummaged in the pantry for the last of the kibble. She had bought one small bag the other day because she was between paychecks at the library, her new job search hadn't yet begun and she feared the prospects in Barren weren't that good. "How about…ah," she said, finding a leftover beef patty, which had been Rachel's supper last night, in the fridge. She mixed it with the dry food, then set the bowl on the floor by the counter. "Who doesn't deserve a treat?" she asked Sky, who agreed, doing her happy dance.

Rachel fixed herself some soup from a can. Something good had to happen soon. If Jason was alive, they'd be living in their dream house near Indianapolis, he'd be the same tall, handsome marine she'd married, they'd already have a baby or two. Instead, she'd lost that chance for a family.

As Sky crunched kibble and slurped water, Rachel checked her emails and messages. The rent wasn't her only unpaid bill. The utility company wanted its payment. So did her phone service provider. She scrolled down— and there it was, the newest reminder of her unwise trust, her guilt.

Another text from Chad Whittaker, her brother-in-law—Rachel would prefer to use the term former—his family's golden boy. Jason, the younger of the two brothers, had lived in his shadow. He'd even welcomed that last deployment to Afghanistan, Rachel sometimes thought, as if to prove himself worthy of his parents' love. Jason was a hero, all right; she had the folded flag and a small widow's benefit to show for it.

As she read his brother's latest message, her stomach knotted. Hey, Rach. Why won't you answer me? Just want to know how you are.

On the surface, the words seemed harmless. But in Rachel's view they were not. After her husband's death, Chad's comfort—she and her brother-in-law had both lost someone they loved—had become more and more persistent. And a bit creepy. Rachel loved Jason's parents, but any interaction with Chad was uncomfortable now. She should never have let him in as she had, one of the reasons she had decided to relocate from Indiana to Kansas.

How was it possible that her life, which once seemed so bright, had changed so quickly?

CHAPTER FOUR

"WHAT'S THE PLAN, DOC?" A week later Logan Hunter, a former test pilot turned rancher, straightened from his crouch beside the small brown lump on the stall floor at the Circle H. The little bison calf, which had been born breech, wasn't doing well, but Max wasn't ready to pull the plug.

He hated to give up on any animal and, although he wasn't a pet lover personally, he was rooting for the calf, not only as a valuable part of the herd.

"Let's give him another day or two," he said, also rising to his feet. He brushed straw from his hands.

Logan's deep blue eyes looked worried. He ran a hand through his dark hair. "I believe in second chances, twice over in this case. We've done everything we can, but I know Sam has already named him and I'd hate to see him disappointed." Max had to agree with

Logan. Nobody messed with Sam Hunter, his grandfather, who still presided over the Circle H.

"The loss of a calf is always bad news." Max could hear the mama bison outside the barn, snuffling at the dirt, pawing the ground, wondering where her baby was. "Normally I wouldn't advise you to release this guy from the stall, but maybe his mom will help turn him around. Fresh air, too."

"Either that or she's going to tear down this barn," Logan said. The cow had been pacing the nearby pasture but was losing whatever patience she'd had. "Let's hope the others don't drive out her weak baby."

Years ago, Sam had built a good-sized herd of the blocky brown behemoths and although Max wasn't a fan, he knew that decision had ultimately been a good one. The price of bison meat had soared, seemed to be holding steady now, and with those profits the Circle H appeared to be in better shape than many area ranches that still relied solely on beef. Over the past few years, the fluctuating prices for cattle had meant bankruptcy for several spreads. Logan, a cattleman now to his core, oversaw his own growing herd of Black Angus, though he and Sam still had words over that.

Max followed Logan along the aisle, his friend leading the small calf. At the wide barn doors, which stood open to the chill morning sun, Logan walked toward the partially snow-covered pasture, the agitated bison cow dogging their steps along the paddock fence line. "When I take her calf in, keep an eye on her," Logan muttered, "but I think she knows we're trying to help."

"Probably so. People think animals don't have emotions, but they do."

Logan opened the gate, but as he led the calf into the field, the cow ran at him, brushing Logan and knocking him in the shoulder. He reeled back, then laughed as the mama veered off, her calf trying to keep up behind her. "He's jogging pretty good," Logan pointed out. "Maybe we've been too pessimistic."

"Seems to be my nature these days." Max hadn't been himself since last March when he and Averill broke up for good. He didn't have to tell Logan what he meant.

"You found her yet?"

"Nope. I'm thinking I should drive over to

Farrier, see if her mother will talk to me. Like Averill, she doesn't answer her phone. I'm hoping she knows something, where Averill might be—or if, when, she's planning to come back."

Logan left the pasture and closed the gate. "It's been a week now, hasn't it, since she took off and left you with the baby?"

Yes, but who was counting? "A few days more than a week, actually." Every night, while walking her, Max had plenty of time for reflection, soul searching and wracking his brain about where Averill could have gone. He came up empty each time. "I've talked to everyone I know in Farrier and Barren, including the Girls' Night Out group—" Logan's wife, Blossom, was a member, too "—but no one has been particularly helpful."

"Beyond the worry you must feel, caring for an infant on your own is hard."

"Tell me about it." Sometimes he carried one of the childcare books Sophie had brought from the library in one hand while he jiggled his baby in the other, vainly hoping she'd fall asleep for the rest of the night. Instead, she dozed off, then startled awake moments later to begin the cycle all over again. "I wish I'd studied pediatrics instead of veterinary medicine."

Logan frowned. "I remember those days with Nick—my oldest—especially one night when he took sick during a blizzard. I couldn't get him off the ranch to the hospital. We nearly lost him and I haven't been the same since. Tell the truth, I think that's when my first wife decided to leave me. If it weren't for Blossom now, who's the best mother in the world with our Daisy, too, I'd still be alone." Logan's second wife had come to the Circle H on the run from her abusive boyfriend. Already pregnant then with Daisy, she'd feared for her safety and that of her unborn child. Daisy was now a thriving little girl who doted on all the ranch cats and dogs, and Max suspected she'd make a great vet someday. Fortunately, the old boyfriend had given up his parental rights, and Logan had adopted Daisy. With her and Logan's son, Nick, from his first marriage, it seemed their family was complete. Or so Max had thought.

"I'm happy watching Nick grow like a weed, as he does these days, and, of course, Daisy's a real trip, a daddy's girl for sure, but as soon as Annabelle and Finn announced they were pregnant—finally, some said—Blossom started lobbying for another for us."

"You're not on board with that?"

"Torn," he admitted as they walked back through the yard toward Max's truck. "On one hand, I'd like another, boy or girl, but the ranch has me busy and I have to say, why stir things up?" Logan laughed again. "Daisy's on her mother's side. Keeps telling me she needs a sister to play with. I don't think she realizes that would be years off."

Max clapped him on the shoulder. "Big decision. Mine was made for me, at least for now while everything's up in the air."

"Seriously, how can you handle the baby and your practice?"

"Sophie's feeling a bit better, and she's been trying to fill in here and there, but that's no solution. And I'm still all thumbs with the baby. Clara helps out during the day, which is above and beyond the call of duty, and I've filed an application with Shadow Wilson's agency to find a live-in caregiver, which Sophie suggested, but so far no one's turned up."

Logan gazed up at the hard sun, which had risen higher in the sky. Max needed to get going. When they reached his truck, he fired up his engine, but Logan didn't take the hint and step back. "You know, things happen for a reason. Could be there's a woman out there right now, like Blossom, who needs help herself—a place to stay. And decides to never leave. I'm hoping she turns up for you."

Max doubted that. The last thing he needed was another woman in his life. Another temporary woman who, like Averill, could break his heart again. For some reason, he thought of Rachel Whittaker, whom he'd seen at the baby shop.

He hadn't expected to find her there. Sleek dark hair in a bob, mysterious gray-green eyes. She'd given him a subtle once-over, too, but Max wasn't going there, and from what he'd heard, neither was she.

Which didn't solve his caregiver problem.

SHADOW WILSON SCANNED her computer screen once more, then sat back in her chair. "I'm sorry, Rachel," she said with a sigh. Wintry sunlight streamed through the long windows that overlooked Main Street from her second-floor Mother Comfort Home Health Care Agency office. "There's nothing suitable right now. The only position would be a caregiver for a very ill client in Farrier, but that requires a licensed nurse."

Rachel studied her clasped hands in her lap. In the past week, she had pounded the pavement without success after the hours she still spent at the library while serving her notice. Sophie had had no luck in replacing Rachel, who now reconsidered her plight. Maybe she'd have to ask if she could stay on for another month or two, although how would that help? That wouldn't cover her expenses. She was already being kicked out of her apartment, and there was no other complex in town. "I haven't had any luck, either, finding a new place to live. I have my dog to consider…"

"The most loveable animal—but unwelcome in some apartments, I know. Finn Donovan had the same issue once at that complex because of his dog Sarge. If I were you, I'd live in my car rather than give up Sky."

Rachel agreed. She'd adopted Sky from the animal shelter in Farrier. Unable to spend another night alone, she'd impulsively decided to get a cat, which she thought would be low maintenance. But then, she'd looked into Sky's brown eyes and decided on the spot to rescue her. Rescue them both, really. Two lonely souls. She wouldn't even consider surrendering her dog.

She picked at a chipped nail. "A place to live is one thing. But clearly, there are few, if any, full-time jobs open in Barren. I'd hoped that even after the holidays, Earl might need another clerk at the hardware store, or even Sherry at Baby Things, but apparently everyone is cutting back this year and, according to Sherry, business wasn't that good this past Christmas season."

"I'm hearing that, too." Shadow tucked a strand of dark hair behind one ear.

And Rachel still regretted stopping at Sherry's store to buy the baby shower gift—running into Max. Two unwelcome reminders that her life hadn't turned out the way she'd planned. Maybe it was better that she wouldn't be working at Baby Things.

"My husband Grey says cattle prices have dipped and I'm not getting any requests for household caregivers." Shadow brightened. "What about baby care? I could call all the pregnant women I know, and there are always babies coming in Barren. See if any of them need assistance. Annabelle's due soon—as happy as I am for her and Finn, I don't envy them the wide gap between Emmie and their new little one, which is like starting over as I did—" She broke off. Shadow's daughter and son, both by Grey, were years apart because of the couple's long separation before their reunion. "How are you with newborns?"

Rachel's pulse skipped. She hadn't thought of that job possibility, and for an instant she considered saying, *no experience*, which wasn't true. Taking care of an infant? How could she? Yet she couldn't lie, either. "Actually, I did quite a lot of babysitting in my teens. Weekends, mostly, then several summers as a part-time nanny. I made enough money to pay for my senior class trip to Washington, DC. Then my own cousin had twins. She and her husband were frantic, having two babies at once, their first children. So, I moved in with them that summer during college for a few months. Believe me, I earned those stripes."

"They must have been grateful for your help." Shadow paused. "You've heard, of course, about the baby girl Averill left with Max Crane. He's called me half a dozen times, hoping I'd have someone who could help him."

Rachel stopped breathing. Considering her unwanted reaction to him at Sherry's shop, and her own losses, she said, "I do have experience, but I was really thinking more of working with an elderly person who just needs a housekeeper, someone to cook, drive them to appointments, remind them about medications and so on."

"We've already determined that no one fits that bill, Rachel. Of course, things change on a dime, and I'll keep looking, but I'm afraid you're out of luck there for now."

"Yesterday I even asked Jack if the Bon Appetit needs a server—something I've never done—or a hostess, but like everyone else he said no." She rose from her chair in front of Shadow's desk, fearing again that without a suitable job she'd have no choice but to move away from Barren and the friends she'd made here. Her new sense of belonging. "Thanks for trying."

Shadow's voice stopped Rachel before she reached the door. "Max is offering a very nice package—good pay, clean quarters and the hours you're looking for. He's desperate. Why not give the job a try?"

Rachel's chest felt tight, and the palms of her hands had gone damp. Her childcare experience had all been long before she married, before she became pregnant, before she lost… And to live in Max's house? Hold *his* baby day and night, feed her, rock her to sleep? The constant reminders of what she'd lost would be unbearable. Her heart was racing now. A panic attack. She couldn't breathe. And how could she work for Max, who had recently stirred emotions in her that she thought had died long ago? Being virtually alone with him in that house on Cattle Track Lane was not going to happen.

"I…can't," she managed to say. "I can't." Then she bolted from the office, probably leaving Shadow to gape after her in shock.

"HELP ME OUT HERE," Max said that night, the baby on one arm, a book of names in his other hand. Juggling both, he paced his living room. And reeled off a short list to Sophie, who held a book of her own. "Poppy, Abigail, Fleur…" None of them seemed to fit.

"Wish I knew what names Averill put on the birth certificate."

Considering their breakup, had she used her last name, McCafferty, rather than Crane for the baby? In any case, in the state of Kansas those records were not for public view. Max had checked, then filled out a simple form as required to get a copy, or abstract, for himself of the original registration from the Office of Vital Statistics within the state's Division of Public Health. He was waiting for it to arrive in the mail—if it existed. "What if she gave birth outside a hospital?" he asked. "At home or somewhere?"

"Or if she left the hospital right after giving birth, there might be no official record." Sophie ran a finger down one page, ignoring the take-out bag she'd brought of his favorite fried chicken.

Sophie wasn't eating, and Max cast her an assessing look. "You're wasting away."

"Don't nag. Let's get this done."

"There are too many choices. Maybe I should just name her after Mom."

"Bonny? Not exactly in fashion."

"But that's cute, right?"

Sophie shook her head. "I've always liked Fiona."

"Nice but sounds British. No, she's a Kansas girl." He gazed down at the baby, who pursed her lips, then made nursing motions at the air. "Beautiful, too. She needs something equally pretty."

"But maybe temporary," Sophie reminded him, her eyes weary with dark circles underneath. "Once you hear from the state or if you find Averill first, we'll know." She studied the next page.

"What if I never find her?" And why hadn't she at least called? It had been over a week. Pretty soon he'd have to talk to the sheriff. He tossed the book onto the sofa as he passed by. Max made another lap around the room, jiggling the baby.

"At least you're all set with the convertible car seat/stroller."

"Ready to jog," he agreed, breaking a smile, remembering what Sherry had said. "Also, I have diapers, bottles and a crib."

Sophie reached out to touch his arm. "Everything will work out, Max."

He raised an eyebrow. "How can you be that sure?"

Her tone was soothing. "Because you're a capable person. As a vet, you know more about babies—animal ones, I admit—than you think you do. And you practically raised me, didn't you?"

"Sophie, you were a teenager when Mom and Dad died." Hit head-on by an unlicensed driver going the wrong way. The shock of that, the double loss, still rattled him. His struggles afterward with Sophie had been those of the adolescent variety. Suddenly, with the baby, he was again responsible for another human being.

"You finished their job," she said. "Beautifully, Gabe might say."

He stopped pacing to drop onto the sofa beside Sophie. "And decided not to have kids of my own." Briefly, he'd considered marriage, a family with Averill, though that conversation hadn't gone his way. Perhaps that had been the start of the decline in their relationship. In the end, he and Averill hadn't worked out. Max doubted he had what it took to be a true partner. He wondered if he could even be an effective parent—at the same time he had no choice. Now, it seemed, he had the family part but no wife.

"You have a child," Sophie said, leaning over to kiss the baby's cheek.

But for how long? "What if I get attached to her—" he already was "—and then Averill just shows up and wants her back? I have no idea whether she meant for me to take over for a day, a week or forever."

Getting the birth certificate was one thing. He also had to find Averill.

"Sophie, how hard is it to locate someone's address?" He'd been to Averill's apartment numerous times before their last, dreadful argument in March. Even then, there'd been a final attempt to reconcile, one more time together… "I really need to talk to Averill's mother."

"I'll see what I can do about an address at the library tomorrow."

"Thanks." He hated to bother her. Sophie not only had morning sickness; she had a full-time job, would soon be without her assistant and was searching without success thus far for Rachel's replacement. Still, she had better resources than he did. The baby fussed, and Max took a deep breath. Looked like another sleepless night ahead. "I guess my first order of business is to retrain this baby. Any suggestions?"

"Retrain?"

"According to Sawyer McCord and the books I've read, her days and nights are mixed up." The first day after he'd found her on his porch, Max had taken the baby to see the doctor, who'd pronounced her in perfect condition. He'd guessed she was roughly two weeks old and given Max a starter supply of the formula Sawyer preferred for newborns plus a hearty clap on the back. But he hadn't been able to hide his grin. Max Crane, baby daddy. The news had been all over town before he walked into Sherry's shop and saw Rachel Whittaker.

"I have no suggestions," Sophie said at last. "I'm a newbie—even more than you."

Which hardly seemed possible to Max.

Shutting off any thought of Rachel, whose image kept reappearing in his mind, he shifted the baby to a more comfortable position. His left arm had fallen asleep. Sophie handed him a chicken leg and a packet of fries. "Eat," she said, wrinkling her nose in distaste. "I can't stand the smell."

"You're not gonna be sick, are you?"

"If I don't take a bite myself, I'm fine."

"I'm sure glad men don't get pregnant."

Sophie didn't respond. She rummaged in her purse, then pulled out a sonogram. "I can't wait to see our little one. Look, Max. Isn't she—or he—the cutest thing?"

Max couldn't make out anything but a blurred shape. He'd seen images of puppy litters that looked clearer. "Uh, yeah. I'm going to be an uncle," he said, echoing Sophie's comment that first day about being an aunt. To his relief Max's baby had stopped snuffling and fallen asleep. He flipped pages in the name book. "How about Ashley or Ashlyn? Either one goes good with Crane."

"I'd be thinking of Annabelle all the time. Too confusing with all those As."

"Caroline?"

"Um, Cass and Kate. More of my friends."

He turned another page. "Then why not Gabrielle?"

"Max, no. Gabe is your best friend."

"Wendy," he tried.

"Willow," she said.

"With all your friends and Gabe, we're running through the alphabet. Who cares if these names remind you of your pals?" He was on the last page now. "Zsa Zsa," he murmured, which was too reminiscent of an old movie star, then, "Wait. What about Zoey?"

Sophie smiled. "I like it. It's familiar enough. And I have no friends whose names start with *Z*."

Max trailed a finger along the baby's cheek. "Then Zoey it is."

"Of course, she'll also need a middle name."

"Are you just teasing me now?"

She grinned. "It's too much fun to resist."

Sophie had been right, though. He'd think about a middle name later. For the moment at least, the baby—his baby—had a name.

He gazed down at the tiny girl in his arms. Felt another strange rush of warmth, which he'd never experienced before that morning on his porch, as she opened her eyes again and looked up at him. Uber-focused, it appeared, even when he was sure she still saw mostly lights and moving shapes. She had homed in on his face, though. It was as if she were looking into Max's soul.

In a near whisper, he said, "Hi there, Zoey Crane."

CHAPTER FIVE

"I HAVE NO idea where my daughter is."

Max didn't believe the woman. Sophie, excellent research librarian that she was, had come through with an address for Averill's mother. The day after they'd named Zoey, he'd driven over to Farrier, but Carol McCafferty didn't seem inclined to cooperate. Standing in the half-open doorway to her apartment, wondering if the neighbors down the corridor could hear, he shifted his weight. He wasn't surprised by the cold welcome.

Averill had told him enough about her background to expect as much. She was mostly estranged from her mother and had never wanted to visit even when she and Max were serious, but he had no other leads. "Anything you can tell me," he began again. "I'll take it from there."

Carol's ice-blue gaze, so like Averill's in color if not warmth, didn't waver. "If I didn't know she was pregnant, and I haven't seen her in months, what makes you think I could tell you where she is now?"

"I understand you're not close—"

She ran a hand through her short-cropped dark hair, threaded with silver. "Do you? Because of Averill, I lost my own baby. Lucie was in her care—a *five-year-old child*, completely dependent upon her older sister—when she 'disappeared' at the mall. Is that what Averill told you? That there was nothing she could have done to prevent that? She always liked to play the victim herself."

"I'm sorry for your loss."

"It's not only a loss! That was the tragedy of my life." She started to close the door.

Max stuck his foot in the gap. "Please, hear me out."

She glanced at him. "Will listening, talking bring Lucie back? I'm not surprised to hear Averill is in more trouble. She wouldn't have dared to tell me about a baby. Even she knew how I'd react."

"But Zoey is your granddaughter."

A burly man appeared in the doorway behind Averill's mother. "What's all this?"

She turned into his embrace, burying her

face in his barrel chest. "Averill's boyfriend wants to know where she is." She gave a bitter, muffled laugh. "Isn't that rich?"

"We don't know," he said. "What's more, we don't care. For the first time in years, Carol can sleep through the night. She's doing her best to be happy again. Now you turn up and want to rip open old wounds? Expecting us to *help*? You have nerve, buddy."

Max tried to ignore him. "I didn't realize how strongly you felt, Mrs. McCafferty."

"Her name's Sullivan," the man said. "We're married now."

"Congratulations," Max muttered. Averill had been right, then. She'd told him about her mother's new boyfriend and feeling like a fifth wheel, one reason she'd moved to Barren in the first place. She'd expected them to wed. Yet he'd underestimated the extent of her mother's resentment, her anger. Max appealed to the woman's husband after all. "Then family must be important to you. Relationships." He held Sullivan's gaze. "Look, I'm sorry to bring up old heartaches. I wish Lucie had never disappeared, that she was here with you now, but she's not. And you still have another child."

"If I'd had any money, I would have dis-owned her," Carol said, still not looking at him. Her voice trembled, and Max, who'd lost his own parents, could understand some-thing of how she felt about Lucie. The words dropped like stones.

His mouth tightened. He hadn't expected this to be easy. "With all due respect, I think you're being too harsh on Averill. She still feels guilty for what happened—and how must she have felt when she discovered she was carrying my child? Alone, and perhaps heartbroken herself. She should have been able to turn to you. I lost my parents when I was in college, but there are times still when I need them—like when Averill left our baby on my doorstep." He took a breath. "I could have used my mother's support, my father's advice. My sister and I try to help each other, but it's not the same as a parent."

Carol's new husband gazed at him. "Your child. Are you so sure the kid is yours?"

BABIES DIDN'T MUCH interest Lauren Anderson. The next big story did. As a reporter for the *Barren Journal*, she was all about headlines.

Lauren focused on the laptop in front of

her as she sipped coffee at a table in Barren's one café. In the hubbub all around, the rattle of cups and plates, the chime and clink of silverware, the voices that lifted and fell, she eavesdropped on the other patrons. Her daily stop-in offered the opportunity, however slight, for her to mine gold, uncover a great source of material for an upcoming *Journal* feature that could set her disgraced career—never mind her personal life—in motion again. She strained her ears to hear every word from the next table.

"I was taking my morning walk last week when I saw Maxwell Crane carry a dresser drawer into his clinic," one woman said, and Lauren's ears perked up. She recognized Bernice Caldwell, a virtual study in brown—hair, eyes, clothes—and a town gossip. Which suited Lauren fine. Such people could be her best sources.

Claudia Monroe, Bernice's friend, patted her carefully styled hair, a more flattering shade of brown than Bernice's but with too many highlights. "A drawer? Is he redecorating that clinic?"

"No. You'll be shocked when I tell you—

it had a baby inside and there was that sweet little face peeking out. A baby!"

"What's he doing with an infant? Maybe one of his patients—"

"There were no other cars in the lot except his truck. Oh, no, it must be his all right. I understand Averill McCafferty dropped the baby on his *porch*. Wonder where she went after that. No one has seen her since she quit as his receptionist at the clinic—and poor Clara stepped in to fill the gap."

"Clara fills any gap that opens up," Claudia murmured, stirring a third packet of sugar into her coffee. "She's practically a saint."

The two women exchanged knowing smiles.

"I never thought Max would fall for anyone—he's married to his vet practice—but if you ask me, Averill was a temptress, like Cleopatra or Salome. Even Delilah."

"Giving her too much credit," Claudia pointed out. "She may have bewitched him temporarily, but Max is no fool. I'm guessing he came to his senses, then sent her packing."

"Before he knew she was expecting."

"Or did he?"

"Ladies," a cooler voice seemed to chide as

well as greet them. Lauren looked up to see Nell Ransom, part owner of the NLS ranch and a bona fide cowgirl, standing over their table. She and her husband, Cooper, an ex-cop from Chicago and now local cattleman, were quite the power couple in Barren. Nell, Lauren knew, was tough and had no use for gossip. "How are we this morning? Have you heard, there's a blizzard on the way? But then, isn't there always in January?"

"Nell. How's that adorable baby of *yours*?" Bernice wanted to know.

Nell's eyes lit up. "She has Cooper wrapped around her finger. He's such a dad."

Lauren, eager to hear more, wished Nell would get her coffee, then go. Writing her weekly column—"Who's Who in Barren"—wasn't much of a challenge and, frankly, boring. A year and a half ago, she'd thought she had the scoop of the decade on Gabe Morgan, the then-foreman of Sweetheart Ranch. But her story of his connection to Brynne Energy and its huge oil spill in the Gulf hadn't gone to press before the national news broke—Gabe was the millionaire son of Brynne's CEO—and Lauren's dream of leaving town for the brighter lights of the big city, a desk at the *New York Times* or *Washington Post*, had crashed and burned. Lauren had begun to fear getting stuck in this little burg forever.

But what if…? Her lack of interest in children aside, there could be a major story right here and now. Which happened to include a baby.

Bernice had waited until Nell left the table to place her own order. "Max has been trying to find childcare, I hear. Bringing a baby to the clinic every day, with all that noise, dogs barking, cats whining, germs everywhere… not an appropriate place for such a little one," she said with a nod for emphasis.

Claudia, who preferred to focus on herself, agreed. "It's never easy. I've had problems with my Lizzie even though she's a grown-up now. Leaving her husband, trying to cope on her own with three children, then remarrying that *cowboy*—who names someone Dallas?—and having a fourth baby, practically out of wedlock—"

"You've been spending quite a bit of time with them," Bernice pointed out.

Claudia bristled. "They are my grandchildren. I feel an obligation to be part of their lives. I've even come to tolerate Dallas. He makes my daughter happy, but there are times when I wish I'd had more than one child myself. I have too much invested in her."

Lauren wondered if that was doing Lizzie Maguire any favors. Still. Who was she to question other people's motives? Except, perhaps, Maxwell Crane's, and when Bernice spoke again to redirect the conversation, Lauren seized upon that part of the story.

"I've heard other concerns. A single man, always caught up in his clinic, working long hours and answering emergency calls in the middle of the night…" Bernice trailed off with a pointed look at Claudia.

"I see what you're thinking." Claudia reached into her Kate Spade tote for her cell phone. "We can't let this lie. I'm going to call someone myself who can follow up on the situation. Right now."

Lauren's heart beat faster as she keyed in some notes on her laptop, her cold coffee forgotten as she listened to the one-sided phone conversation.

"There." Claudia ended the call and sat back in her chair. "We've done all we could."

"For that child's sake," Bernice agreed. "We're not the only ones worried. Mrs. Higley told me she stopped by the sheriff's office about the same matter. He didn't seem concerned, but then he never does. I do wish Finn was still wearing that badge. So, it was up to us to intervene."

And to me. Lauren made another note in her new document. With any luck, she would not be writing a "Who's Who" column this week.

In Barren, an abandoned baby made much better copy. A heartbreaker, for sure. Her next stop would be at Travis Blake's office to get his reaction. At last, she had another chance.

There wouldn't be a dry eye in town when Lauren finished her story.

WHEN MAX GOT back to the clinic after his visit with Averill's mother and some morning calls at various area ranches, he found Clara in a dither. The waiting room was empty, though, and no cars except hers and his truck were in the lot. Max checked his watch. "Sorry I'm late, G. Let me get more coffee in the break room, then I'll be ready for my one o'clock."

Clara held a bunch of what appeared to be bright red paper hearts. She'd been decorating again, filling the clinic walls and the tops of tables, the front desk, too, with Valentine's Day decorations. In January. But clearly that wasn't what bothered her. "Max, there's trouble."

Her distress rattled him. She was one of the most stable people he knew, and normally unflappable. She'd taken over Zoey's care that first morning like the pro she was, reducing Max's stress to a manageable level.

"If there's something wrong, we've had plenty of practice with crises, haven't we? What is it?" He added, "If you need money for more hearts and flowers everywhere, just ask." Not that Max intended to observe the upcoming romantic holiday, but he didn't care if other people did. Spreading cheer in a place where they brought their sick and injured pets wasn't a bad idea. He only hoped Clara wasn't doing too much. Sometimes he worried about her health. Clara was no longer young, and he noted the too-bright flush in her cheeks now.

She was almost gasping for breath. "The sheriff was here."

"Travis Blake? Why?"

"Apparently someone—I'm guessing Mrs. Higley because she was here that first morning, though Travis wouldn't say anything except 'a concerned citizen'—reported Zoey being in a dresser drawer then. As if she were somehow being deprived of proper care. I told him we're doing the best we can, that you'd bought the appropriate things for her afterward."

"I stuffed my truck with baby items, everything on your list—and more. I could have opened a baby shop myself. It's all set up at home now. Too bad Travis didn't show up there instead. He could have seen for himself. So, what's the problem? He should track down Averill. She's the one who needs to explain."

Clara patted his cheek. "I know, dear."

"What else did Travis say?"

"Not that much." She pulverized one of the hearts in her hand. "He's always closemouthed. At first, he seemed almost amused, and I got the impression he didn't believe that 'concerned citizen,' but by the time he left... Max, I'm worried that the authorities are involved. Can you *prove* Zoey is yours?"

He drew a deep breath. Good point. He'd been meaning to talk to Travis, and after speaking with Averill's mother earlier, he'd realized he needed the sheriff's help. Hoping

Averill would turn up on her own, he hadn't wanted to make a missing person report until now. Clara was right about Zoey, too.

"I've filed that application to get Zoey's birth certificate, but it may not be enough. Averill might not have used my last name as the father. When I went to see her mother, her new husband implied the baby might not be mine."

"Could that be true?"

"I guess anything's possible. Averill and I were on the verge of breaking up, an exclusive relationship, I'd thought, when we—I mean, counting on my fingers, the timing is perfect."

Clara briefly put a hand across his lips. "You needn't explain further to me."

"Did the sheriff ask me to stop by?"

"Yes," Clara murmured, "at your earliest convenience."

"I'm not in a very good position, am I?" If Max didn't hotfoot it over there, Travis would surely be back, but he did realize what he had to do first. "I need to take a paternity test."

Clara turned, possibly to hide her red face, and began to drape the chain of hearts across the front of the reception desk. "I think that would be wise. There's no telling when or if Averill will return. And if she *didn't* put your name on that certificate…"

"I know." The issue of paternity hadn't seriously crossed his mind before. He'd hoped to find Averill and clear things up before the matter arose. But now Travis was involved. What if Averill had already been seeing someone else when they broke up? Max stood there with his jaw clenched. For the first time since he'd found Zoey on his porch, his concern for Averill's whereabouts, for her, was eclipsed by anger. He hoped she was all right, wherever she was, but it was her fault he was in this mess.

Clara cleared her throat. "Max, I believe our pharmacy sells home test kits. I'm not sure how accurate that would be, but as a start…"

Max wasn't going to the local drugstore. In Barren, gossiping, spreading rumors, stirring things up by people like Mrs. Higley were kind of a town sport. People did care. They just got carried away, poking their noses where they didn't belong. He needed to be discreet.

"I have a four o'clock near Farrier," he said. "I'll get one over there."

Clara finished taping the heart chain in place. When she looked at him again, he could see that a Valentine's Day celebration, the likes of which had begun to spring up all over town, was no longer on her mind. "I'm afraid there's more," she said. "I hate to tell you this, but after Travis left, a van pulled in—from Child Protective Services."

CHAPTER SIX

LAUREN HAD HAD an unexpected hard deadline on a last-minute feature for the *Journal*'s editor in chief—the library auxiliary was having a big rummage sale in April and needed volunteers. Didn't they always?—which put Lauren's own piece on hold. She'd never seen so many committees for this and that, so much bustle in Barren like a bunch of busy bees. But then, she was a big-city girl. And wanted to be one again. It was midafternoon before she entered the sheriff's office to interview Travis Blake.

"Have a seat." On his feet, he waved a hand at the hard chair in front of his desk, then sat again. They'd first met at a county commission meeting where Travis had spoken about his need for more funding and body cams for his deputies. Not exactly the scoop of the century, and as soon as he finished, she'd left.

The few inches of copy she'd filed then had bored her to tears.

No one would be bored when her story about the Front Porch Baby hit the stands.

Because of people like Claudia and Bernice, everyone in town must know about the baby by now, so Lauren needed a different slant for her piece.

As soon as she broached the topic, Travis leaned back in his chair, tilting it on two legs against the wall behind him. He crossed his arms over his broad chest. "Didn't you learn your lesson a while back?"

Lauren blinked. "I don't know what you mean." But her innocent act didn't work with the sheriff.

"A year ago last summer. Eighteen months. Citizen of the Year. Annual award. Does that refresh your memory?"

He knew it would, not that she needed the reminder. Lauren had slaved from May until July on her blockbuster article about Gabe Morgan, who'd lied to everyone in Barren. Some people, though, came up smelling like roses. It was Lauren who'd lost out then to Sophie Crane on becoming Citizen of the Year, Lauren who was avoided on the street these days, who could no longer seem to get a table at the Bon Appetit. If she'd had any friends before, she didn't now. Everyone liked Gabe, who had since married Sophie, the town librarian, and settled down for good here on their own ranch.

"You can't blame me for trying," she said.

Travis studied her. "What's your angle today?"

All right, since he wasn't one to beat around the bush either, she'd come straight to the point. "What do you know about that abandoned baby? Sheriff." Just to keep things sounding official.

"She wasn't abandoned. She was left at her daddy's house. And, of course, your journalist Spidey senses told you there's a story there."

"Maxwell Crane doesn't strike me as the nurturing type—except with cows or horses. Maybe he's not the father."

"Do you always make such quick judgments on other people?"

"I've been here long enough to see what's going on." On the other hand, the sheriff himself was an enigma. She waited a beat before saying, "What's *your* story?"

Travis ignored the question. His bottle-green gaze met hers. Clearly, he wasn't about to tell her anything personal. "Are you writing a piece on Max? Already?"

"People in town are talking. I'll give them the facts." But Travis himself had also piqued Lauren's curiosity, her bloodthirst for the even bigger story. Maybe she'd almost missed it. "Fine. Let's put Max aside for now. I've heard you were FBI before you came to Barren and ran for office. I wonder what happened in the Bureau to make you cut and run."

"I didn't run. I drove," he said without a smile at his little joke. "I've always liked small towns. I was ready for a slower pace."

Hmm. Perhaps, or not. Lauren tilted her head to give him a once-over, from that shock of light brown hair, those eyes and the tan shirt he wore, the dark uniform pants. His gold badge glinted in the overhead lights as if to remind her that he was law enforcement. "Come on. Why don't you save me some time? Tell me all about it. Because I'm certain there's a juicy story there. The more you try to block me, the more interested I become."

The chair legs thumped back onto the floor. "How do you look in your mirror? Always trying to put someone else on the spot like you do."

She almost smiled. She'd made him lose his temper, start to reveal himself. She'd hit pay dirt or dug the first shovel full anyway. "It's my job. I'm a reporter."

He said mildly, "And I realize you need to redeem yourself after that disaster about Gabe. Which was only the beginning. Talk about a story. Yours, I mean."

Lauren didn't want to share any details about the past mistake that had brought her here.

When she didn't respond, to her relief Travis seemed to abandon the personal topic. "Maybe you haven't noticed that Gabe's just fine and so is his wife. Sophie's expecting— am I scooping you here?—so why not do a feature on her as a first-time mom? That'd be heartwarming."

Lauren stiffened. "Forget it." For now. "I did come to talk to you about Max. Are you aware that Child Protective Services has paid him a call?"

"Yes, ma'am." There was no respect or manners in the short sentence. "There's not much that happens in this town that I don't see or learn about." His mouth had tightened, the words like a warning. He stood behind his desk. "If you want more, go speak with Max. Get your 'scoop' straight from the horse's mouth."

"Ha ha," she murmured, taking her time to rise from her chair. Travis Blake was jingling the keys in his pocket, eager for her to leave. To slide away from any probing questions she might ask about him personally? They didn't know each other well but Lauren knew herself. She didn't give up. "I'm hoping we can work together. We'll talk again. About Max, too," she added. "I'll get the story. And yours. Count on that, Sheriff."

Travis saw her to the main doors. She could feel him watching her as she stepped out onto the sidewalk. "Thanks for coming in," he called after her.

She raised a hand in the air and laughed.

But the sheriff of Stewart County, Kansas, was not off her radar. In a professional, and personal, way.

TRAVIS TURNED FROM the front window that looked onto Main Street and Lauren Anderson's retreating back. He caught the curious glances of the desk sergeant and the dispatcher, held up a hand to prevent any inquiries, then went back to his office. Slumped in his chair, he tried to quiet the rapid beating of his heart. *Lauren Anderson, you are a dangerous woman.*

He hadn't guessed how dangerous when she went after Gabe Morgan. Now, she had violated Travis's inner sanctum, his hiding place if he opted to call it that. And he'd heard those rumors about Lauren. Disgraced in her last job, fired for failing to fact-check an important story, relegated like him to this small town and its non-Pulitzer Prize–winning newspaper rather than a beat at the *Boston Globe*. He was surprised, though, that she was still here. Lauren wasn't winning any popularity contests, yet she doggedly kept on, apparently hoping to prove herself once more before she moved on to bigger things. Travis had to respect that. For different reasons, they seemed to be in the same boat. Sinking, in his case.

Now she had her sights set not only on Max but on Travis. It wouldn't take much for her to find out that his last posting had been in Wichita. Making a connection with the kidnapping case that had brought him down might take a bit longer, but he had no doubt she'd get there, too. Ask more questions he didn't want to answer. Learn the truth about why he was here as sheriff when he could have become the agent in charge of the Wichita office or eventually moved on to DC, possibly at a more senior level.

Normally he was good at fending off people he didn't want to talk to. He didn't court trouble if he could avoid it. Yet he'd just given a poor performance, lost his cool, and Lauren had picked up on that. He needn't speculate on where that would go, yet he wondered. How could he prevent what he'd always known was coming?

Still. He didn't mind seeing a pretty woman in his office now and then.

Under other circumstances, he might have indulged her, laughed at her questions, even asked her out because, even though she had a nose like a bloodhound, she was an attractive woman. Dark-haired and blue-eyed with the kind of sassy mouth he liked. Travis could have let her end his long dry spell, welcomed the dance of a possible new romance.

But, no. Blocking her moves might almost be more fun.

Someone rapped at his door and, grateful for any interruption, Travis called, "Yeah?"

His dispatcher, a matronly woman, poked her head in. Her appearance always shocked him. She had nondescript brown hair except for streaks of violent blue in the supposed fashion of the day. "Everything okay, Sheriff?"

"Sure. Why not?"

"There's usually trouble when that Anderson woman turns up."

"I can handle it." *Her,* he added silently. Besides, he wasn't about to supply Alvie with gossip fodder.

"Next time I'll try to stop her before she marches straight for your office."

"Her visit was kind of a surprise. You do that, Alvie. Thanks." For a second, she appeared to have another question, but Travis quelled that with a look. He rose from his desk, then grabbed his hat from a hook on the wall. "Think I'll patrol Main Street before rush hour." Which was a stretch. Barren never had much traffic.

"I can ask Sarge to stop her, too."

"I'll tell him myself, but the press is always a thorn in the side of law enforcement."

He got no argument there. Alvie gave him a quick salute, then sauntered back to the phones, the blue streaks gleaming in her hair. Travis might not be that popular in town, or accepted yet, but his staff watched his back well.

The problem was, how to keep Lauren from learning just how unsuited he was for this job—or any other in law enforcement?

Travis clamped his hat on his head, then stepped out onto Main Street as if there'd be any reason to write a few tickets.

BEFORE HIS NEXT appointment that afternoon, Max ordered a burger and fries to go at the café, but as he headed for the door, he met Sheriff Blake coming in. "Hey, Travis. Just the man I need to see."

"Same goes. Clara tell you I went by the clinic?"

"She did." Max had to discuss a shoeing problem at an area ranch with the farrier, then get his paternity test, but he had a few minutes. He found a table, then waited for Travis to join him with his own food. "Late lunch," Max said.

"Early dinner." Travis lifted one eyebrow. "Then you probably know one of our finest citizens paid me a visit, upset to have seen you carrying that baby around in a dresser drawer."

Max swallowed a bite of his burger. "The first morning after I found Zoey on my front porch that was all I had. She was warm, comfortable, safe…"

Travis snatched a French fry from Max's plate. "Lot of people in this town like to gab, and I was obliged in that case to listen. I kept meaning to stop at the clinic before today, but one of my deputies has been away so I've been shorthanded. Sorry I had to bother you. I think I scared Clara half to death."

"You're not the only one. CPS dropped by, too."

"I heard."

"I wasn't in the office and Zoey was with my sister, so nothing came of that, but I suppose I'll hear from them again."

The sheriff grabbed another fry. "Well, I saw nothing to be alarmed about. Which I told our concerned citizen by phone afterward." As a starting point for their discussion, Max decided to show him Averill's unsigned note about the baby. Travis said, "You're sure this is from her?"

"I know her handwriting." *I can't take care of her. There's too much going on right now. She's yours.* "You're not going to ask me if Zoey's really my child?"

"I figure you'd say if she wasn't." He added, "I'm assuming you and Averill…" His other eyebrow went up.

"We're not still a couple. We broke up last March. Just long enough," Max pointed out, "for her to be pregnant with Zoey after our last time together—which ended in another, final fight."

"Doesn't seem that likely she'd leave the baby with you, then. Have you tried to contact her? Ask for some explanation? Is it possible she took off on a lark—"

"Right after giving birth?"

"You have a point. And from what I know about Averill she doesn't seem the type to give up a child."

"She has a lot of guilt about her sister's disappearance. The only reason I can come up with for her leaving is maybe following some new lead on Lucie. Averill didn't want kids herself, the responsibility for a baby." Max picked up his burger for another bite but ended up putting it back on his plate. Even though he'd stopped in for lunch, he didn't seem to have any appetite. He said, "On the other hand, I did want a family. I'd never thought much about that before Averill and I got together, but then…"

"Her pregnancy might have been a shock to her at first, but Averill had months to change her mind. She carried to term. Could be she developed postpartum depression and panicked. She may think things over, come back, even try to reconcile with you. That seem possible?"

"We went back and forth for months before our last breakup. Which hollowed me out. No, I wouldn't want to try again."

"Which means what? If, or when, you do find her. What if she wants the baby back?"

"I'll face that when I come to it. In the meantime, I'll take care of Zoey, do my best with her." Which still included finding a full-time caregiver. For today, Zoey was with one of his neighbors, an old friend of his parents.

Travis leaned back in his chair. He'd polished off his chicken sandwich while Max just moved his burger around on the plate. "You should have come to me sooner. Filed a missing person report."

"I know. That's what I wanted to see you about today."

"All right. Once you do, I'll dig into some of my databases, see if I can find mention of her." He paused. "You have any reason to suspect foul play?"

"No."

Travis blew out a breath. "I'll do whatever I can, Max, but if I were you, an unmarried dad, I'd establish paternity as soon as possible."

"I'm working on that," he said, "a DNA test." And told Travis he was waiting for Zoey's birth certificate to arrive.

"That's good because right now you have no legal rights regarding custody, visitation, decision-making for Zoey, and so on. That proof will settle any question of whether she should be with you—in the event CPS or the court has doubts. It will also preserve Zoey's rights, making her eligible to receive benefits through you, financial support included. I assume you're okay with that."

A lump had formed in Max's throat. "I'll do anything I can for her."

Travis nodded before he finished his coffee. "I didn't expect a different answer."

Max pushed his plate toward him. "You want my lunch? I'm not hungry."

"I wouldn't mind half of that burger."

There was silence while Travis ate the rest of Max's food. He'd pick up something later after he'd digested their conversation. His ex-girlfriend, missing as if she'd stepped off the edge of the world. No legal rights to the baby sleeping in his house. CPS, the gossips in town. The sheriff.

"Averill and I may not be together anymore, and I feel some anger about this situation, but I also care about her well-being."

"You wouldn't be Max Crane if you didn't. That head-in-the-clouds expression you get sometimes doesn't fool me." Travis rose from his seat. "Part of my job is reading people's faces, their tells. I'll get back to you as soon as I can. Try not to worry so much."

Max couldn't help that.

But top of his worry list was to find a care-giver. Fast.

AT THE LIBRARY, Rachel filled a box with the belongings she'd kept at work. Her favorite coffee mug, her warmest sweater—the old building could be drafty in winter—her tattered guide to the Dewey decimal system, her worn copy of *Rebecca* by Daphne du Maurier…her frayed nerves.

This was her last day at the library, and Sophie, hovering nearby, must have sensed how hard it was for Rachel to leave without a safety net in place. "I'm going to miss you at the front desk. I know I keep saying this, but I wish you were staying."

With another week left to serve on her notice, Rachel was also out of a job sooner than expected. Sophie had decided to promote one of the pages to take her place. The girl was on a gap year after her high school graduation last spring, and because she'd already been doing many of the tasks Rachel had, Sophie wouldn't need to train her replacement. There was no reason for Rachel to stay any longer.

Plus, even though Sophie was saying all the right things, over the past week the under-the-surface tension had gotten to them both. Sophie had agreed, though, as a goodwill gesture to pay Rachel for the full two weeks.

Rachel said, "I'm sure Patty will be great."

She shifted a half package of snickerdoodle cookies around to make room in the box for the little elephant figurine she'd kept on her desk in this cubbyhole near the Biography section of the stacks.

Sophie must know she regretted her decision. Rachel had no new job waiting in the wings. What if she'd never given her notice, tried harder to manage with this part-time job? Not possible, of course. But as of now, she had no other options.

They were standing there, Rachel on the verge of tears, when the main doors opened, and Max Crane headed straight for them. He stopped long enough to kiss Sophie. "Scoot, will you? I need to talk to Rachel."

Sophie sent him a puzzled look. "Use my office. I'll be at the front desk."

She had to feel as confused as Rachel did. Why was he here? Max took his sister's chair while Rachel sat in the hot seat facing him.

She soon realized this must be about her job search because he'd brought what appeared to be her short résumé with him. "I talked to Shadow who tells me I should give you a chance," he said at last, "convince you to try." He glanced up from the paper he'd been reading.

"You mean caring for the baby?"

Rachel worried her lower lip. She badly needed a job—any job at this point—and a place to stay, but she'd run out of Shadow's office before in a panic, and now she'd be jumping from the frying pan into the fire. Remembering her unwanted reaction to Max at the Baby Things shop, that lightning-quick awareness of him, she couldn't possibly consider the position.

Max didn't seem wild to hire her, either. With a slight frown, he scanned the sheet again. "Sophie says you're a crackerjack worker at the library here but—"

"This is my last day."

"And you know books, not babies. Am I right?"

But Shadow must have added Rachel's experience to the résumé. Wasn't he reading closely? "I did a lot of babysitting when I was younger—some of that with newborns. And I'm very responsible," Rachel murmured, a flash of unwelcome memory causing her voice to crack. She'd never had the chance to hold her own baby, and a fresh wave of sadness threatened to overwhelm her. It would be so hard to cradle Max's tiny daughter, to change diapers and prepare bottles, to walk the floor with her at night when she became cranky from teething and not think about the baby she'd lost. What if she simply couldn't do the job without losing her own sanity?

Still, at this point she could hardly afford to be choosy unless she left Barren, which Rachel didn't want to do. "If I could, I'd suggest a trial run without pay, but I'm scraping the bottom of my finances right now." She'd run out of dog food for Sky again, and Rachel's emotions were close to the surface. She didn't want to cry in front of him. "I have to be out of my apartment tomorrow."

She paused, knowing she was about to shoot down her own chances, but she had to be honest. "Besides, how awkward would it be, us bumping into each other every morning, having coffee in our bathrobes in your kitchen? Two strangers. And what would people say? You know how it is in Barren. They talk. Endlessly."

Max agreed. "For some reason, I seem to be the focus of many conversations. Every woman in town has tried to fix me up." His eyebrows rose. "It's a full-time job fending them off."

Or maybe he had too high an opinion of himself.

"I'm sure you're the catch of the day," she said half to herself. But Max heard and broke into a smile.

"Sorry, that sounded…narcissistic, didn't it, which couldn't be further from the truth. I've always been kind of a nerd, my head in the clouds. Oblivious, Sophie says, as to whether I've remembered to shave or change my clothes."

He did sport a five-o'clock shadow, becoming as it was.

Max said, "I can take the chatter, but you're right. I wouldn't want to see you in the cross-hairs of someone like Bernice Caldwell or Claudia Monroe. That would be unfair to you." His dark gaze met hers. "By the way, you'd have no reason to worry about me."

Rachel didn't respond. She worried about every man she met. She'd trusted Chad, and her brother-in-law had betrayed her trust. Or rather, Rachel had let him.

Max said, "I'm sure you've heard about my relationship with Averill—the baby's mother. I'm still trying to deal with that train wreck of my life…" He let the rest trail off. "Plus, Zoey demands most of my attention, the reason, of course, that I need childcare help in the first place." He gave her another, thinner smile.

She stared at him, tempted to beg for the full-time position even though she feared it wasn't the right choice for her.

He stood, as if he'd suddenly remembered another appointment. "Sorry, Rachel. You were right. It might be better for me to hire someone older…"

Again, he didn't finish. His gaze slid away from hers, and Rachel saw faint color in his face. Had Max reacted to her in the baby store as she had to him? This wouldn't work at all, then. Staying in his house, seeing him all the time, even sometimes having meals together. No, he was right too.

Max turned toward the office door. Rachel had been dismissed. The rejection, oddly, troubled her. This was the strangest job interview she'd ever experienced. Why had he come if he wasn't prepared to offer her the job she needed so badly? It seemed he'd talked himself out of it. Maybe for the same reasons Rachel had all but sabotaged the interview.

He held open the door, and Rachel had to follow.

"It probably wouldn't work anyway."

Max stopped, turned quick enough that she almost ran into him and held up the copy of her résumé. "Who am I kidding?" he asked. "I'm at the end of my rope. Someone from Child Protective Services stopped by the clinic today. Freaked Clara out. Do you want the job or not?"

Rachel swallowed. "I do," she managed.

"Okay, let's give it a try. With full pay. If you need an advance on your first check, that's fine." Which told her how desperate *he* was. But then, so was she. The advance would cover her back rent. "When can you start?"

"Tomorrow morning?" Rachel had to finish packing. A local moving company would transfer her few pieces of furniture early the next day to a small storage unit. "I think I can be at your house by nine."

They shook hands, and at the front desk

Sophie and Max spoke for a few minutes while Rachel returned to her cubby.

She shoved a last book into the box. She'd spent the better part of her time in Barren here. She'd been safe, useful. A part of things. She valued Sophie's friendship. Even when they'd disagreed, mainly when Rachel had overstepped the boundaries of her job while playing detective after Averill "borrowed" those books, she'd still been happy here. She closed the flaps on the box, then taped it shut. Now, leaving the safe harbor of the town library, she was about to drift into some likely rough seas.

She only hoped she didn't drown.

Lugging the carton, she walked over to the counter. She couldn't accept the job without being completely honest. Hoping Max wouldn't change his mind, she said, "I'd be bringing my dog."

CHAPTER SEVEN

IN MAX'S HOUSE on Cattle Track Lane, Shadow Wilson's teenage daughter, Ava, was curled up on Max's sofa, scrolling on her iPad and obviously wishing she was somewhere else. This had been Rachel's move-in day, the beginning of the new job, and she was a bundle of nerves. Out in the backyard, Sky whined while Rachel wondered how Max would take to having the dog here, too.

Shadow had come to help Rachel settle in once she'd reached the house and unlocked the door with the key Max had put under the mat. He was due to show up any minute with Zoey, who'd gone with him early to work.

Sky yipped, begging to come inside, but Rachel wanted her to inhale the outdoor scents, imprint them on her mind so she could find her way back to this house if she ever strayed. And having spent months in the shelter before Rachel had adopted her, Sky could still be wary of strangers. Rachel had also heard Sophie's stories about her own dog and her brother's reluctance to have a pet. What if Max couldn't tolerate Sky? Rachel couldn't imagine anyone not falling in love with her, but she planned to introduce her gradually, hoping Max would be unable to resist her lovable mutt.

Ava's voice was sulky. "Mom, when can we leave? I'm losing my whole day here, and I have homework."

Shadow said, not batting an eye, "If you have enough time to be on social media all morning, your schoolwork should be a cinch later." Today the schools were closed for a town-wide educational conference.

Gaze still glued to her tablet, Ava said, "My little *brother* got to do what he wanted. Why couldn't I?"

"He had a regular play date with his friend— and would have been running all over this house if he'd come with us. Don't be rude. We won't stay much longer." Shadow turned to Rachel. "Chaos follows me everywhere." She fluffed the white lace skirt of a bassinet, a gift from her and her husband. "Ava's upset because she wanted to go with Grey to a cattle auction in Wichita."

Ava was a beautiful girl, dark-haired like her mother with her father's blue-green eyes. Wearing jeans with strategic holes in them and a loose top that sloped down on one shoulder, she looked like the typical teenager she was, and Rachel couldn't help but think of the daughter she might have had. How hard would it be when Max came home with the baby? Rachel glanced at the front door.

"Relax." Shadow stopped her. "As soon as Max gets here, he can carry this bassinet upstairs to the nursery."

"It's hardly that," Rachel murmured. "A crib, a nightstand piled with boxes of diapers—and an old blind at the window. Part of my job will be to furnish the room."

A car pulled up in the drive and her pulse began to hammer. Sky barked her head off from the rear yard. What if Rachel couldn't do this job after all? And Max kicked them both out? She could be literally on the street and in worse shape than she was yesterday. Footsteps sounded on the walk, the porch, and the bell rang.

Shadow nodded toward the entry. "You've got this, Rachel."

"I hope," she said.

But it wasn't Max, who wouldn't need to ring. Clara stepped inside, carrying a small bundle in a soft pink blanket. "We're here. Rachel, Max says he'll be back soon. I've been tending Zoey at the clinic while he was in Farrier on an emergency." She gazed down at the little face that barely showed above the blanket, then held out the baby. "Take her, dear. Be prepared to fall in love."

Instead, Rachel had to look away. A flood of memories nearly swamped her. The first time she'd met Jason, tumbling head over heels for the tall, tough marine with a gentle spirit. Their wedding day, Jason in his dress uniform, the arch of sabers over their heads. Their first home together, then the moment she'd told him they were pregnant, holding up the test stick. His delight over the coming baby. Jason leaving for his last deployment, his love for her in his eyes. His promise to return, safe and whole. The pair of soldiers at her door with solemn faces... Her miscarriage, feeling alone then, and frightened. Chad's unexpected comfort. Rachel's search for another place that felt like home, another place where she might belong.

She could sense Shadow and Clara watching her averted face until the silence became awkward and she had to turn and look at them. Clara was still holding the baby. Shadow gently pulled the blanket back so Rachel could see her better.

Feeling as if she were having an out-of-body experience, she gazed down at Zoey, then smoothed a trembling hand over the baby's dark hair, looked into her blue eyes, half-ready to grab her things and run.

Shadow hugged her. "It'll be all right."

Before she could say anything around the lump in her throat, Ava bounded off the sofa, appearing interested for the first time since she'd followed Shadow through the door.

"Let me see." Ava studied the baby, then glanced at Rachel. "She's so little."

Clara laughed. "I'd love to stay and help, but there are appointments at the clinic to see to, and Candi—our vet tech—is with a post-surgical patient. There's no one to man the front desk." She thrust the baby into Rachel's arms.

And Clara was gone, bustling out the door

to her car. Holding Zoey's sweet weight for the first time, Rachel glanced at the large bag Clara had left in the entryway. The baby was beginning to fret.

"Rachel, I imagine she's ready for a bottle." Her tone gentle, Shadow plucked one from the diaper bag, then headed for the kitchen. "We'll warm this, then you can feed her. Bonding time," she added.

Shadow had given Rachel a lot of moral support, but when she left a short time later, ushering Ava outside after a last hug for Rachel, the house echoed with emptiness. Zoey's eyelids were drooping. As the baby finished her bottle, Rachel shifted in the living room chair, the tension in her arms making them quiver. It wasn't as if she had no experience with babies. She knew how to change a diaper, how to feed and bathe an infant. She could do this. She had to.

Still. She was glad when she finally heard Max's truck in the drive.

"DIDN'T MEAN TO keep you waiting," Max said to Rachel as he came through the front door at midday. Outside, the promised blizzard was brewing, fat snowflakes beginning to settle in the tracks his truck had made on the driveway.

Max could hardly hear himself over the baby's wailing, and from the sound of it, she'd been working herself up for quite a while. Out back a dog was barking, and Max bit back a sigh. He took off his muddy boots, hung his stained coat on a hook by the door. "Horse over near Farrier tore through a barbed wire fence, cut himself bad. I stabilized him, but we had to ship him to Wichita for advanced treatment." He eyed the entry hall but saw no suitcase, no boxes. "You get settled all right?"

"Yes, thank you. The room is very nice."

"You can do whatever you want with it. Paint, hang wallpaper…"

In Rachel's arms, Zoey let out another ear-splitting cry that made Max's head pound. The dog outside howled.

Rachel averted her gaze. "I've fed her, changed her, walked this floor, but she keeps crying. Zoey did sleep a bit after her bottle, but I don't seem able to soothe her." She paused. "I shouldn't say that when I convinced you I was worth a trial run in this job…"

"We're all on a trial run." He took Zoey from her, bouncing the baby lightly in his arms, trying to quiet her with a soft "Shh, it's okay." But once she got started, almost nothing made her stop except, "The rocking chair," he said, heading for the stairs. "Come with me. It's the one way I've found to lull her to sleep. From my limited experience, I've learned this is her tired cry so she must need another nap."

Max still had his doubts about Rachel. She didn't exactly exude confidence, but neither did he. Or no, Rachel seemed uneasy with the baby. He carried Zoey upstairs to the make-shift nursery, which wasn't exactly from the pages of *House Beautiful*. It had been his mother's old sewing room, then Max's study cubicle when he was in college, even Sophie's bedroom at one time when as a teenager she'd wanted a better view. He'd guessed that meant being able to talk to her boyfriend from the rear window where she thought Max couldn't see them. He plopped onto the old rocker that had been his grandmother's and laid a blanket over his lap. "Zoey usually likes this," he said, keeping his voice low.

After a few minutes of rocking, the baby gradually quieted then fell asleep. And Max let out a breath of relief. "Now you've had a preview of what my nights have been like. Want to change your mind?"

"I promised I'd stay. I will."

He half smiled. "Don't make promises you can't keep. I'll ask you again tomorrow morning."

"My answer will be the same. I've cut all ties—the job with Sophie, handed over the keys to my apartment this morning, put my furniture in storage. I'm all yours," she added, then seemed to think better of what she'd said.

"I know what you meant." He turned his head toward the window. "That your barking dog?"

Rachel swallowed. "Yes. Sky. She's feeling a little unsettled, but she's usually a sweetie and she's easy to get along with. She'll do anything you ask."

Max thought of telling the dog to trot down the street to his clinic, open an empty kennel and shut herself in, eat whatever she liked from the feed room. But he'd agreed, reluctantly, that Rachel could bring her dog. Ordinarily, that would have been a deal breaker for Max, but even Sophie agreed that he'd survived his nephew-dog Remi's house training.

"I'd ask her… Sky to just quiet down before she wakes Zoey."

Rachel said, "I'm sorry, Max. I'll go out, reassure her that I'm still nearby. She must think I've abandoned her."

"No, better just bring her inside. The wind's kicking up and the snow has started. You can put her dog bed in the mudroom. I've taken the rest of the day off. After I clean up and change clothes, I'll head to the store for groceries while the roads are open. We could be socked in here by tomorrow."

Rachel looked alarmed by that, and she and Max were on tenterhooks all day. He did his best to help keep Zoey as happy as possible. Max would have forgotten to eat dinner—which he often did—but to his surprise Rachel cooked. Their first night together, an awkward meal he would have avoided if he could. He guessed she would, too.

They faced each other across his parents' old dining room table, Max occasionally rocking back on his chair's rear legs, which always drove Sophie to make some comment about his lack of manners, and Rachel staring at her plate of spaghetti and meatballs, clearly with one ear alert to any cries from the second floor, where Zoey was asleep.

He buttered another roll. This weird breaking of bread with her had ironically restored his appetite. "Zoey will be up again soon. I thought I was making progress in changing her schedule, but not much, it turns out."

"You should sleep tonight. You hired me to take over. I'll stay up with Zoey."

"You don't know what you're asking for."

"I can learn," she insisted when he merely raised one eyebrow.

Max forked another meatball into his mouth, chewed, then swallowed. "I opened today's mail while you were bathing Zoey. The state sent the copy I'd requested of her birth certificate."

Rachel had stopped eating. "That's good, right?"

"Yeah, but unfortunately my last name isn't on it. Neither is Zoey's first. For now she's Baby Girl McCafferty. So, as far as I'm concerned, her name is Zoey." Yet Max wasn't ready to petition the court to change that on the registration. He'd like to have Averill's agreement.

"Have you had any luck finding her mom?"

He hesitated, unsure whether to confide in Rachel, a near stranger. Still, she did live here now. "Nope. I talked to Averill's mother, but she wants no part of her or the baby. Weird, I thought, when the disappearance of her younger child shattered her. You'd think she'd need Averill. Instead, she blames her for what happened."

"That's sad."

"Yeah," he agreed, "but I still have to find Averill." Max tilted his chair back again. "Before you ask—yes, I'm sure Zoey is mine. In the meantime, I, uh, took a paternity test yesterday." He'd done a cheek swab and somehow managed with a crying Zoey to collect her DNA. "The lab results will take a few days." The home test he'd bought at the pharmacy in Farrier claimed a 99.9 percent accuracy rate according to the included literature.

"Everything will be okay," Rachel said, her gray-green eyes briefly meeting his as they'd done only a few times since he walked into the house.

For tonight, after some negotiation, he and Rachel agreed to take shifts with Zoey. After his first one, Max fell into bed and dropped off into a dead sleep. He hadn't had more than a wink here and there since he'd found Zoey on his porch. Tonight, she seemed to be holding to her plan—sleep a little, then wake up wide-eyed and alert to suck down another bottle and get her diaper changed. But there was no falling back to sleep once she'd been fed. Max knew she would soon start to fuss a little, then a lot, then burst into loud cries again that no one, including him, could quiet.

Not long, it seemed, after his head hit the pillow, he woke with a start. It was 3:00 a.m., according to his glow-in-the-dark fitness tracker. He'd certainly put in a lot of steps as a newborn's dad. Bleary-eyed, he stumbled from bed, across the hall and into the nursery, where Rachel was walking the floor, humming softly to the baby but with a harried look on her face.

"Every night?" she asked. "I'd forgotten. My cousin's twins were like this. Two at once."

"Every night. Rachel, let me take another turn."

When Max reached for Zoey, his hand brushed Rachel's arm, and she recoiled with lightning speed. She moved so fast Max didn't know what was happening until she was halfway across the room, and he was holding

Zoey, one side of her blanket trailing to the floor. "Sorry," he said for perhaps the tenth time that day. He and Rachel seemed to be taking turns with apologies. "Didn't mean to take you by surprise."

"You didn't. I…" Her gaze shot toward the doorway and she took another step.

"Go to bed. I'm good here. Thanks, Rachel. See you in the morning."

She was gone before he finished speaking. He glanced out the nursery window. The snow was coming down horizontally, and by morning the roads would be a mess. He'd be lucky to catch another hour or two of light sleep before he had to get up again, shower, dress and head to work. Unless they were canceled, those appointments he'd rescheduled to be here this afternoon with Rachel and Zoey would be waiting for him as soon as the clinic doors opened. He didn't envy Rachel alone all day with the baby, but that's what she had signed on for—and so had he.

Max sank down on the rocker, kicked it into gear and nestled Zoey close to his chest. She seemed to like his body heat, maybe his heartbeat and now-familiar smell. As the snow fell outside, and Rachel's dog yipped a few times from behind the mudroom door below, he fed Zoey a bottle, and finally there was blessed silence. The baby lay snuggled against him, her mouth partly open, pink rosebud lips still making half-hearted suckling motions. Max stroked a hand over her silky dark hair, inhaled the sweet baby scent of her, and knew he would do anything to make sure Zoey had a happy, healthy life. But would that be with him? "My little girl," he whispered, and Zoey's mouth turned up in a faint smile. Gas, her doctor Sawyer would say, but Max didn't believe him.

In the darkened room, lit only by a small giraffe-shaped night-light, he rocked and rocked, his heart full of love for the sweet, helpless being in his arms.

And wondered. He had reassured Rachel Whittaker that he had no interest in another relationship, that she could trust him to keep things between them strictly business. So why had she jumped like some scalded cat at the mere brush of his hand against her?

CHAPTER EIGHT

IT WASN'T EASY to avoid Max, but Rachel tried. Ashamed of how she'd flinched from his touch last night in the nursery, she also felt guilty yet anxious for another reason. At their brief contact, a wave of warmth had run down her arm. Masking her awareness of him, which went beyond being his employee, wouldn't be easy. Why did she feel this way when, to her regret, she'd already let Chad under her guard? Rachel hadn't replied to her former brother-in-law's recent text. *Why don't you answer me?* And she still hadn't told her in-laws, whom she loved, that she'd moved away to escape him.

In the kitchen she poured fresh coffee into two cups. Sophie had plowed through the foot of snow that had fallen overnight to come visit this morning, bearing gifts and cooing over Zoey.

Rachel gestured at the unwashed breakfast dishes in the sink. "Excuse the mess. I haven't had time to pick up today. This house looks like a bomb struck during the night. At the library I thought I knew what I was doing, but here... Shadow says chaos is part of being a new parent—or caregiver. There's certainly that."

At the table Sophie added milk to her coffee, an occasional treat during her pregnancy that she'd told Rachel she cherished. "You've already won the first battle. Max was more than glad to see Remi move out, and here he is, having let you bring Sky." Which told Rachel how desperate he was. The dog was lying at their feet under the table, head between her front paws. "Big points for that. Huge."

Rachel cracked a smile. "Sky is reliably housebroken."

"And will be a big support here for you." Sophie added, "Don't forget the Girls, either. We always have your back. By the way, we're meeting soon. Annabelle's shower, remember? I'll text you the time and place. I think Kate's tied up right now so Sweetheart Ranch is out. I'd host instead but, honestly, Gabe and I are still living out of boxes. I don't know where anything is." She grinned. "Maybe we'll come to you this time. I know everyone's dying to meet Zoey."

Rachel made some excuse to beg off, then changed the subject. "How's my replacement at the library doing?"

"Great, I'm happy to say. Patty always was a good page, and she's stepped up as my temporary assistant until she starts college next fall. I miss you, of course, but we're good. You're doing fine here, too, Rachel."

She wasn't as sure as Sophie. "I'm not exactly a novice, but I'm always afraid I'll do something to harm Zoey."

"Babies, I'm told, are tougher than they look. Has Max heard back about the birth certificate?"

"Yes." Rachel explained about Max's name not being on the registration.

"And there's nothing new on Averill? I hate to keep asking him."

"Nothing," she said. "Averill didn't even give Zoey a first name, period."

Sophie sipped her coffee, then set it aside. "When I was born, my parents couldn't agree on a name so that's what they did. Baby Girl Crane. A month or so after they corrected that, they got my official birth certificate with Sophie on it."

They were speculating about Averill's whereabouts when the front doorbell rang, and Rachel went to answer. She wasn't expecting anyone. "I wonder who this can be," she said, "especially in this snow." She swung open the door, half expecting to see Bernice Caldwell or Claudia Monroe. Rachel hadn't even combed her hair.

Instead, a petite woman wearing a plain dark coat stood there with a hesitant smile. She held out a hand. "Good morning. I'm Deborah Neal with Child Protective Services."

Remembering that Max had mentioned the agency, Rachel fought an urge to shut the door as they shook hands. "Rachel Whittaker." She hastened to add, "Dr. Crane isn't here right now."

"I missed him at his clinic the other day, but we've had a complaint, which I have to follow up on." She mentioned the dresser drawer, the lack of proper equipment for an infant. "I need to check on the baby. May I come in?"

With a sinking heart, Rachel held the door

wider. She could hardly refuse. Sophie had risen from her chair at the kitchen table. She came up behind Rachel and put a hand on her shoulder. "The baby's sleeping," Rachel said.

"Then I'll just peek in on her."

Sophie cleared her throat. "Maybe it would be better if you came back another time."

"And you are?"

"Dr. Crane's sister. Zoey's aunt." Her grasp on Rachel's shoulder was firm. "Rachel is his baby's full-time, live-in caregiver."

"I wasn't aware that Dr. Crane had hired someone. With the proper qualifications, I presume."

"Um. Well, I don't have a nurs—"

Sophie spoke up again. "My brother would not have anyone in this house without knowing she can do the job. Rachel is devoted to Zoey, as if she were her own child, so you have nothing—the county has nothing—to be concerned about." She took a breath, then plowed on. "She's also a friend of mine. I can vouch for her. Rachel used to work with me, and she's the best. You can ask Shadow Wilson at the Mother Comfort agency, which handled her job application. Zoey couldn't be in better hands than she is with Rachel."

Sophie was doing her best, but Deborah Neal was still insistent about seeing the baby. Rachel led the way from the kitchen along the hallway past the living room, where before the incident in the nursery, last night's chip bag, empty dip container and soda glasses littered the coffee table, then upstairs. The nursery looked stark to her. The new baby monitor sat in its box on the nightstand, an open package of diapers spilled out on the floor. A yellow onesie had somehow gotten draped over a lampshade. A haphazard pile of laundry had been dumped on the rocking chair—and the bear she'd bought Zoey that played soft, soothing sounds, among them a maternal heartbeat mode, was also still in its carton, but thank goodness the baby was sleeping peacefully. Of course, she would be; she'd been up most of the night.

"As you can see," Rachel said, "everything she needs is here, but we're just getting organized."

Deborah Neal took a visual tour of the room, as she had downstairs, seeming to miss nothing on her way through the untidy house, her expression neutral. She leaned over the crib, inspecting Zoey without comment.

Shredding Rachel's nerves, she made notes in a small book. Finally, she glanced up and started to speak.

Before she did, Rachel held up one finger. "Let's go downstairs before we wake her."

In the living room, she didn't invite the agent to sit down. They all three stood there in an awkward silence as Deborah Neal surveyed that room again, her mouth pursed. Then she closed her notebook and studied Rachel for a moment. "Thank you for letting me check on Zoey. One more question. Dr. Crane is the baby's father?" Rachel assured her that he was, and Deborah turned toward the entryway, not looking entirely convinced. "Please tell him I'll be in touch."

Rachel and Sophie watched her go, waiting until her van had disappeared down Cattle Track Lane. Then Rachel let out a breath. "What did that mean? Oh, Sophie." Rachel put her face in her hands. "I may have made things worse for him."

"I'm sure not." Sophie paused. "But we'll soon find out."

MAX HADN'T SHUT the front door behind him that evening before Rachel rushed from the kitchen, her face a mask of distress. His first thought was of Zoey. "The baby sick?"

"No, she's fine. Even sleeping." A small frown between her eyes, Rachel wrung the dry dishtowel she was holding. "I tried to reach you, but you didn't answer, and I didn't want to leave a message on your cell or with Clara. Upset you when you were working."

He hung his jacket in the entryway. "I turned my phone off. I was in surgery all day. This is my weekly spay/neuter clinic, and some of those Christmas puppies and kittens, a lot of rescue animals, too, were due to get fixed. So, what's happened, Rachel?"

"Child Protective Services was here." Rachel repeated their conversation, Deborah Neal's concerns, her own fears, which were enough apparently to make her break her obvious vow to avoid Max.

Clara had warned him that the agency was looking for him, and he'd told Rachel, but he should have been better prepared. "What did Ms. Neal say?"

"That she'd be in touch with you. That's all, but she inspected every inch of this house, which looked like a disaster area. I'm so sorry, I should have cleaned up earlier, organized the nursery, but Zoey was fussy, and I didn't expect company."

"I'd bet that was on purpose. If she'd given warning—"

"And that's not all." After Deborah Neal had left, Rachel had seen a small article in today's newspaper under a familiar byline. "Lauren Anderson wrote about Zoey, about you, plus some barely veiled insinuations," she went on. "Sophie was here with me this morning. She tried to convince the woman from CPS that I'm a qualified worker with references, but all I could see was the mess around me. Deborah Neal kept giving me the once-over. And I thought here I am, as Lauren wrote, a single woman living with you, a single guy, alone now in the house together... What if that woman reads the article? Or Lauren writes another?"

"Lauren phoned me for comment but I wouldn't give her one. Nothing's going on."

"You and I know that, but Deborah Neal doesn't. What if that's grounds for taking Zoey? And you'd have to go to court to straighten everything out?"

"We'll see about that."

Rachel twisted the towel again. "I'm sure

other people are already talking, which won't look good. Sophie told me not to pay any attention but—"

"Rachel, forget Ms. Neal, Lauren Anderson and the people in this town. If they want to talk, they'll talk." He bypassed the stack of mail on the entry table and picked up the landline phone. "If it'll make you feel better, I'll give Travis a call, see what he thinks." He might know the ins and outs of CPS.

He put the sheriff on speaker after explaining about the visit as well as Lauren's article. "Ignore the newspaper thing, if you can," Travis said. "Complaints of possible neglect cases are made to the Kansas Protection Report Center. I don't know who made one, maybe not even the person who came to see me about the dresser drawer business, but Neal was right. That complaint had to be investigated."

"If she wasn't satisfied with her visit, can they take Zoey? Simply because we hadn't put away the diaper supply or set up a baby monitor before she came? Because unwashed dishes were left in the sink? The living room? That's not neglect—"

"Max. I doubt that's the impression she

had. Everybody's home has bad days. That call they must have gotten was what I term a nuisance complaint—like the person at my office when this all began. But CPS does not have authority to remove Zoey from your home without your consent or a court order. I doubt it will come to that. What's the word on paternity?"

"Still waiting for the DNA results."

"I doubt I can do anything to expedite that, and the fact that you're not on Zoey's birth certificate is a factor but let me try."

"Thanks, Travis."

"In the meantime, don't panic. Go about your business. You, too, Rachel," he murmured with a smile in his tone. "Try to have a good evening, you two."

RACHEL DOUBTED SHE could follow the sheriff's advice. She had let Max down, but that wouldn't happen again. Tomorrow, although she'd done the dishes today, she'd sweep through the whole house, tidying up and cleaning until it gleamed and looked as sterile as a hospital operating room. While holding Zoey in her baby carrier, Rachel had already installed the monitor in the nursery after Deborah Neal left, put the laundry away and arranged the disposable diapers on the nightstand. She'd sanitized the trash can, then put in a fresh liner for the dirty ones.

"Rachel." Max had bent his head to look into her eyes.

"Sorry, I was wool gathering. Planning for tomorrow."

"Travis was right," he said. "We need to focus on Zoey, not Lauren or some bureaucrat who hasn't a leg to stand on as far as the baby's concerned. Zoey isn't being neglected—never was—so why are we worried?"

"Clara was, too," she pointed out.

"And what's more…" He moved a little as if to grasp her shoulders, then dropped his hands. Again, as she had the night before, Rachel had stepped out of reach. His mouth tightened. "Hey. What's this about, anyway? I know you're worried about people gossiping, but you have nothing to fear from me. And that's what this looks like. Am I right?"

"I'm nervous, that's all. About doing this job well."

"This has nothing to do with baby care. Last night—your first night here—you flinched when I touched you. I would never—"

"I know you wouldn't. I just…" Rachel looked away. "I'm not very comfortable around men because—" She couldn't tell him, even when Max's eyes darkened.

"Did someone hurt, abuse you? Attack you?"

"No, nothing like that. But as you know, I lost my husband some years ago and I, well, ever since I've been on my own. Before I came here, I lived by myself. I haven't been around other men, I don't date, I don't belong to any singles groups, I don't do the online match thing… I've kept to myself and for now that's what I want to do."

"Which doesn't explain recoiling from me. There's something else. Why not tell me?"

Rachel tried to meet his gaze but failed. "I made a mistake—not that long after my husband passed away—" As if Jason had simply died in his sleep, and the horror of his death in battle hadn't come home to her. "I regret that, and I don't intend to repeat that mistake. It has nothing to do with you, Max. I'm just jumpy. Let's leave it at that, can we?"

"We can," he said, but he sounded as if he really wanted to keep probing.

Sitting in the living room with Max later,

both pretending to watch television, as they had the night before, didn't ease her tension. Making the excuse that she'd like to rest before Zoey woke up for Rachel's first shift tonight, she went upstairs to finish unpacking and better arrange her room. If CPS showed up again, she'd be ready.

She was climbing into bed when her cell rang, startling Rachel as she glanced at caller ID. Oh, no. It was Chad. He had never phoned before; he'd limited his approach to texts until now. Should she answer? She hadn't responded to any of his messages and she didn't want to speak to him. But Rachel also didn't want him ringing her cell at all hours of the night, waking Zoey. Bringing Max across the hall into her space with more questions she wouldn't answer.

"Hello."

"Rach, how are you?" His tone eager, Chad laughed a little. "I've given up on texting—for obvious reasons. But I won't give up on you. You know, Mom and Dad ask about you every day. When are you going to come home, see everyone? See me," he added as if they'd parted as best friends.

"I'm not coming back. I'm…happy here, and I have a new job."

"Oh, yeah. Doing what?" He'd always thought she needed a keeper, and soon after Jason died, he'd been right. Her first mistake had been believing Chad had a strong moral compass. Yet to be fair, there'd been a time when she'd found him charming, fun, easy to talk to. A time when he'd been as vulnerable as Rachel was.

"Nothing you'd be interested in," she said. "Just…housework for someone. Was there a reason for this call?"

"Sure. Catching up. How long has it been since we talked?"

"Not long enough," she said.

He only laughed again as if she wasn't serious. "Rach, you keep resisting the adventures we could have together. Housework? What fun is that? Say, what if I hop a plane, come to *Kansas*," he said as if it were the end of the earth. "We could grab your stuff, then head off somewhere. On safari, or to Paris in the winter, which could be a trip. Kansas?" he said again. "Must be snowy there, just like here in Indiana so maybe somewhere warmer instead. What do you say?"

Rachel gazed out her bedroom window at the yard blanketed in white. The roads after the blizzard weren't clear, but the last thing she wanted was to travel with him. "Don't you have a job?" It wouldn't surprise her if he still didn't. "Chad, I have responsibilities." She bent down to pat Sky, who lay asleep on the rug. "And I don't want to go anywhere with you ever."

Shaking, she hung up.

Not that he'd go away.

And someday she'd have to deal with him…before he showed up in Barren.

CHAPTER NINE

GIRLS' NIGHT OUT was normally a fun time for Rachel. In the past year and a half, she'd attended most of the meetings, and tonight—Annabelle's baby shower—should be no exception. Here at Wilson Cattle, Shadow and Grey's ranch, she was among all the new friends she'd made in Barren, an accepted part of the group now. And what could be better tonight than a celebration of coming new life?

Yet the phone call from Chad a week ago kept running through her mind. So did CPS and Lauren Anderson's short piece implying, among other things, that Max might have no rights with Zoey. And what if Chad made good on his notion—or had that been a threat?—to come see her? Rachel had never been physically afraid of him, but that, too, could change.

Annabelle sat near the fireplace surrounded

by gifts and the rest of their friends. Blossom Hunter, Shadow Wilson, Logan's ex Olivia McCord, Jenna Smith, Lizzie Maguire, Willow Jones, Kate Bodine. And Sophie, of course. They'd all come tonight, plus Sherry from the Baby Things shop, who sometimes joined them, and Shadow's mother-in-law, Liza, who spent part of her time in Texas, was also here.

Nell nudged Rachel. "Where are you, kiddo? You're sitting right next to me, taking small sips of your wine now and then, but you're not really here."

"Just preoccupied," she said. "Feeling inept maybe at caring for Max Crane's baby."

"I doubt that. I do know you, and you do everything well."

"That's a stretch," Rachel murmured. In her family people didn't brag about their accomplishments. They didn't pat each other on the back. When she'd first met Jason, she'd found it hard to believe how open his parents were, how accepting of her. Ironically, it was Chad who'd been the easiest member of Jason's family for her to relate to. His friendly manner and his almost puppy dog behavior were, at first, irresistible. Tempted to tell Nell about his phone call, she remained mum.

"Where's Zoey tonight?" Nell asked. "We were hoping you'd bring her."

"Not this time. Max is home." She added, "Maybe I'm just sleep-deprived. He and I take turns at night when that should be my duty with Zoey, but I honestly can't refuse his help. Between us we manage to get three or four hours each, at least dozing, so we're only half-exhausted most of the time. I wonder if Zoey—who's a darling, believe me— might have colic."

"How old is she?"

"One month or so."

"Ask Sawyer, but my little one started around three months. Just after Cooper and I had decided she was the world's most perfect child."

Rachel tried to laugh but the sound caught in her throat. "I'll give Sawyer a call. Probably I'm expecting too much of a newborn." Not that Rachel had any experience in her own life. She didn't want to tell Nell about her miscarriage years ago, either. They'd become friends at Rachel's first GNO get together, but they weren't yet at the stage where she felt she could confide her deepest sorrows, although everyone did seem to know about Jason.

Rachel forced herself to brighten and changed the subject. "Oh, look. What an adorable bathrobe." Annabelle had just opened another gaily wrapped package. "I love the kitten face and ears on the hood. How cute is that?"

"Very." Nell was still looking at her instead. "So. How are you and the hunky doc getting along?"

Rachel flushed, remembering the night she'd winced at Max's neutral touch and the brief discussion they'd had on the night Chad called. Partly her reaction had come from her natural reserve, her background, partly from her memories. "It's kind of awkward, but of course our primary focus is on Zoey. Not that I was looking for more. Neither is he. I mean, after Averill…"

"And your husband. I'm sorry, Rachel. That's a lot for anyone to deal with. Has Max had any luck finding Averill? I still can't believe she'd just dump the baby on his doorstep and disappear. I realize Averill had her problems, but I never thought she could be that cold."

"We weren't on good terms, really, but I don't want to say anything negative about her. And I know how concerned Max is. After all, she is the mother of his child."

"I hate to say this, but I'm hearing rumors—which I hate—that he's not Zoey's dad."

"Then I imagine you saw Lauren Anderson's article. Max took a DNA test. The results should come soon."

Her tone of voice must have told Nell to back off. "Sorry. I do love Barren and everyone in this town, but the gossip can get out of control." Nell had once told Rachel she despised people who told tales. "I did read the paper but I also know Lauren Anderson will stretch the truth to get her story. Still," she said, "I admit I'm curious. What's going on with CPS?"

"Sheriff Blake tells us not to worry. Once Max establishes paternity, he'll have parental rights no one can argue with."

"Hey," Shadow called out. "What's the big secret?" She waved her hands. "We're all over here. Come join us." Annabelle was starting to open Rachel's gift, the comforter.

Nell pulled her up from the sofa. She slung an arm around Rachel's shoulders. "Just remember. I'm always ready to lend a listening ear. I won't betray your confidence."

But Rachel had grown up with people who believed in keeping your own counsel. It wasn't seemly, her parents had said, to air personal laundry for the whole community to see. Which had included Max.

She sure wasn't about to tell him, Nell or anyone else about Chad Whittaker.

THE NEXT MORNING, Max drove over to the Circle H, where Logan Hunter wanted him to take another look at the spindly calf they'd been trying to save. to his surprise, he found the undersized bison playing in the paddock closest to the barn. "What have we here? A miracle?"

"He's eating well, moving around. Guess that second chance finally worked."

"Logan, that was a third chance. Tell the truth, I'd about written him off."

Logan punched him in the arm. "Thanks, man. I think that tonic you left for him did the trick."

"Or he has a strong will to live. Anyway, I'm glad and I imagine Sam is, too. Let's hope this calf starts to grow now. So why did you really want to see me? You could have told me about the bison on the phone, saved me the trip."

Logan looked shame-faced. "Sorry to interrupt your busy day. I know life's complicated right now with the baby, too. How are you coping?"

"We're coping." He remembered Logan's advice before. Max had indeed found a woman to help since then, but "I had my doubts about Rachel, yet she seems to be settling into the job. At least we're both trying hard." Besides, he had no other candidates if he even thought of replacing her. Their conversation last week was eating at him, though.

Their slight brushing of arms on her first night in his house had been innocent enough, but the way Rachel had jumped back as if he were about to harm her still bothered Max. She'd never said anything negative about her husband—about anything at all, really, which seemed to be her way—but there had to be a reason why she'd reacted like that.

He doubted Rachel would stick around, as Logan had hoped someone would for him. Sometimes Max thought she couldn't wait to leave.

"Is that all? The job?" Logan asked, re-capturing Max's attention. "I think you're at-tracted to her."

He blinked. "How can you tell?"

Logan grinned. "The way you say her name. I was like that with Blossom, trying to ignore my feelings for her even years after my first marriage to Olivia had blown up. I was concentrating on my boy Nick's welfare but not my own...sound familiar?"

Max shrugged because he wasn't sure he could speak. There was no use denying he found Rachel attractive, yet he didn't wel-come that feeling. And Logan's mention of his failed marriage with Olivia reminded him about his own breakup with Averill. Like Logan with his son, he had to consider Zoey. His attention had to remain on her and on the clinic that supported them. He didn't have time or the inclination for another relation-ship that might go as wrong as his and Aver-ill's had. A relationship with Rachel that she clearly didn't want.

"I do like her," he managed to say. Far more than he'd expected to. "Doesn't feel as if she likes me that much. But it's probably for the best. For both of us. I need to think of the baby."

"Kids change everything," Logan agreed. "I know Nick did. Daisy, too, for sure. Now I'm still struggling with our daughter and Blossom's campaign to have another child in our family."

"How's that going?"

"It's not." Logan rubbed his neck. "In fact, I'm in the doghouse today—or rather, the barn, which is where I intend to stay until Blossom cools down. You're right, the bison calf was an excuse to get you out here."

"What else are friends for?"

Logan shook his head. "It wasn't that she threw a pot at me last night or something, but she made her position clear. She wants a baby. Daisy does too but not one that's so little, she's now decided, which I could have told her in the first place. The baby wouldn't be a real playmate for years. I can't begin to think what to do."

"Join the club." He wondered if he should even try to breach Rachel's gates—because Logan was right. Max's issue wasn't only about the baby but his own unwanted attraction to Rachel, which surprised him. Considering her reaction to his first touch, nothing good could come from another, even in friendship. He should avoid her as she had him. "Good luck with Blossom. That's a big decision."

"One I've made before. When I finally realized how good we are for each other, and got on board with having Daisy, adopting her, things worked out. Until now. It's not a matter of not wanting another baby, which is always a blessing, but that, like I told you, we're doing okay with the four of us. Blossom, Nick, who's like a son to her, Daisy, who's my child now, and me… I love them. Why start over with an infant, up all night, having to work all day around dangerous animals on two hours' sleep—"

"Hey, you're playing my song."

Logan laughed a little. "Yeah, listen to me gripe when my situation's a lot simpler than yours right now. Baby sleeping through at all?"

"Not yet."

"But Zoey's a blessing, too, isn't she?"

"You got that right." Max started to say that another child might be good for Logan, but Logan already knew that, so he kept his mouth shut. It was Logan's problem to work out with Blossom, and he had no doubt they would. They had one of the most solid marriages in Barren, which seemed to specialize in them. "Well, I better get going. I have appointments at the clinic all afternoon."

But Logan had more to say. "Before you go, come take a look at my gelding. Seems off to me. Make the trip from town worth your while." Logan was probably making work for him so he could pay Max for the visit, which Max as a friend would try to refuse, but he went along into the barn and ran a hand over the horse's hide.

"Feels a bit warm. Let's take his temperature." The gelding had a slight fever and Max soon discovered a small abscess in his left front hoof. He gave the horse a bolus of antibiotic, left more for Logan to administer later, then walked with him out of the barn. "Should feel better by tomorrow. If he gets worse, give me another call."

"Sure will, Doc. Thanks."

Max clapped him on the shoulder. "Now stop hiding out in the barn and go talk to Blossom." One way or the other, those two had the kind of loving marriage Max would want. If he wanted one at all.

"RACHEL," SAID A SOFT, deep male voice as someone gently shook her shoulder. "Hey." That night, in Zoey's room, she roused from a deep sleep in the rocking chair to find Max bending over her. As soon as her eyes opened, he straightened with a jerk and moved closer to the changing table as if he expected her to leap up from the chair and rush out of the room. But Rachel had been in a near-coma, Zoey at last cradled against her chest. The afternoon had been rough, and she hadn't gotten anything done except to walk the floor with the baby.

"You're home," she said in a drowsy voice, stifling a yawn, and not fully aware that she'd referred to the house as if it were theirs.

"Got tied up at the clinic longer than I expected."

He'd called earlier to say he'd be late, but he'd never been this late before. Rachel had put Max's dinner in the oven on low to keep warm. "How's your patient?"

"Touch-and-go," he said. "Dog crashed after surgery. Yesterday she looked good, but just before closing tonight everything went haywire. I'm trying not to feel guilty when there wasn't much else I could do. She's stable now, but if she makes it, I'll be grateful."

"It must be hard to lose a patient."

"Animals or humans." He sent her a sympathetic look. He'd lost his parents and she had lost Jason, their baby. "Never gets any easier. Let's hope it doesn't come to that."

"Did Candi help you?"

"She'd already gone home. I called but she couldn't get away. Said the dog was fine when she left and had even eaten some wet food. Clara came in, though, bless her. She's not a tech but she did help with the crisis. Stuff happens," he said in a weary tone. "I was tempted to sleep on the couch in my office tonight but I'm hungry. And I wanted to see... Zoey. Things okay here?"

Rachel rested her head against the chair back and gazed up into his eyes, remembering Nell calling him the *hunky doc*. The name suited, and she should keep her distance, but tonight she was too tired to jump up from the chair. To resist even the slight contact when he'd touched her shoulder. In fact, she felt boneless, unable to move. Whispering, she cupped the baby's head. "Zoey drifted off after a particularly bad session of crying. I think my ears are getting used to that, but nothing seemed to soothe her. I decided to try giving her a few more ounces in her bottle, which did help, but she didn't give up until, in pure exhaustion, she closed her eyes as if she couldn't keep them open another second. We may want to try a different brand of formula."

He hunkered down in front of her, his voice still low and, it felt to Rachel, surprisingly intimate. Sky, whose feet had been moving in some doggy dream, lay by the rocking chair. She opened her eyes to look at Max, her tail thumping. He gave Sky a quick pat. "Thanks for pulling double duty. I'll take the rest of the night."

"No, you will not." She glanced at her watch. "Max, it's nearly midnight." He'd left the house before eight o'clock that morning. "You already worked a sixteen-hour day. I can stay up with Zoey." As if they were a couple who eased each other's burdens.

Rachel smoothed a hand over Zoey's back, relishing the warm feel of the baby's weight on her chest. For the first time, she didn't feel close to crying over the loss of her own never-to-be-born child, and a strange, new softness had settled inside her. It was impossible not to cherish this little one, even though she belonged to Max.

"What's all this?" he asked, gesturing at the new mess she'd made in the room.

Rachel straightened enough to look around at the paint samples, fabric swatches, a pile of decorating books she'd gotten from Sophie. She'd have to put them away in the morning. "I got brave this afternoon. When the Girls' group met last night, Nell asked why I hadn't brought Zoey. I worried that she'd be unhappy in those bright lights, with so much noise, past what you and I laughingly call her 'bedtime,' and I wouldn't know how to cope in a different setting—without this rocking chair. This morning I realized I've been hiding out in this house since I got here when I need to get other things done." She yawned behind her hand. "So, we set off for town while Zoey was in a good mood. Thanks for putting her seat in my car—just in case. We stopped at Earl's hardware to get these samples."

Max studied the array of paint chips. "They all look pink to me."

"Various shades," she murmured, stroking

Zoey's hair again. "I'm thinking this blush one for three walls, using the darker one—not that dark or it wouldn't be pink—for an accent wall. I like the rich contrast against the pure white baseboards and trim."

"You lost me," he said with a smile. Max stood, his knees popping. "I'm sure Zoey will love whatever you choose."

Pleased that she'd done something right, pleased him, she sat up, trying not to jostle the baby, who was beginning to stir. Rachel didn't feel as groggy as she had when she opened one eye to find Max right there, inches from her. Which didn't alarm her. Maybe she was starting to trust him, mainly because he wasn't Chad.

She gestured at the fabric samples. "What do you think of this cute plaid pattern with some green in it too?"

"Fine by me."

"Or would you prefer the paisley?"

Max grinned. "I don't even know what that is. You pick. I said you can do whatever you want with this room. Yours too. Go for it." His index finger rested between the pretty plaid swatch and the paisley, which although lovely, looked "older" to her. Rachel had seen an adorable, huge stuffed giraffe in a catalog with a big bow in the same shades as in the plaid or paisley. She liked its playful effect. Perfect for the far corner of the room beside some bookshelves.

"Okay," she said. "I will."

Rachel and Max gazed at each other, his brown eyes warm, her heart feeling oddly mushy, before she abruptly broke the stare, handed Zoey to him, and he looked away. Rachel stood. In the glow of the nursery's nightlight, she hurried toward the hallway with Sky padding after her. Away from Max, from a sense of something new between them that coursed through her veins.

She wasn't here to imagine the house or Zoey might be hers, that she and Max might do more than temporarily bond for practical purposes over his child. Or to fall for a man who still had another woman on his mind as she did with Jason. Averill might well come back, repentant because she'd left Zoey for a short while, and Rachel should hope that she did. Despite his promise to avoid another such complication, Max might decide to reconcile with her. And then, with their family intact, Rachel would be looking for another job.

"I'll get your dinner," she called back to him. "Rachel."

She couldn't afford to indulge in even a casual fantasy. With Jason, their plans for a family, a home, a future had also died. Even her in-laws seemed off-limits to her now because of Chad. She wasn't close to her own parents, who weren't exactly supportive, and in fact Rachel rarely spoke with them. As for Max... She needed to make sure that long exchange of looks didn't happen again. Rachel should be like him with Sky, tolerant but basically aloof.

She went down the stairs, hoping his meal hadn't dried out in the oven. She would decorate Zoey's nursery. Do her job here for as long as it lasted.

And that was all.

She needed to remember that.

CHAPTER TEN

"THIS IS WHAT I have to look forward to, huh?" At the WB ranch the next day, Max lifted Cody and Willow Jones's toddler into his arms. The chubby little guy, who had his mom's flaxen blond hair—and his dad's merry dark eyes—immediately wriggled to get down. A second later, he was tottering across the yard, laughing as he chased one of the barn cats.

Cody grinned. "I have to tell you, I'm head over heels about that kid. I don't know what Willow and I did before he came along." He rolled his eyes. "Except have time for us. Our love life's suffering these days, while her mom's already asking when we're going to have a second one. Jean wanted a girl."

"After raising her two boys, why not," Max said. "Zach and Noah were handfuls."

"That's what Jean says, but she's only joshing. She loves them, too." Cody whistled through his teeth. "Harper, leave that kitten alone."

The boy didn't listen. Harper Jones had a mind of his own. Just like his dad. Willow was strong-willed too, so it shouldn't surprise Max that their firstborn had followed in their footsteps. Harper, still learning to navigate on the uneven ground, stumbled and lurched, giggling, up the slight hill toward the house. Willow appeared in the kitchen doorway and waved at Max. Then, with Cody watching as if to make sure his son reached her safely, she scooped up Harper and shut the door.

"She's got him," Cody said, sounding relieved. "I worry."

"What parent doesn't? I've been a basket case since Zoey came into my life. I don't want to think about when she starts walking. She's growing so fast I can see it happen."

"That's how it goes," Cody agreed. "So. How's Rachel Whittaker working out?"

Max didn't know why that subject had come up, as it had with Logan yesterday, but he supposed the whole town must be talking. "Good," was all he said.

He was still thinking about last night when he found Rachel sleeping with Zoey in the nursery, both of their faces so unguarded, peaceful. His heart had melted like ice cream dripping from a cone. What was that intense stare he and Rachel had exchanged about? Only the day before when he'd talked with Logan, Max had realized his feelings for Rachel weren't quite so simple as he'd thought. His track record had shown him that he wasn't relationship material. He'd reminded himself then that he wasn't looking for anyone—except Averill, of course.

"The arrangement's okay, then?"

"Sure. Rachel's great." But the taut statement sounded hollow. He and Cody were friends but not close enough for him to confide in about Rachel. Which wouldn't be fair to her. Max thought about her plans to decorate, the way they'd ended up talking… and how she'd rushed from the room again just when he'd thought they were more comfortable with each other. Max would never harm her, or any woman. He'd be a fool to try something she didn't want, then be charged with harassment on the job. Not that he would even think of pulling a stunt like that. Cody's grin had widened. "What?"

"From the instant I first saw Willow, I was a goner."

Max knew their story hadn't been all moonlight and roses. Cody had gotten on the wrong side of the law years ago, stealing cattle from Grey Wilson's spread with two other guys, and no one had faulted Willow's dad for insisting that his daughter drop her then-boyfriend Cody like a hot rock. But after some time in prison, Cody had turned his life around and eventually, he and Willow had reunited, fallen in love all over again and married. Like Logan and Blossom's marriage, theirs seemed to be a good one, and Max felt a twinge of envy so unfamiliar that he almost didn't recognize it. "We're not like that," he muttered.

"Why not?"

How did his friends, Logan and now Cody, both pick up on those feelings Max didn't welcome? For that brief time the night before, he'd felt a real connection between him and Rachel. She had also commiserated with him about his sick patient, his long hours, but that must all be because of Zoey. It had to be. She'd stayed up with the baby afterward to let him sleep, struggling this morning as she made coffee not to let him see how tired she was. Just as he didn't want her to see how their conversation had unsettled him.

As if they had a real relationship when he'd vowed not to get involved with anyone.

"Cody. I have enough with Zoey, and looking for Averill… Why would I start something with Rachel Whittaker?"

"Why not?" Cody asked again.

Max didn't answer. Rachel wasn't the only one who had fears. For one thing, he doubted he could provide enough emotional support for whatever was troubling her. Certainly, he hadn't been able to with Averill. What if he did express these fragile feelings for Rachel and, horrified, she left?

He started toward the nearby corral and Cody followed. Max had come to reexamine a mare he'd performed a hysterectomy on last week. "Star looks good," he said after a brief inspection of the bay. "Incision's healing nicely. I'd let her out a bit close to home in another couple of days. Don't send her off with the others too far or too soon."

Cody nodded. "You did a great job, Doc." He paused before going on. "But about you and Rachel, I have a suggestion. Does she ride?"

There was no him and Rachel. "Not that I know of," he said.

"Bring her over sometime. We've got a real gentle gelding here. I bought him for Harper, but that was premature. Should have known better. Willow wanted to kick me clear into next Sunday. Our boy's not ready for a pony, either. She doesn't even want me putting him up on my Diva in front of me, but the new horse could use some exercise."

Max said, "I don't think—"

"Free of charge. Rachel must need a break now and then." Cody described the horse. "If she spends an hour or two on this ranch, gets acquainted with Buck, hops on, you could even join her. You can't work all the time either."

Max shook his head. Spend time together like that outside of work? Away from his clinic and her duties with Zoey? He suspected that idea would never fly with Rachel, but he wouldn't know unless he ran it by her, and it held a certain appeal. It wasn't as if they'd be alone.

Cody said, "Just a thought."

Max thanked him, but as he drove back to the clinic, his mind was all over the place. He shouldn't encourage any activity with Rachel other than those centered on Zoey. He was her employer, nothing more. Yet the memory of last night in the nursery rode with him. So did that sight of her in the rocking chair, her face smoothed out in sleep, her body relaxed as she rarely seemed to be around him.

Whatever had happened to her to cause that anxiety wasn't his fault.

And Max didn't want to push her too far. Still. It hurt to watch her jump back from him like he'd done something wrong. What harm could there be in at least passing on Cody's suggestion?

"Buck?" Rachel stared at Max, who'd come home earlier than he normally did. "You think I'd go anywhere near a horse with that name? Cody Jones must have some grudge against me that I don't know about."

"He thought you might like a change of scenery, that's all."

"You hired me to take care of Zoey and run this house, not to hang out in some barn. What am I not hearing?"

Max picked through a pile of mail from the entryway table. "The horse may have an off-putting name, but Cody claims he's gentle. He's sound, not too large for you, has a kind eye. I bet he keeps all four feet on the ground. You wouldn't have to pay to ride. Cody was insistent about that. He offered in part because Buck's been out in the pasture or stuck in his stall since Cody bought him." Max explained about Harper being too young to ride yet, even on a pony. "He'd like to see the horse get more exercise."

"In my spare time?" Rachel murmured. There hadn't been any from the first day she'd stepped into Max's house. Tonight, in part because he'd come home early, she hadn't started dinner yet. Zoey would wake up any minute now from what had, thankfully, turned into a two-hour nap. The little night owl would probably be wide awake for half the night. Rachel had used the unexpected interlude this afternoon to straighten the rooms, dust furniture and mop floors. She half expected Deborah Neal from CPS to show up again, especially after Lauren's article in the paper. "I appreciate Cody Jones's suggestion, but I won't be taking him up on it. There aren't enough hours in the day and I've never—"

"—ridden?"

"A few times when I used babysitting money to pay for a trail ride with friends. But not like Cody or Willow, Nell or even Annabelle when she's not pregnant…any one of a dozen people here who own ranches and ride every day." She waited until Max looked up from the stack of mail he'd been sorting. "And what about you? If Cody wants to exercise his horse, you should do it instead of me."

Max avoided her gaze. "I'm a vet. I take care of animals that other people ride."

"You're at barns every day. You don't like horses?"

"I do," he said, "but I leave them—except for giving shots or treating illness, injuries— to their owners. More than a few people have tried to turn me into a cowboy, and Gabe keeps telling me to buy some cattle, but I'm not interested right now. When would I find the time?"

"Are you afraid of them?"

"Gabe, Cody, even Logan can be prickly at times—"

"I meant horses, as you must know." He was trying to distract her. What wasn't he telling her? Rachel smiled anyway. Sometimes he was very cute, not only in a physical way with that boyish cowlick in his dark hair. She liked his wry sense of humor.

"You are, aren't you?"

Max frowned at an envelope in his hand. "Averill is—was—afraid, I'm not. If I were, any horse can sense fear and get the upper hand. Sophie, who was never around horses, has actually learned to ride, which is a good thing because now she's married to a cowboy and living on a ranch."

Rachel still thought he wasn't telling her everything but was enjoying herself. "I think I'll call the WB, let Cody know. I have to admire you, though, for trying to transfer his offer to me when it must be for you instead."

"That's not what I was doing." Max was silent for a moment. "Rachel, no one's forcing you to do anything. I'm sure not. We agreed that—" He broke off, staring at the envelope in his hand as if he'd just realized who it was from, then tore it open.

For one instant, Rachel feared it was a letter from Child Protective Services, a report on Deborah Neal's visit, even a court order about Zoey. Max would be devastated to lose her. He'd have to hire a lawyer, petition for custody… "What is it, Max?"

His voice quavered. "The DNA results. Zoey's mine," he said, shaking his head as if he couldn't quite believe what he'd read. "I always thought—I *knew*—but this makes it official. We're a perfect match. I'm Zoey's dad." Rachel saw tears in his eyes.

She snatched the page from his hands to see for herself, then let out a happy cry. "Oh, Max, what wonderful news." Before she recognized the impulse to throw her arms around his neck, she'd done just that. Max's arms came around her waist and he kissed Rachel on the cheek. Then, when he should have stepped back or she should have pushed him away, he lowered his head and touched his mouth to hers. The brief kiss went through her, flowed along her veins like warm honey, along with the memory of last night in the nursery, the long look they'd shared that had seemed to mean something important, and new, to both of them.

In a flash of sanity, Rachel came to her senses and so did Max.

Quickly, he turned away and she all but ran into the kitchen. She began pulling ingredients for dinner from the fridge, the pantry, her heart beating a quick tattoo. She should race upstairs, see to Zoey, but couldn't seem to move in that direction. When she turned around, he was leaning against the doorframe, a grin lighting his face before it vanished and he frowned.

"Rachel. Should I apologize? I never planned to—"

"No, it's fine," she said, desperate to restore the balance of their relationship as caregiver and official dad. "We should celebrate," which didn't sound right, either, as she reached for the lone bottle of wine on a shelf. "Your DNA results," she clarified.

Max obviously agreed. He opened the bottle and poured two glasses, his hand trembling a little, then they toasted. "To Zoey."

"To you," she added, taking a sip. "I'm so happy for you, Max. She's safe with you now. You won't have anything to worry about—except Averill's whereabouts."

"I'll talk to Travis Blake again. See what else needs to be done now before—if—Averill comes back. Or I find her."

Rachel touched his shoulder before she thought better of it. He was about to speak, warmth in his eyes, when the baby monitor on the kitchen counter squawked, and she heard

Zoey cry out from the nursery. Ten minutes more, and Rachel would have had dinner cooking. Now that would have to wait. Zoey would need a diaper change, a bottle had to be prepared…

She was halfway to the stairs when Max spoke.

"I'll get Zoey," he said. "Don't bother with supper. I'll call for some takeout. What if we have Jack deliver a feast tonight from the Bon Appetit?"

"Fancy," Rachel said.

"You wanted a celebration, that's what we'll have."

As if they were indeed a couple, a family with Zoey, and Rachel was truly, permanently, a part of their lives. Tonight, she could almost believe in such a fantasy after all. Almost.

"Béarnaise sauce," she said, her mouth already watering. She loved Jack Hancock's petite filet. She'd set the table in the dining room with the best silver, the good china that had belonged to Max's mother, the sparkling crystal glassware that resided in the high cupboard. She and Max—with Zoey as an interested observer—would share a festive meal.

And Rachel would try to forget that kiss. She hoped Max did, too.

At least she'd forgotten Cody Jones's offer—and Buck.

CHAPTER ELEVEN

TRAVIS HAD SPENT the next morning in court on a traffic case. Afterward, he drove back from Farrier to Barren, picked up lunch from the café, then left the restaurant to find Max leaning against the passenger side of the Stewart County SUV. Travis raised his eyebrows. "Don't tell me. I'm under citizen's arrest for parking past the time on the meter." He grinned. There were no meters in town and all spaces were free.

Max didn't smile. "I need to talk to you. Here okay or should I meet you at your office?"

"Here's fine. I need a break. One of the townsfolk decided last Saturday night to ignore the red light—the only light in Barren—after an evening spent at Rowdy's bar. I pulled him over, then gave him a Breathalyzer test, which was off the charts, only to have the guy resist arrest. He got off today in court with community service plus a mandatory stint in

AA. A repeat offender…" Travis trailed off. He could see now that Max appeared shaken. "You hear again from CPS?"

"No."

"What about the DNA?"

Max nodded. "Zoey and I are a match. Father and daughter. The baby's mine, although my name's still not on her birth certificate."

"Which was Averill's right." Travis pushed his Stetson back farther on his head. "I dug into those databases but came up with nothing about her. However—"

Max had turned pale. He blurted out the words. "I just heard from her."

"What?"

"Averill. I was in surgery earlier when she called, but afterward when I checked my phone, she'd left a voice mail." His tone hoarse, he repeated the message. 'I'm sorry, Max. I'll explain soon. How's the baby?'"

The news shocked Travis too. "So. Considering the note you got before, and this message, it seems Averill definitely left town of her own accord. As an adult she also has that right to go anywhere she pleases—and not come back if that suits her, too."

"Even when she clearly abandoned Zoey?"

There was a short silence. Travis had just gotten a glimpse of Lauren Anderson coming out of the Bon Appetit then going into a store next door. She had been at the courthouse earlier, too, but Travis had avoided making eye contact with the pesky reporter who was obviously sniffing out another story. Not about him, he hoped. She'd gone into the courtroom then next door, thank goodness, but it had taken him the entire drive back to Barren to stop having palpitations. He was having a hard time now keeping his attention on Max's problem, which did concern Travis.

"Willful abandonment," he said at last. "The definition varies from state to state, and I'd have to look up the timing here, but that could be defined as anywhere from six months to a year. If Averill has really given up her child and hasn't supported her in that time, it's better that Zoey has been with you, Max. As her biological father caring for her in a responsible manner, you'd get full custody."

"So, what do I do now as far as the state's concerned?"

"You'll want to petition the court, get that birth certificate amended, establish your proof of paternity, which you now have. I believe there's another form to fill out—no surprise." Travis saw Lauren leave the store next to the restaurant then march toward her car, which was parked across the street in front of the Baby Things shop. He laid a hand on Max's shoulder. "You really love that little girl, don't you?"

"Yeah." Max smiled. "Now, if she'd only sleep through the night."

They exchanged a few more words before Max seemed to remember that he had an appointment at Wilson Cattle. As he drove off, Travis saw Lauren turn. She spied him, too, then started across the street. "Sheriff Blake."

He felt his stomach take a nosedive. "What can I do for you?"

"Stop avoiding me. You ducked into the courtroom over in Farrier before I could even say hello."

"I didn't know you wanted to." But if he'd been standing on the driver's side of his SUV while talking to Max, he would have gotten in and gunned it down Main Street. Now he was trapped. Travis leaned against the passenger side of the truck. "Start talking because my lunch is getting cold."

"Maybe we could picnic at the park. Get better acquainted."

"Haven't you already eaten?"

"Jack didn't have a table. I don't need to eat. I'll watch you." And ask questions.

"I don't see the point," he said, studying his boots. "I have no information on Max—or rather, Averill McCafferty, to share."

She batted her eyelashes. "You just don't want to."

He didn't disagree. Was she flirting with him? He was out of practice with women, and he had no interest in striking up a friendship with Lauren, much less getting involved.

"I wasn't happy about that little hit piece you did on Max."

"All right, then. Business." She shook her head. "I kept wondering why you were so dis-interested—personally, it seemed—in help-ing me write that story for the *Journal*. So, I've done a little research. And guess what? You're not just a small-town sheriff—"

"County sheriff," he said.

"—who spends all his time writing traffic citations and appearing in court on DUI/resist-ing arrest cases. No, your history's far more interesting."

Travis crossed his arms. The palpitations

were back, stronger than before. He could be about to drop dead right here in the street, but he kept his voice cool. "I wouldn't call my background interesting."

"FBI. Special agent, Wichita office. Glamorous stuff, Sheriff."

"If you had the job, you wouldn't think so. It's mostly pushing paper around."

"And I've only gotten started."

Like a lifeline, his phone buzzed, and Travis glanced at the screen. "I have to respond to a call." He brushed past Lauren, around to the driver's side of the SUV, and hopped in. "Step back," he called out, not meaning just from the vehicle.

"Not on your life," she said, seeking safety on the curb.

There'd been an accident down on Cottonwood Street. Sounded like a fender bender, but he wouldn't tell Lauren about that or she'd show up at the scene. He was still shaking when he turned the corner a block down and saw an old pickup's front end jammed against the rear of Clara McMann's car.

RACHEL WASN'T A fan of Lauren Anderson. She didn't know anyone in town who was. So, when Rachel came out of the Baby Things

shop with Zoey and saw the town's star reporter about to get in her car, she tried to
hurry the other way through the icy slush.
After her previous outing with Zoey, she'd felt
brave enough to do more shopping. As tiny as
she was, the baby had grown enough to need
new clothes and after buying several packs
of onesies and an irresistible peach-colored
outfit, Rachel needed to pick up her weekly
check at Shadow's agency, which handled the
pay for her clients.

Unfortunately, Lauren had seen her pushing, or rather shoving, the convertible stroller
along the frozen sidewalk. "Rachel Whittaker."

"Oh. Lauren." Caught, she stopped and
turned. "Nice day, isn't it?"

"If you like twenty-degree weather."

"I'm a Midwesterner, used to winter—and
snow."

Lauren, who claimed to be from New
Mexico originally, wrapped her scarf tighter
around her throat. "If I get my chance, which
I believe I will, I'll see this town in my rearview mirror. I'd prefer sunny California, the
LA Times, or Arizona, the *Republic*, except
for the summer heat in Phoenix. Frankly, I'd

accept another position in either place. As long as the newspaper offered me a tempting package. How's your new job? Miss the library?"

Rachel imagined that Lauren was in no position, like her, to be choosy. "I do miss it, seeing people all day, but Zoey's a darling."

"And Max?" Those two words seemed loaded with innuendo.

Rachel tried to push away the memory of their easy conversation last night, that shared kiss. She should think instead about watching Max with Zoey, the tender way he held her, the look in his eyes when their gazes held. "He's a good dad."

"If that's true," Lauren murmured.

Rachel didn't want to air Max's private business, especially with a reporter who was always looking for the next story, but Lauren had already written about Max so Rachel decided to set her straight. "He got the DNA results yesterday. Proof that he and Zoey are father and daughter." She hoped that would satisfy, and silence, Lauren.

"I do wonder about Averill's take on all this, and when she's coming back. The courts claim to be neutral about parents' rights, not preferring to give custody to one or the other, but in my experience, they tend to favor the mother. What will he do—having adjusted to fatherhood so beautifully—if Averill decides to sue for custody?"

"I'm sure he'll cross that bridge if he comes to it." Rachel leaned over to refold Zoey's blanket and had to smile at the baby, not only to ease her own discomfort.

Lauren was studying her when Rachel straightened from the stroller. "If Travis Blake doesn't, or can't, find Averill, perhaps I can. I have my sources, too."

Rachel didn't respond. She could see why others in town avoided Lauren, and why they'd been happy to see Sophie win the award instead two summers ago as Citizen of the Year. In the end, there hadn't been any contest. In Rachel's mind—and she wasn't alone—Sophie was by far the better citizen and, equally important, a better person.

"You have to admit," Lauren said, "there's a real story here. The poor abandoned baby, the mysterious missing mother who left her behind so soon after giving birth, the belea-guered dad who, if I've heard correctly, did not intend to have a child." She waited a beat before adding, "And then there's you. Living in his house, or is that playing house?"

Rachel stiffened, and their kiss was suddenly center front in her mind again. She could feel her face heat. "There is nothing between me and Maxwell Crane. I believe you already covered that subject." But even Lauren's tone had hinted at a juicier story than the one she'd already published. Rachel pushed the stroller forward, but its wheels got stuck in the slush piled at the edge of the sidewalk. So much for her dramatic exit.

Lauren bent down to free the wheels. "Done," she said with a smile. "See you in print."

She headed back toward her car parked in front of Sherry's store.

"Oh, dear," Rachel told the baby. "Now what have I done?"

She had no doubt that Lauren would use the little information she had given her.

Not in Max's favor.

BACK AT THE clinic after his off-site appointment at Wilson Cattle, Max discovered Clara missing from the front desk. The phone was ringing, and he snatched it up. His trip to Wilson Cattle had been a bust. By the time he got there, after talking to Travis about Averill on the street, Grey had had the situation with a rank horse under control, and thankfully the animal hadn't been injured after sliding on ice in the barnyard. "Crane Veterinary," Max said to the caller.

He heard a woman's panicked voice. "I'm traveling through town to California, and Cuddles, my ferret, is having trouble breathing. Can you help him?"

Max didn't hesitate. "Bring Cuddles in. I'll see you now." He gave the woman directions, then called out for Candi, his vet tech. Where was she? Max was ready to admit that she wasn't the best he'd ever hired. Her recent excuse that she couldn't come in to help with the dog that had crashed after surgery because she had to run to Farrier for the last night of a sale at the mall hadn't set well with Max. Maybe he'd have to let her go. Not that there were people standing in line to take her job.

He thought about how lucky he'd been to find Rachel. Yet maybe he shouldn't have celebrated with her last night. Certainly, he shouldn't have kissed her, even when she'd put her arms around his neck first. He'd hoped that having Rachel in his house wouldn't prove dangerous to his peace of mind, but their kiss—and his unexpressed feelings—had changed things. Max didn't know how to deal with that.

He needed to focus on his work.

The dog he'd saved after a postsurgery crash seemed to be holding its own today in the rear kennel area. Comfortable, and eating well. Which satisfied Max, leaving him the ferret to deal with now. "Candi!" he yelled. Besides that emergency on the way, Max had more appointments scheduled. They would soon be arriving.

Candi appeared in the doorway to the kennels. "Sorry, I was feeding Mrs. Higley's cat."

"Beauty? Why is she here?"

"She came in after you left the clinic. Mrs. Higley is certain she has a sinus infection."

"Which requires hospital care?" Max rolled his eyes. "Prepare room one for an incoming emergency." He issued instructions for the equipment he might need, not that ferrets were his area of expertise. He'd started for his office when the main door opened, and Clara came in, looking white-faced.

"I'm late," she said, her voice shaking. "I

stepped out for lunch, then to change an appointment at Doc Sawyer's—and got rear-ended on Cottonwood Street. Then the sheriff came. Max, I didn't mean to leave you so long without someone at the desk."

"That doesn't matter. Sit down, Clara." He guided her to a sofa in the waiting room and tried, without appearing to, to conduct a visual exam for any injuries, even illness. Lately she'd seemed flushed, short of breath, and now she looked frighteningly pale. "Were you wearing your seat belt?"

"Yes, of course."

Which didn't reassure him. The restraints were necessary, but whenever airbags went off, they carried a lot of force and many people ended up bruised anyway. Clara might even have whiplash or a possible concussion. "Why didn't you go to the emergency room?"

"I told Travis Blake I felt fine. He tried to insist, but I was already overdue at work."

"Clara, you're a lot more important to me than this front desk."

"Don't fuss." She tried to change the subject. "Did you and Rachel have a nice dinner last night?" Max had been so excited about the DNA results, he'd called Clara to tell her, too.

"We did, but..." What was he going to do about that kiss?

"I'm so glad things are working out well for you both. And how is Zoey?"

"She actually slept four straight hours last night." Leaving him and Rachel to pretend to ignore each other as they watched TV. "We're—I'm hopeful that she's starting to turn around. I can't imagine what it will be like when she sleeps all night."

"You have Rachel to help, and what a lovely person she is."

"She's doing a great job."

"And personally? I'm sure you've noticed by now that she's also a very pretty woman."

"Clara." As if he were so dense he couldn't see how attractive Rachel was. "Neither of us wants a relationship—beyond that of employer/employee." A reminder that he obviously needed himself today.

"Maxwell Crane, just because you and Averill didn't work out, you mustn't shut yourself off. I doubt Rachel would even think of breaking your heart."

"Clara, quit. Stop matchmaking." How had he let her switch topics when a car accident was nothing to ignore? Especially if she had some underlying health issue? "I want you to go home, rest, take it easy for a while." He didn't like her lack of color. "No, I'd rather you saw a doctor first. Travis was right. Let me have Candi drive you over to see Sawyer."

Clara started to protest. "You may be right…" she said in a weak voice, then didn't finish. She pressed one hand to her chest, said "Oh. It hurts," then passed out on the sofa.

CHAPTER TWELVE

BARREN DID NOT have a hospital, but Rachel reached the emergency room at Farrier General in record time. She'd still been in Barren after her troubling talk with Lauren when Max called. As she rushed into the waiting room, lugging the baby carrier, she spied him pacing the area, which was all but empty. He looked stricken, his face as white as bleached flour. "How is Clara?" Rachel asked.

"She's being stabilized. I hope." He ran a hand over his face. "When she collapsed, I thought my heart would stop. You should have seen her, Rachel. And where was Candi, my tech? She was supposed to be setting up for an emergency patient. Instead, she was on the phone with her boyfriend. I would have fired her on the spot, but that would mean leaving the clinic unattended. Heaven knows how she's managing now. I had to refer that patient to a vet here in Farrier—not ideal, considering the extra drive, and assuming Candi gave her the right directions."

"I'm so sorry, Max. Is there anything I can do?"

"Nothing for either of us right now. She's in Sawyer's hands." Clara's physician, Max told her, had rushed to the hospital to confer with the emergency room doctor as soon as he heard about her collapse.

"Capable hands," Rachel assured him. "He's wonderful at the clinic with Zoey. Come, sit down." She pulled him toward a sofa, then set the baby carrier at his feet. "Let me get you some coffee."

Max nodded, his gaze fixed on Zoey. By the time Rachel returned, juggling two coffees and a plate of doughnuts, he was standing again, carrying Zoey back and forth across the room. "Here, Max, let me take her. You need caffeine—and carbs."

He took one sip, then set the cup down on the coffee table. He reached for Zoey again, as if she were his comfort. "I thought Clara was going to die right there in my waiting room. I've never been so scared in my life." He hesitated. "Except when my own parents were killed," he said, shaking his head. "I realized today that I see Clara not only as a friend or coworker but a kind of surrogate mother. When Averill left my clinic, Clara stepped in to take the job, but that's not all she does. It was Clara who organized me the day Zoey was left at my door, she's the one who soothes my patients, keeps the clinic running like a clock…" He trailed off, as if there were something to add but he didn't want to.

"I know," Rachel murmured, patting his arm.

"She's the mainstay of our town. Single-handedly she helped Hadley Smith turn his life around, gave him a place to live, the love he'd never known as a kid. Years later as an adult he came back like a homing pigeon, re-paid Clara by saving her ranch—which had lain fallow after her husband died—and with his wife and children has given her an ex-tended family again."

As he spoke, the waiting room doors swished open again and Hadley himself stormed into the waiting room. "What's the deal?" he asked Max. Right behind him his wife, Jenna, ap-peared, crying.

Rachel guided her to a chair. A tense si-lence settled over the small group that had gathered to keep vigil for Clara. Hadley's normally steely blue eyes were filled with concern, his big frame seeming too large for the small waiting room space.

"I can't lose her," he kept saying, then, "Where's Sawyer? What's taking so long?"

Jenna did her best to calm him, but she looked shattered, too. Rachel knew Clara was like a mother-in-law to her and doted on Jenna's small daughter as she did Hadley's twins from his first marriage.

"She's the kindest person I know," Jenna said with a sniff.

The inner doors finally opened, and Sawyer, who had privileges at Farrier General, came out, his eyes serious. They all rushed over to him. "She's stable, but not out of the woods yet. She's being admitted and I've asked for a cardio consult." He tried to smile. "Wouldn't you know, though, she's in there trying to solve everyone else's problems? Giving the nurses advice on their love lives." He smoothed a hand over his dark hair. "She's had what appears to be a mild heart attack from the tests we've run. She already had an appointment scheduled with me. Has she been complaining of chest pains, fatigue?"

"No," Max and Hadley said at once, and Max added, "Not until today." Then, "No complaints, but I have noticed some shortness of breath and that she hasn't seemed quite well."

"Knowing Clara, maybe she's been hiding symptoms. The cardiologist will be able to tell us more. I wouldn't assume the accident is related, although that stress wouldn't help, and she can't have visitors right now. You all might as well go home."

"We're not going anywhere," Max said for the group.

Hadley got in Sawyer's face. He pointed a meaty finger at the closed doors to the exam rooms. His powerful build loomed over the doctor. "Listen to me. You have the most important patient in there that you've ever had—get that? If anything happens on your watch to Clara—" His voice broke on her name.

"Hadley." Jenna touched his shoulder. "Sawyer is doing everything he can." She sent the doctor an apologetic look. With her quiet manner, her soft blue eyes, she was a perfect fit for the rougher, often blunt Hadley, who did have a tender heart but a tough exterior.

"No, I understand," Sawyer said, his tone gentle. "We all feel the same way."

He disappeared through the swinging doors to the exam rooms and for the next few hours everyone huddled together in the waiting area.

Rachel said a few prayers and, with Zoey in her carrier again, sat close to Max. In a distracted tone, he told her about Averill's voice mail message, but that didn't seem to matter at the moment. Eventually, her hand crept into his, the gesture feeling natural. Even Lauren Anderson's prying interview today on the street finally left her mind.

She would have to tell Max. But later. Not while he was so obviously hurting about Clara. Even Zoey seemed to know that her daddy needed her to keep smiling, cooing, just being there. She hadn't fussed at all.

It wasn't long before the word had spread, and the entire waiting room filled with citizens of Barren. The women brought positive energy, the men their strength and quiet understanding. Rachel saw more than one cowboy with tears in his eyes.

"There isn't a person in town who doesn't love Clara," Max said, blinking.

That included Rachel. She didn't know Clara as well as he did but liked her immensely.

When almost everyone had left except Rachel, Max and the Smiths, Hadley sent a reluctant Jenna home too. Their children had stayed at the NLS ranch with Nell's grandfather and his wife, who were neighbors, but they would soon need to be put to bed at home.

After Jenna had gone, Hadley was the first one on his feet as Sawyer came through the doors again. Rachel couldn't tell from his expression whether the news would be good or bad, and Max, gripping her hand, looked as taut as a strand of fence wire.

Sawyer blew out a breath. "She's doing better and, although still in some danger, I'm hoping further tests will indicate only minor damage to the heart muscle. It was good she reached the hospital as quickly as she did. In other words, her prognosis may be good. The cardiologist has seen her, and she's been moved to a room upstairs. Not ICU," he added as if that might fully ease their minds.

Rachel sagged in Max's arms, and Hadley looked as if he wanted to do the same.

No one seemed able to say anything but "Thank you," repeatedly.

It wasn't until sometime later when Rachel stepped outside into the chilly night that she could think of anything except Clara. She buckled Zoey into her car seat, then got behind the wheel, her mind spinning with the events of the day as she checked her phone.

And saw a new text from Chad.

RACHEL HAD GOTTEN to the house before Max did. Worried about Clara, he wasn't in the mood to eat the quick meal Rachel had prepared. His stomach was in knots. While she went upstairs to settle Zoey for the night—part of the night anyway—he picked at his food. What if Clara's prognosis didn't prove to be as hopeful as Sawyer had said? Maybe he'd been trying to allay everyone's fears and her test results would be worse than expected. A year and more ago, Max wouldn't have dwelled on the matter like this; if he remembered, or Sophie reminded him, he would have sent Clara flowers, dived back into his work at the clinic and gone about his life, which then had included Averill.

He tried to occupy his thoughts by checking on the ferret, which had survived. The Farrier vet would transfer the woman's pet to Max's clinic in the morning.

His phone beside him, he was still sitting at the kitchen table, pushing around a gray veggie burger on his plate, when Rachel came downstairs.

"Stop fretting," she said. "Clara is a strong person. She'll get through this."

Max didn't answer. Normally, Rachel might persist as she did whenever he lost confidence with Zoey, but now Max could see she felt troubled, too.

"Can't help worrying," he murmured. "Everybody in this town must feel the way we do tonight. Clara's always been the most energetic woman I know, especially at her age. She keeps going like the Energizer bunny."

"Which, according to Sawyer, may or may not have contributed to her heart attack." Rachel sank down onto a chair, then pushed her plate away.

"You don't like veggie burgers?" Max asked.

"My attempt to feed us more healthily, but I'm not hungry. It's hard to believe she's lying in that hospital bed tonight."

"It's the best place for her right now."

"It felt like the whole town turned out—even when they couldn't see her yet."

Max eyed Rachel. "So, what else is on your mind?"

She toyed with her unused fork. "I hate to tell you this, but I ran into Lauren Anderson today. I didn't want to bring that up before, but she seems overly interested in Zoey, but even more about you and me." Rachel told him what the woman had said. "If she writes another story, Max, she's going to put an even more negative spin on this situation. It may not bother you that people talk, that some in Barren will think we're 'living in sin,' but CPS may agree that it's not a good home situation for Zoey."

"Deborah Neal's report cleared me," he reminded Rachel. He'd shown her the positive result of the visit from CPS as soon as it arrived. "And Zoey's a *baby*," he insisted. "She can't know if we're single, married, just co-workers of a sort or whatever."

"I know, but I'm sure you haven't forgotten how Lauren went after Gabe Morgan, how driven she is to find that next big story, to resurrect her former status as a hotshot reporter on the move, ready for the biggest market in this country. Remember, she was fired in Chicago for falsifying a story—"

"Failing to check the facts," he said, which wasn't the same thing. Still, Lauren had botched her job and fallen from grace.

"I realize Sophie might say I have a penchant for judging people unfairly, being too quick to 'do the right thing,' but I've heard Lauren often enough, boasting about her dreams of the *LA Times*, or another prominent newspaper. It's no secret she's unhappy being stuck in Barren. And Zoey's story—we—could still be her ticket out."

"I doubt that." But his stomach had flipped over. "I think you're overreacting. Maybe she's just nosy. Besides, CPS inspected this house. And I've talked to Deborah Neal since I read her report. Now that I have proof of paternity, what else can she or anyone do?"

"I have no idea, but I don't trust Lauren. Half the time these days news reports seem slanted—and she's a features writer. She could also say anything she wanted in her weekly column, and whether it was true or not, you'd have to defend yourself. I don't know how much real influence she has, but she can stir up trouble."

Max slumped in his chair. She had a point. "Travis Blake tells me I probably can't claim what he calls 'willful abandonment' of Zoey by Averill for some time." His mouth hardened. "I wish I could find her, straighten out any possible custody issue. Who knows what will happen if Averill does turn up? Even her voice mail message didn't clarify things."

"Can't Travis help with that search?"

"Not his jurisdiction. Her last known address was just outside Stewart County. He's trying to find her unofficially, but—" Max broke off. "What if he does? What if Averill decides she wants to be a mother after all? I could end up in a real battle for Zoey then."

"Don't borrow trouble." Rachel was frowning, though.

"You're not upset only about Lauren or Clara. Even Zoey. What is it?"

She tried a shrug. "I heard from my brother-in-law," she said, moving her full plate back and forth on the table. "He and I have a 'unique' relationship. It always throws me to have any contact with him."

"Is this guy what you wouldn't talk about?" Rachel was skirting the issue, not meeting his gaze. Had she moved to Barren to get away from him? "Rachel. Whatever this is about could affect Zoey, too." He was worried now about Rachel and Zoey as well as Clara. Sophie would be amazed by his sensitivity.

"It's awkward. He…doesn't seem to understand," Rachel said. "My life is different now when he wants it to be the same—or the same as it was soon after Jason died. Too soon," she added with what Max interpreted as a guilty look. Maybe it wasn't only her brother-in-law she worried about but her own part in that relationship.

She rose from her seat, gathered their dishes and went to the sink.

"That's all you have to say?"

"Tonight, yes." Case closed. Again. He could almost hear her mouth snap shut.

Max wanted to press her but for now that seemed futile. Still, the last thing he or Zoey needed was the threat of a domestic disturbance in their home. Then, after all, Max would have to worry about CPS again.

RACHEL STOOD AT her window, peering out into the night, her fingernails pressed so deeply into the palms of her hands there must be half-moon indentations in the skin. She hadn't been able, couldn't bring herself, to tell Max everything about Chad. That wasn't his obligation. He needed to protect Zoey. But she also had to consider the risky situation she might be putting Max and Zoey in. After all, she was living in their house. What exactly could she do about Chad?

There'd been a time when she would have welcomed him with open arms. Which was a big part of the problem. From the first, she'd liked his open personality in contrast to her own, more guarded outlook. Her need to do things the right way, to please others. She'd liked the fact that Chad, like Max now, didn't care what others thought, that he felt confident in himself. Then later, her guilt at what she'd done with Chad had made things uncomfortable for Rachel.

Now, she saw no way to deter him.

What effect could he have on her job here? On her relationship with Max? Not that she had any intention, after their kiss, of letting that become more than it already was. She may have stopped flinching most of the time whenever he came near, and she did trust him, yet Rachel had learned before they met that she couldn't trust herself. She'd made a terrible mistake once before, one that had forced her to relocate from Indiana to Kansas, to rebuild her life here alone. For a while she'd been able to keep her guilt under control, and she'd concentrated on working with Sophie at the library, but here, in Max's house, that part of her past was now coming to haunt her.

She leaned her forehead against the cold window and could almost see the words of Chad's latest text reflected in the glass.

Headed your way. Can't wait to see you. Put on your best dress. Date night.

CHAPTER THIRTEEN

TRAVIS WAS PLAYING solitaire on his phone a week later when Max walked into his office. He wore a frown and as he removed his Stetson, the cowlick in his hair stood up. Max was no cowboy, but he lived and worked among them, so he seemed to share the same status. Travis assumed he was en route to an area ranch this morning.

"Hey. What's up?"

Max dropped onto the chair in front of Travis's desk, as if he were settling in for a long chat that Travis told himself he didn't have time for. Not that he'd been doing anything useful except sharpening his cognitive skills with a game. There were days lately when Travis would even welcome an attempted bank holdup, dangerous as that could be.

He shifted in his seat. "I told you the other driver in Clara's accident has been charged, right?"

"Yeah, and I should have come in sooner, but I needed to get my thoughts in order. I want to run a couple of other things by you—about Rachel, for one."

"I thought she was doing okay," Travis said. The rumors around town claimed a lot more than that, which he tried not to pay attention to. He liked Max. They were becoming better friends. He liked Rachel, too. He didn't care for wagging tongues, people who should stick to their own troubles. "Shoot," Travis muttered, hoping he wasn't about to get an earful about Max's love life.

Instead, and to Travis's relief, Max told him about his talk with Rachel, which he'd obviously been brooding about for the past week, his fear that she'd gotten in too deep with some guy who wouldn't leave her alone. "Just a hunch," he finished, then sat back in his chair. "She wouldn't say more, but I'm wondering. Is there anything you can do?"

"Not unless she wants a restraining order." Assuming there was cause for one.

"I'd hate to sweep my conversation with her under the rug, then something happens and I didn't try to protect her." He looked at

Travis as if for some magic answer. "And I have to think of Zoey."

"Where is this guy?"

"Don't know. She wouldn't say."

"Then this seems premature, Doc. Tell her to come in, talk to me. I'll see what I can find out then—oh, and by the way, I've come to the end of the road as far as Averill's concerned. Nothing has come up in the databases since I spoke to you last." He glanced at the screen on his phone, his unfinished solitaire game. "I'm guessing that, whatever her reason, she googled 'how to disappear without a trace.'"

That didn't seem to satisfy Max. Rachel's possible stalker, which might be an exaggeration, and Averill's whereabouts weren't all he wanted to talk about.

"Then there's Lauren Anderson," he said. "She accosted Rachel on the street last week. Implied that we're carrying on, together, in my house."

Travis didn't find that worthy of comment. Wouldn't be the worst thing for Max to develop a relationship with someone new. Still. Not his business, and Travis knew, too, how difficult forgetting someone could be.

"I think she's writing another story about us for the *Journal*. I'm surprised it hasn't come out yet. What can you do?"

"Lauren," he said, the name rolling off his tongue more easily than Travis felt comfortable with. "Pesky journalist, dedicated member of the fourth estate, a pain in my side—but no, there's nothing I can do. Zip. Zilch. Nada."

"Why not? Whatever she writes would be conjecture, gossip and untrue. Isn't that slander? Or libel? Defamation of character or something? I won't have Rachel smeared in the press. I had reservations before I hired her, but she's good with Zoey and I like how she fits into the baby's life and mine."

Travis's brows went up. Maybe not just gossip after all. He struggled not to smile.

"Look, when I have a chance, I'll talk to Lauren, okay? Not officially because there's no cause. Yet." Travis shut down the solitaire game. "But sometimes this badge speaks volumes. Let's see how she reacts." The fact that Lauren had published information at her last job without checking the facts and gotten canned was always uppermost in his mind. Well, almost. He thought of that swingy dark hair of hers, those sharp blue eyes, her willowy frame... Travis jerked upright in his chair. "That okay with you?"

"Yeah, thanks," Max said, then rose and started for the door.

"I'll get back to you. Take it easy, Doc."

For a few minutes after Max left, Travis stayed in his seat. Fiddled with his phone. Listened to the silence. Another dead day in the sheriff's department of Stewart County, Kansas. Except for Max's visit, his concerns, there'd be little to keep Travis awake for the rest of the day.

He sighed. At least he would stop in at the *Journal* offices later. In the meantime, he had routine paperwork on his desk to finish, which he'd been avoiding, including his final report on Clara McMann's accident. There were times when he missed Wichita, being a federal agent. Yet there he'd run into too much excitement, and this job was his penance. His safe space, too.

He picked up the first paper, half wishing Lauren would walk through his door.

Which gave him another, better idea that involved her and might help Max. Travis, too.

AFTER LEAVING ZOEY with Sophie, Rachel met Max that afternoon at Farrier General, where, to everyone's relief, after a week in the hospital Clara was doing well today. Sawyer had said, "Her test results look better than I even hoped for." Ensconced like a queen—which she richly deserved to be—in a private room loaded with floral arrangements, she was holding court with several townspeople when Rachel and Max walked into her room.

Rachel hung back, feeling awkward and out of place. Ever since their quasi-talk about Chad, she'd felt edgy, spooking at shadows, inspecting every car that passed by on the street, trying to see if Chad was at the wheel, headed for Max's house. He could easily have gotten the address from his parents.

Max stepped forward to hand Clara the spray of red roses he and Rachel had bought in the downstairs gift shop. The flowers were wrapped in cellophane with a pretty design of hearts. Barren and the surrounding towns appeared ready for Valentine's Day soon, and the displays of candy, cute stuffed animals and roses were everywhere. Max claimed

Clara's decorations at his clinic had made it resemble a float in a Rose Bowl parade.

"Goodness," Clara said, clearly pleased with all the attention, "I've never gotten so many flowers in my life. I woke up this morning and wondered if I'd died overnight."

"Heaven forbid." Max kissed her cheek. "What would we—I—ever do without you?"

Clara blinked as if she didn't recognize this version of Max. "I imagine each passing day must remind you of how I'm needed at the clinic. Is Candi covering the desk while I'm gone?"

"Shadow Wilson sent someone over." Over the past few years, her home health care agency had expanded its reach. There weren't that many requests for in-home caregivers in Barren, so Shadow also managed office workers and the like. "A temp," Max hastened to add because Clara's face had fallen. "Nobody can replace you, G."

Rachel knew the older woman didn't like Max using that nickname, his abbreviation for *gorgeous*. She edged closer to touch Clara's hand. "I'm glad you're feeling better." Clara's color had improved, and Rachel didn't want to remember the time spent in the ER waiting room, praying for her survival. "Any idea when you'll be released?"

"Sawyer refuses to tell me. So does the cardiologist he forced on me." Clara grimaced. "I don't know why there's all this commotion." She waved at the flowers that surrounded her bed, the sweet stuffed bear and kitten that sat on her window ledge. "I'm ready to go home and back to work."

"You listen to Sawyer," Max said with a frown. "None of us wants another scare for which I feel responsible. I could see you weren't feeling well. I shouldn't have let you help with the dog that crashed that night, which by the way went home a few days ago. Thanks again, Clara. Together we turned that around."

"That's lovely news, Max." She sank deeper into her pillows. "Rachel, could you put these beautiful roses in some water? The nurses can give you another vase—if there are any left."

Rachel took the opportunity to leave the room and get away from Max, who kept darting glances at her. He surely remembered their brief conversation about Chad last week. Rachel had stayed as much as possible to herself ever since and wished she hadn't said anything then. She'd been too tempted to tell him the whole story, which could only change his opinion of her for the worse. She was guiltier than her former brother-in-law, and Rachel dreaded his imminent arrival because he probably wouldn't heed her own text telling him not to come. She was surprised he hadn't shown up already.

When she returned to Clara's room, Earl from the hardware store and a woman she hadn't recognized had left. They'd been replaced by, of all people, Sam Hunter, who'd brought more flowers. The older man, still whipcord lean with hair that was now more gray than brown, was familiar with hospitals. He'd once suffered a stroke, then after recovering from that broke his leg while trying to resume his ranch work too soon. In partnership with Logan and Sawyer, his grandsons, he owned the Circle H.

"Don't let this blip on your radar throw you, Clara," he was saying, his hard blue eyes looking softer than they normally did. "Look at me. I should be dead twice over, yet here I am. You'll be right as rain in no time."

"You're a dear, Sam." Clara patted his cheek, blushing. "And thank you for the flowers."

She looked at Rachel, who had just set her and Max's roses on the last space left on Clara's nightstand. "I'll get another vase," Rachel said, then brushed past Max.

Unfortunately, this time he followed her into the hall. "Rachel. Wait."

She turned and nearly ran into his chest. "What?"

"I wanted to tell you. I spoke to Travis Blake earlier. He's going to talk to Lauren."

"And do what? I don't like it, but she has every right to print any story she likes."

"Which would be a ginned-up scandal of sorts that's completely false."

"Didn't you notice? Even Clara was giving us looks—back and forth as if she were at a tennis match."

He sighed. "Before her attack, she did do some matchmaking, which I objected to— and if I hadn't told her not to keep trying—"

"Her coronary wasn't your fault. Whatever brought that on, it had probably been brewing for some time, as Sawyer thinks. She's not a young woman."

"And works too hard. Maybe I shouldn't have let her take over Averill's job. The clinic can be a madhouse, and some people aren't patient or kind or polite. Answering those phones can result in verbal abuse. While I understand my clients being upset when their pets are ill or injured, I hate them taking that out on Clara."

"She is a lot sweeter than some people in this town—Claudia, for instance. Every time I see that woman, I'm just waiting for her to make a snide comment. She sure wouldn't hesitate to scapegoat me."

Max looked alarmed. "What are you saying? Claudia wouldn't make you think of leav—"

Rachel softened her tone. "No, I'm not quitting—I couldn't leave Zoey." Sophie had offered to keep her overnight, but to her own surprise, Rachel couldn't bear the thought of being separated even when walking the floor held no appeal. She'd only been taking care of Zoey for a short while. Was she getting too attached? Yet who could not. Every day Zoey changed, becoming more alert, responsive to people, and displaying some new little skill like following Rachel's finger with her eyes. "I mean, I can't leave now. One day I'll have to." She looked away from Max's steady gaze. "When I'm not needed any longer."

If Max found Averill, and they reconciled for the sake of their child, or if Max met someone new, fell in love… The notion made her heart twist. She wasn't ready for that, either, when she hadn't dealt with Chad and worked out her own feelings for Max.

At the nurses' desk, someone handed her a vase and grinned. "If Ms. McMann gets another bouquet, I'll have to go down to Maternity. We're out at this point."

Rachel returned the nurse's smile, then headed back down the hall. Again, Max kept pace with her. When she glanced over, she noticed a look on his face she'd never seen before. The warmth she'd become used to in his eyes but also a touch of…was that regret, sadness?

"Rachel, I know the rumors bother you. I don't want you to feel uneasy. About Lauren. Because of me. The house, us together…" He hesitated. "I wouldn't want to lose you."

She didn't know what to say to that except, "Really. It's fine. If Lauren writes another story, we'll decide what to do then." Surely, CPS wouldn't enter the picture again. Would they? Still, Rachel's arrangement with Max didn't look…proper, as her own mother might say. As old-fashioned as that seemed, and as much as society had changed over time, there were those in Barren who, like her mother, would disapprove.

Her thoughts short-circuited when she stepped back into Clara's room with Max and saw Sam Hunter's head bent close to Clara's. The two jerked apart, their faces flooding with color. "Oh," Clara said, a hand pressed to her throat.

Max turned ashen. "Everything all right? Should I call the nurse?"

"Everything's…fine." Clara put space between herself and Sam. The two of them looked befuddled, as if that closeness had surprised them as much as it had Rachel.

"Clara, you'll be home in no time. Let's go," she said, grabbing Max's arm.

He was still looking back over his shoulder when they reached the elevator. "You think… Did I see what I thought I saw?"

Rachel was sure from the guilty looks on the older people's faces that she and Max had interrupted a near-kiss, however innocent that might have been. She punched the button to go down to the lobby. "I bet Clara and Sam have known each other all their lives. They're friends."

"They were…canoodling," Max said, then wrinkled his nose. "Now I sound like Claudia Monroe. You're right."

Rachel laughed. "I think they're sweet."

She even felt envious. Did Clara have a boyfriend? A Valentine? Well, why not?

In the gift shop, as she and Max had sorted through the roses, Rachel had wondered what it would be like if he'd been buying them for her. And despite her concerns about Lauren, about Chad, that was almost enough to make her believe in…love again.

LAUREN STRETCHED, rolling her head to ease the crick in her neck. She closed the document she'd been working on. She'd gotten lost in the article that she hoped would exonerate her so she could move forward again. Her chat with Rachel Whittaker on the street last week had given her enough to start, and she felt pleased with the result so far. Averill, missing. The baby. Rachel living with Max. What if it was even more complicated than that? She'd use just enough facts as a teaser, enough questions to make people in town want more. This could become a whole series.

When the main door opened, she startled. The rest of the staff had gone home, and it was after six. Alone in the building, she reached for the silver letter opener on her desk. "Who's there?"

Then a deep voice she recognized said, "Burning the midnight oil?"

Travis Blake. A little rush of heat ran across her nerve ends, which should have been a warning rather than a blast of awareness. The tall, good-looking sheriff of Stewart County—why couldn't he be old and ugly?—sauntered in to lean one broad shoulder against her cubicle's frame, his green eyes dancing. "Sorry," he said, not sounding sorry at all. "Did I scare you?"

"You always scare me. Still. There's something about you that makes my typing fingers itch."

He grinned, but his eyes grew wary. "That something is for me to know."

"And for me to find out."

Travis sighed. He dragged out a metal folding chair and sat. He gestured at her computer. "What's the hot deadline about?"

"None of your business."

"This town and everyone in it are my business."

"Reporting is mine. I had a column to finish."

"Listen," he said, "I got a visit this morning from Max Crane. He tells me you've been harassing his baby's caregiver."

"Harassing? We had a little talk, that's all."

"You made insinuations about the two of them. Further insinuations." He stared her down. "Lauren, I don't care if you keep chasing the next big thing that will get you out of this town until a hundred years from now when you drop dead at this computer. But leave the doc and his housekeeper alone. There's no story."

"Oh, but there is. And I mean to cover it."

"What, now you've become a gossip columnist? Like Ann Landers?"

"She was an advice columnist. Get your facts straight, Travis."

His expression faltered. He wasn't as sure about Rachel and Max as he wanted her to believe. "Like you did in Chicago?" he said coolly.

As if Lauren needed the reminder. "Well.

If you must know, I didn't just lose my job, I lost something else. My editor there was also my fiancé."

"Ouch," Travis said, looking a bit ashamed of himself.

"You can guess how that turned out."

"Okay, I shouldn't have said that. Let's get back to business here. You probably know that I don't have any authority to try to change your mind about printing some cheap-shot article, which I hoped you'd gotten out of your system with the first one. But for your own good I'd advise you to drag that document you stayed late to work on into the trash."

She looked pointedly at him. "Averill McCafferty. No one has found her."

"Max filed a missing person report, but I've exhausted all my sources. I've driven over to Farrier, then half a dozen towns in the area looking for Averill myself. I've alerted other departments. I've disappointed Max—and questioned my own ability to track someone down, which was part of my job before this one."

"Yes, and I'm so curious about that," she said with a smile. "But, speaking of stories—and Averill—why don't I put a small item in the paper? Something to bring her out of hiding. A direct appeal."

"No," he said. "That could end up hurting Max. If there was no response…"

"Then tell you what. If you give me *your* story, I'll hold back on Max and Rachel. Averill, too. For now. I'm betting yours is even better. I know this much already—you got fired, Travis, after blowing some case, any mention of which seems to have mysteriously disappeared."

He shifted in the chair. "The Bureau and I parted ways. They don't tend to publicize such events, or the cases that brought them about."

"So, I am right." She held his gaze. "I'm thinking something above the fold. Headlines. I can see them now."

Travis looked as if he wanted to strangle her. "Can you just, for one minute, forget your egotistical need to destroy someone for your own gain?" He paused. "So. Different angle. Different approach." His next words stunned her. "What do you know about Averill's sister?"

"She vanished years ago—"

"Ten, to be exact. Is she dead, you think? Or is she alive, living another life?"

Now he'd seriously piqued her interest, diverted her from the baby story, if not his own.

"Like maybe she was abducted by someone who simply wanted a child they couldn't have themselves? Did that happen with your case? In Wichita?"

He shook his head. "Uh-uh. This is *not* about me. What if you do your best work here? Help me find Lucie McCafferty? Think of all the good that would do. For Averill, too. Think of the heartwarming headlines."

"Help you? Meaning what, exactly?"

Travis's green eyes sparkled. "There was a lot of press around that incident. The articles are readily available. I'm sure that, like me, you've read them. First, we go through those again. I hate to admit it, but you have a different take as a reporter on things like this than I do as a cop. You might even bring a woman's insights to the search."

She leaned back in her chair, grinned at him. "You see me as a woman, not just an aggressive journalist hunting down that next blockbuster story?"

"Oh, you're aggressive, all right." He didn't address the rest of her question, which only made Lauren certain he had a similar awareness of her as she did him. "That's why I came knocking on your desktop tonight."

She laughed. "I have to agree, this could be fun." Not to mention the breakthrough she needed. Yes, for her own gain. It wouldn't be a hardship, though, to work with Travis Blake. She'd enjoy the eye candy and have a better chance to crack his facade. She sobered. Her skills as a reporter, his as a bloodhound. Win-win. "You're on, Sheriff."

"Good. Because the rest of my theory is, if we're lucky, we'll find both of them. Averill and her sister. You eat dinner yet?"

"No, and the café's open."

Travis had lost his usual look of ennui. After being with the FBI, he must find his job as sheriff in this small Kansas town a bore. Which gave them something in common. He seemed excited as he said, "We can strategize while we eat."

CHAPTER FOURTEEN

A WEEK LATER as she tidied the nursery, Rachel patted Zoey's back in the baby carrier, reaching for her phone with the other. She hadn't expected to hear from Jason's mother who'd hung up on her in tears after their last call. That had been before Rachel began to work for Max.

"Hey," Rachel said, staring out the window at the ever-falling snow, "how are you?"

"Fine." Kathy Whittaker's tone was clipped, even cold. "Is Chad there?"

At the sound of his name, Rachel's heart was already in her throat. "No, I haven't seen him."

Every day Rachel had expected to look out the window and find his car in the drive. This was to have been a snowy, indoor day for Rachel and Zoey, who'd already taken her morning nap, but she wondered if going downtown to have lunch at Jack's might be a better idea.

"I'm worried," Kathy said, and Rachel's

last hope that he'd realized there was no future for them and stayed home died. "He didn't check in each night as he promised to do, and he was in a strange mood when he left here."

"When was that?"

"A week ago."

So, he hadn't left home right away. Rachel had received his text two weeks ago, texted him not to come. And Kathy was a world-class worrywart, an anxious mom at the best of times. Rachel could understand that.

She'd always been the type to fret over things herself, and since she'd come to Max's house to live, she'd fallen in love with Zoey. She felt orders of magnitude more concern now at the baby's slightest cry. Despite Rachel being her temporary caregiver, Shadow called that First Mom-Itis. Rachel's fear of dropping Zoey had gradually vanished with experience, but her worries only morphed into other areas. Had she given Zoey too much formula this morning? What if Zoey choked from crying so much? What if the stroller collapsed one day because, in a rush, Rachel hadn't converted it properly?

She wasn't a real mother, yet she understood Kathy's mindset, and although Chad was in his thirties now, as Rachel was, Kathy still called him her baby. Rachel wondered why he hadn't dated other women—which he'd told her—rather than fixating on her. If Jason had tried to prove he was worthy of his parents' approval, what was Chad determined to prove? That, in their lifelong competition as brothers, he could win over Jason's widow?

"Kathy, I told him not to come here."

"Why not?"

Rachel remained silent. She couldn't share her reasons with Kathy.

"Chad was never anything but kind to you. He loves you, Rachel, as we all…do." The slight hesitation didn't surprise Rachel. In the past year or so, her relationship with Jason's family had grown increasingly tense. They couldn't understand why she'd left their hometown for another place that, to them, seemed similar. And Rachel could hardly tell them she'd moved away because of Chad. He was the son who could do no wrong.

But then, they didn't know what he'd done, why he was coming to see her—what Rachel had unwittingly fostered before she realized the path they were going down. Because she loved them, she would not cause the Whittakers any more grief if she could help it. She didn't want to hurt them. Compared with her own parents, they were candidates for Family of the Year. Getting caught between Chad's mother and father and him made her angry as much as it grieved her.

"I'm sorry, Kathy. I don't know what else to say. I did what I had to—for myself. That may seem selfish, but without Jason I felt… well, there were too many reminders there of when we'd been happy, and our future seemed bright," which was true. Tears welled in her eyes. "I had to go. I miss you. All of you—"

"Please let me know when Chad arrives. I've lost one son. I'm afraid of losing him, too."

Rachel's pulse skipped. What was she saying? Kathy had told her Chad was in a "strange" mood. Had he become depressed simply because she wouldn't let him take their presumed relationship to a new level? Or had he played the victim for his mother? Jason's father would see through that, but maybe Kathy could not.

"Please don't worry," Rachel said in a calming tone. Zoey gazed up at her with clear adoration in her eyes. At least that's what Rachel wanted—needed—to see. How could she let Chad in this house? Risk Zoey's well-being if, indeed, his persistence about Rachel had deepened into some dark obsession. Maybe she should have talked to Travis right away, but Rachel hadn't wanted to think the situation was that serious, that she could handle her former brother-in-law. "If Chad turns up, I'll tell him to call you."

But that wasn't all Kathy had to say.

"Please reconsider about living so far from us. I understand about the memories, but, Rachel, you belong here. I'm sure that's why Chad took off as he did. He wants to convince you to come home. To be near us again."

Near him, Rachel added silently. She couldn't tell her mother-in-law that, either. How much longer would it be until Chad rang the bell on Cattle Track Lane?

By the time they hung up, Rachel felt even guiltier than she already had. She didn't want to trouble Kathy, yet because of Chad that had become impossible. She hugged Zoey tighter against her, as if holding on to this new life she was making here for herself.

Even though the snow was still drifting

past the nursery window, Rachel bundled up Zoey, gave Max a quick call then hurried out to the car and drove into town.

IT WASN'T UNTIL that night, after Zoey had been tucked in her crib, that Max decided to push Rachel for answers he hadn't gotten earlier that day—and two weeks ago. Whatever troubled her could affect Zoey, and when he'd answered Rachel's call that morning, he'd heard her anxious tone. "Is Zoey all right?" he'd asked.

"She's…yes," Rachel said, "but could you meet us at the Bon Appetit for lunch?"

Max had finished with his next patient, then left his temp and Candi to hold the fort until he got back. Rachel's tone had reminded him of that first night when she'd flinched from Max, and he hadn't forgotten their brief conversation about her brother-in-law.

"Okay. Tell me," he said once they were downstairs again in the living room, seated beside each other on the sofa.

Rachel hesitated. He could almost see her mind spinning, sorting through options.

Max said, "At lunch you made a good attempt to show me there was nothing bothering you, but I think I know when you're not okay."

Rachel's lips pressed tight. "It's Chad. My brother-in-law. He's supposedly on his way here, so you do have a right to know something about him." She paused. "I should give you some background first. My parents were strict, even stern, and in our house, growing up, I toed the line, believe me. I learned to do 'the right thing,' to behave the proper way, which is why I must seem rather rigid to people. When I worked at the library, Sophie asked me once, 'Is it more important for you to be right than to be fair?' Which, I came to realize, it was. I still feel that Averill stole those books from the library, even though she returned them. But I had a gut instinct about her." She shrugged a little, as if to apologize for dissing his ex-girlfriend.

"Your instincts may be correct. Keep talking. I won't judge you, Rachel."

She paused again before going on. "When I met Jason, this dashing marine in dress whites at my best friend's wedding, I knew right away that he was The One. And his family... They were like this model of how a family should be. Jason was the younger of their two sons, and I've always thought he tried too hard to win their love when he had that all the time—if not as obviously as Chad, who never had to work for their approval."

"He was spoiled."

"He has this sense of entitlement. Since Jason died, he's assumed that includes me."

After their previous conversation, Max had figured out that Chad wanted the same relationship with Rachel that she'd had with his brother, even though she hadn't shared any details. "How so?"

"At Jason's funeral I thought Chad's extra attention was just normal…comfort, and I was grateful for it. I was shattered by grief, and I was also…pregnant at the time."

Max winced. "Rachel, I didn't know." Where was her child?

"So you see, I was doubly vulnerable then. We'd conceived right before Jason left on his last deployment, and the whole family was thrilled. Kathy, my mother-in-law, bought baby clothes, pictures for the nursery, and so did I. The day we learned about Jason, she and I were painting the room. Way ahead of schedule, but maybe we sensed that everything would go wrong, and we were both pretending we could prevent that tragedy."

"I'm sorry, Rachel."

"So am I." Her gaze met his. "I coped then as well as I could, which wasn't that well. And Chad was always there to hold me up or lend a shoulder to cry on. He'd gotten compassionate leave from the military—he was a marine, too, then—after Jason's death and was able to tack on extra time to be with the family. Kathy was a mess, terrified that her older son might face the same fate on his next deployment. Chad was great at reassuring her. He was our rock. I trusted him, too."

Max had a bad feeling. "But then…"

From upstairs, they heard Zoey in her crib, her soft cries, and waited for a moment until she settled down again. Rachel's face looked hollow, bleached of color.

"I hate to relive this," she said. "But just before Chad finally went back on duty, he asked me out to dinner, just the two of us, he said. I assumed we were still buddies, both trying to manage our loss, but at the restaurant I began to feel unwell. Chad took me to the hospital, where I later lost the baby."

"Ah, Rachel." He put an arm around her

shoulders, and to his surprise she nestled against him. He thought he could see where this was going. She'd started to tell him two weeks ago. "If this is too painful—"

"No, I do want to tell you now. Get it off my chest, maybe." She shrugged. "Anyway. More grieving for the baby, more of Chad's devoted attention. Until I realized that his invitation to dinner alone, his constant being there for me, had become something else. When he told me he had feelings for me that went beyond being my brother-in-law, I was shocked. I told him how inappropriate I felt a romantic relationship between us would be. Chad wouldn't listen."

Max's jaw tensed. "Inappropriate, yeah."

"I thought I'd made it clear how I felt. But a year after Jason died, and Chad had served another tour of duty, he came home again on leave to his parents' house, and I could hardly avoid him. I'd considered leaving, moving back to my family's house, but I stayed instead. With the Whittakers, I could be more relaxed than with my parents." She paused. "If I could have chosen a family, it would have been Jason's. All of them. That turned out to be a mistake."

Max understood her better now. "I imagine things didn't stay comfortable."

"With Chad around, he kept asking me out. I kept saying no and that his parents would also find that odd. Chad claimed I was channeling my girlhood, my strict parents. He made me feel foolish."

"Then what?"

"He decided to leave the military. There'd been trouble with a superior and he was, well, weary of war. He hated his mother worrying, he said. And once he was home for good, he was there all the time. But I still didn't leave, in part because Kathy needed me, until Chad and I had a huge fight. I think even his parents overheard because they were in their bedroom, and we were below in the great room. He…tried to kiss me, didn't want to take no for an answer. Chad said that he'd always loved me and why did I keep resisting? I told him it was just weird for him to be chasing his dead brother's widow."

Max's mouth hardened. "I agree."

"I knew then that I *had* to leave Indiana. It was one of the hardest things I've ever done, and it nearly killed Kathy. Certainly, that affected our friendship, which is still iffy, but all I could think about was getting away from Chad before things got even messier. I was shocked that he would betray Jason's memory, that I had betrayed him, too…"

There was something she wasn't saying, but when she trailed off, Max let it go. He knew the basics now of her relationship with Chad Whittaker.

"Are you frightened, Rachel?"

She shook her head. "Not for the reasons you may think." Rachel looked up into his eyes. "Thanks. I needed to get that out. You're a far better listener than people believe, Max. I'm more worried about Zoey, about you, than I am about Chad. Perhaps I *should* quit. I don't want to bring trouble into your home."

"We talked about that after Lauren bothered you. You're staying," he said, surprised by the vehemence in his tone. Max had felt a swift kick of panic, a sense of impending loss that shocked him. In less than a month, he'd come to depend on her with Zoey, but he'd also come to enjoy Rachel's company. Then there was that brief kiss they'd shared, which they'd been trying to ignore ever since. And his own reluctance to express his tangled feelings.

Max thought of the gossip, of Lauren Anderson's story. He thought of Chad, whose car might turn into his driveway at any moment.

"Rachel. I won't let anything happen to you, understand?"

"This isn't your problem, Max, it's mine. I appreciate your concern, but I need to deal with Chad myself. I texted him not to come, which, from what his mother said, doesn't seem to have worked. If I confront him in person now, I can try to convince him to leave me alone—and protect you and Zoey."

He cleared his throat. "Maybe there's another way. What if we use those rumors, even Lauren, to our advantage, let people think we're, uh, romantically involved after all? At the same time, we'll be giving Chad another solid reason to leave you alone." He hesitated. "If he's on his way here, by the time he arrives we can already be…"

When he didn't continue, Rachel blinked. "I don't know what you're saying."

"Engaged," he said, forcing the word out. "You and me. That will quiet the gossips, protect you—I hope—from him. Plus, with a ring on your finger, this town will really have something to talk about. Before you know it, they'll be planning the wedding. So let them. What do you think?" He added, "It's not as if there's nothing there. I mean, we did kiss— once. I thought you liked it, too, although, of course, we wouldn't *have* to repeat that. This would be a fake engagement..." Rachel was staring at him. "My grandmother left some jewelry, and Sophie insisted I take her rings—including an engagement diamond. The design's rather old-fashioned, but Sophie claimed it's the height of style again these days."

"Max, I—I don't know. This makes sense in a way, but do you want people to start planning an event, believe we're in love with each other...then, after Chad leaves and maybe Averill comes back, we split up? Everyone in Barren will feel sorry for you, and they'll hate me." She shook her head. "I don't think this is right."

Max was losing the argument. "That's your parents talking, not you. Or was I wrong, and I'm the only one who did like that kiss, and you can't imagine us pulling this off?"

"It's not that. I've become very attached to Zoey and she's accepted me, too. Leaving her before I want to—must at some point—

wouldn't be good for her. This isn't fair to me either."

"Rachel, I understand. You'd be putting a lot on the line…"

"I do like you, Max—very much—and you make some good points. But—"

Please, he thought. He could sense her weakening. "We can make this work. We'd be playing to people's expectations anyway. But most important, our engagement, pretend as it would be, will serve to quiet those wagging tongues—and keep Chad at bay. We can worry about afterward later." He gazed at Rachel until she nodded, then finally smiled. "Yes?" he asked.

"This is strange, but okay," she murmured. "Yes."

As if to seal the deal, and surely not because he simply wanted to, Max enfolded her in his arms. When he bent his head to kiss her, she didn't resist. He liked this kiss even better than he had their first. Pretend, or not.

CHAD DID NOT ring the bell on Cattle Track Lane that night. Rachel didn't find him on the porch the next morning or see his car in the drive. And there was more good news.

Max told her, his voice jubilant, that Clara had been released from the hospital. When he invited Rachel to come with him on a call to Cody and Willow's WB ranch, she leaped at the chance to get out of the house and preserve her good mood. The roads weren't clear, snow having fallen all night, but Max's truck plowed through the deep white stuff like a hot blade through butter, and his probing looks reminded her of their fake engagement. Had they both lost their senses?

Still, remembering their kisses, she'd gone to sleep last night with a smile on her lips.

Willow and Cody met them in front of the barn where Max had pulled in. Willow immediately moved to lift Zoey from her car seat, tracing a finger along the baby's cheek and blinking back tears. "Oh, and how cute is this?"

Cody stood at Willow's shoulder. "She's been a puddle ever since Harper was born. Now that he's walking, zipping around everywhere, Willow's thinking about another one."

"I didn't say that. My mother did. I just love newborns." With a wink, she baby-talked to Zoey as if the others weren't standing there.

Cody turned to Max and Rachel. "You ready to ride?"

"Ride?" she echoed, her pulse missing a beat. Apparently, there was no veterinary issue here after all.

"Buck has been waiting for you."

"But I—" Rachel broke off. Max must be trying to distract her from her dread about Chad. He'd been so understanding last night, yet she couldn't quite believe that under the gloves she wore against the cold, his grandmother's ring was on her finger today. Despite the pretense, at times Rachel felt she'd known Max all her life, that they'd always been…friends. Would that change when Chad arrived, when Max learned the rest of that story? She was living on borrowed time.

"Come on," Cody said. "I'll saddle Buck for you. I think you'll like him—and vice versa. You can ride in the indoor arena since it's snowy today." He grinned. "Max can borrow my horse, Diva, who has a dream trot. I'll be right there in the ring with you."

Trot? "Max, too?"

"Sure," Cody said.

"I'll get you for this," she told Max, but Rachel had to smile. After their conversation before, Max had little choice but to prove he wasn't afraid of horses.

She followed Cody into the barn. The first smells were a bit much to get used to, but Cody claimed that the aromas of manure, hay and oats were like the nectar of the gods.

"He's a typical horseman," Max said, "and knows his stuff."

His reassurance didn't ease Rachel's fears, but the session didn't go as badly as she'd expected. Max, who clearly wasn't that experienced either, rode beside her. She'd heard that Cody was a fantastic horse trainer, and his business with Willow had drawn clients from all over the state and beyond. He also proved to be a patient, encouraging teacher, and his love of the horses, Buck—who didn't at all—and Diva, a beautiful paint mustang, was clear. She could see they loved him too.

At the end of an hour, her backside ached, but she'd stopped clenching her teeth to keep from shivering in the cool but not cold arena. Rachel had developed a tentative affection for Buck, which amazed her, and managed to dismount without tumbling off the horse. In the stable, Buck nuzzled his face into her gloved hand, then nosed her pockets. "He's looking for a treat," Cody said, handing her a bag of carrots. "Tell him what a good boy he's been."

"He is a good boy," she agreed. Then Cody's mare, Diva, nudged her in the back, making Rachel laugh. "Diva, wait. Don't eat my coat."

Max's ploy had worked. She hadn't felt this good, this free, since she'd left Indiana. Rachel removed her gloves to give Buck and Diva the carrots—and revealed the diamond and platinum ring Max had given, or rather lent, her.

Cody's eyes gleamed. "Wow," he said. "When did this happen?"

"Last night." Max laid a hand on the nape of Rachel's neck, his touch warming her. "We haven't even told Sophie and Gabe yet. If I don't as soon as we leave here, the news will be all over town by nightfall."

"Is it a secret? I won't tell anyone if you don't want me to."

"No secret, and I didn't mean you." Then he kissed Rachel lightly, making her blush. Because of the lie, she told herself, yet she felt the same way she had after Jason had proposed. As if this were real. And for a moment, Max gazed into her eyes, looking as if he wanted to say something, but didn't.

"Congratulations." Cody shook Max's hand,

kissed Rachel's cheek, then invited them up to their new house, which was cozy and gorgeous. Willow, holding Zoey, offered them coffee and got weepy again over the engagement ring.

"Nice people," Rachel said as they walked to Max's truck a little later.

On the way home, they high-fived each other because they'd managed to stay on the horses. Max said, "You saw firsthand that I'm not afraid of those four-legged beasts?"

"You're a regular centaur."

"I'll keep my own legs, thanks." Max reached for her hand on the truck's console. He checked Zoey out in the rearview mirror. The baby was dozing, happily full because Willow had fed her a bottle before they left. "You enjoyed yourself, didn't you?"

"As you intended, Dr. Crane."

"I did," he had to admit. And laughed. "Enjoyed myself, too."

"You were even right about Buck," Rachel teased.

Max wasn't laughing, though, and neither was she when they turned into his driveway and heard Sky barking her head off inside the house. And saw the man standing on Max's porch.

CHAPTER FIFTEEN

"CHAD." IN THE living room minutes later, Max held out his hand, Rachel's brother-in-law's grip clamping down on his as if to show how strong he was. Max didn't bother to add *nice to meet you*. He didn't ask about Chad's journey to Barren. He didn't like Chad Whittaker on sight, which had little to do with what Rachel had told him. If she'd never said a word, he would have trusted his instincts—and Max had to remind himself that Rachel wanted to deal with Chad on her own.

An inch or two taller than Max, he had blond hair cut short and intense blue eyes that didn't go with his easy smile. His broad shoulders and military posture said he could handle himself in any situation. Handle Max if need be.

Max shot a look at Rachel, who was unzipping Zoey's snowsuit, her eyes on the baby. Sky was now in her crate in the kitchen. Unfortunately, her earlier barking, which for once hadn't bothered Max, hadn't deterred Chad.

Max removed his jacket, took the baby from Rachel and sat down on the sofa. He'd be close by if she needed him.

As she spoke with Chad, who seemed in no hurry to leave, Max watched them. They were both standing in the center of the room. Rachel still wore her coat and gloves, and he wondered why she didn't take them off, let Chad see the ring Max had given her. Rachel's stiff stance reminded him of that first night when she'd flinched from Max's touch. He couldn't blame her. Chad's uber-friendly manner barely hid the tension Max could sense inside him.

"Mom and Dad send their love," Chad was saying. He kept his gaze fixed on Rachel's face as if trying to gauge her feelings toward him.

"Your mother is worried about you, Chad."

He laughed. "She always worries. Can you believe? She's still fretting over poor Jason, who isn't worrying now about anything at all."

Max blinked. What a thing to say. A genuine concern for his grieving parent? Or a reminder for Rachel that his brother was dead?

He began to understand the depth of her concern about Chad.

Rachel said, "She and I spoke yesterday. You left home a week ago and she hadn't heard from you when I talked to her."

"I stopped on my way to see a few marine pals."

"And I texted you not to come. Why did you? I won't have your parents think there's anything more between us, especially after losing Jason. Why would you hurt them like that? I'm not happy to see you. I don't know how to make that any clearer. After what happened—"

He glanced at Max. "This is hardly the place to hash over old mistakes. Mine included. You don't understand. I have only your best interest at heart."

Zoey was beginning to make those noises that told them she was hungry, and probably wet. Chad hadn't even acknowledged the baby. "Let's pause this for a moment. I need to warm the baby a bottle," Rachel said, starting toward the kitchen.

Chad reached out to stop her and, in spite of Rachel's wish to deal with Chad herself, Max rose from the sofa, holding Zoey. "Hey," he said. "Don't touch her."

Chad released her and threw up his hands. "What is this? I come to see my sister-in-law, and you're suddenly her protector? There's no law, buddy, against a visit from a close relative."

This was what she'd obviously dreaded, that innocent tone of voice, the words that seemed to hold a double meaning. "Chad," she said, "you weren't invited, and I work for Max. I won't have you barging in, thinking you can take over, make me look bad in front of my…employer."

Max looked pointedly at Rachel, sending her a message. Why didn't she remove her gloves and show Chad the ring? Tell him about their engagement when one reason for it was to get rid of him? Maybe she didn't want to take off the gloves and her coat as if they might send a message to Chad not to stay.

Chad's gaze ran over Max. Dismissing him. "Fine. Then let's discuss our personal business somewhere else, Rachel."

"We have no *personal* business." Her whole body had tensed, but she was holding her own. Max was worried for her. Chad could be charming all right, but Max had no doubt he could also become physical in a New York minute. He needed to be in control. Yet even though Zoey was working herself into a full-on wail now, he wouldn't leave Rachel alone with Chad.

"You heard her," Max said.

Rachel probably didn't want him to witness whatever she and Chad might say, but that didn't matter to Max now. If he had to act, he would. For Rachel's sake. Chad wouldn't get the chance to lay another finger on her.

Chad moved closer to Rachel. "*Dr.* Crane can take care of his own baby. Let him heat up her bottle. Let's take this—us—down a notch. Where's a good place to eat in this town? I asked you to put on your best dress. Let's go—it's too early for dinner but I'm starving—and talk. In private."

Max could see Rachel felt torn between staying here and getting Chad out of the house.

"A quick meal," she said, "but no change of clothes. I'm ready now."

Max couldn't keep from saying, "Rachel."

A minute later, they were gone, and Zoey was screaming. Max had no choice but to tend to the baby, his thoughts in turmoil. He hadn't protected Rachel. She hadn't wanted him to. Or had she been more intent on protecting *him*?

As SHE LEFT the *Journal* office, Lauren glanced out the front window and saw Rachel Whittaker walking past with a blond-haired man. Hmm. Interesting. Maybe she'd been wrong about the situation with Max Crane, they really were just employer and employee, and Rachel had a boyfriend. But right now, Lauren was more concerned with Averill Mc-Cafferty. Or rather, as it had turned out, her sister.

Carrying her laptop, her pulse drumming, she picked her way down Main Street to the sheriff's department through the fresh slush on the sidewalk. If Travis wasn't working late, too, she'd track him down at his house. During their strategy dinner, Lauren had keyed his contact info into her phone. They weren't exactly neighbors, but his address was on her way home. Fortunately, he saved her the trip and was standing at the front counter, reading a paper when she walked in.

"I've found something," she said, stomping the snow off her boots, then plunking the computer down on the counter's scarred wooden surface.

Travis gave her a mild look. His expression reminded her of their dinner when the initial excitement over banding together to find the missing girl, and possibly Averill, had sparked something else. If Travis didn't see the mutual attraction, he wasn't as sharp as Lauren thought. So, considering his demeanor, she would stay in reporter mode. "Remember when we looked at those old newspaper articles about Lucie McCafferty?"

"Sure."

"And saw that last photo Averill took of her on the day she disappeared?"

"I do," he said, his cool gaze warming a bit with interest.

Leaning over the desk, Lauren turned her laptop so they could both see the screen and the group picture of some teenagers huddled together, beaming at the camera. Below them a string of baby pictures spread in a kind of jumbled collage. Lauren pointed to one.

"I'm sure this is Lucie McCafferty."

"The same picture we've seen in the articles," Travis said, his gaze keen now. "But not exactly the same. Is it?"

"You have a good eye. What if this photo was also taken the day Lucie was abducted? Or soon afterward? So, not that long after the one Averill took of her?"

"How did you find this?"

"I monitor the wire services all day to pick up world news for the *Journal*." Lauren took a breath. "In this case, citing an article in the Denver paper. Look at the other girls. This was part of a story on a sweet sixteen birthday party held for the daughter—the girl in the middle—of a very wealthy man. Mega bucks spent, including an entire week of activities, among them a three-day junket to Antigua. And what do teenagers spend a lot of their time doing?"

He shrugged. "Got me. I don't have much to do with kids."

Or anyone else, except the victims or perpetrators of whatever crime happened in Barren. As far as she knew, he didn't date or have a girlfriend. Travis spent his days on patrol or at his desk, his nights at home. He didn't even have a dog. What a waste. Still, his life must be as dull as hers. Today, though, she could barely contain her excitement.

"They're on social media," she said as if to say ta-da. "People their age don't censor what others might see. They display their whole lives, every detail, on those sites. This article is just a start."

Travis studied the group photo. "There's something off here…"

"There sure is. Look closer. As one activity, part of a matching game, all the girls brought these baby pictures to share. You know, to see who can guess which photo belongs with which girl now." Lauren's hand shook as she gestured at the other girls' images. "But one girl didn't contribute a baby photo. It's that of a five-year-old. We know that from Averill's photo of her." She paused. "Why? Because she would have no baby pictures to share. Those would still be with Averill's family. Travis, think what this could mean. Lucie's *alive*."

"Then we were also right that she'd have an entirely different identity now. A new name, possibly a different birth date."

"Yes, but unfortunately the matches aren't shown in this group picture. There are several girls who might be Lucie now. I'm going to check Maura Aiken, the birthday girl's media sites, see if I can find some tagged photos that will help."

"Wouldn't her current 'parents' want to avoid that? We're talking kidnapping here…"

"Once your area of expertise, Travis?"

Lauren's reporter instincts had flashed on high alert. He'd been okay with trying to find Averill, especially for his friend Max's sake, but she'd seen the glimmer of something brighter in his eyes when they started to search for Lucie, a spark from the past when he'd worked for the FBI that Travis had quickly shuttered. The missing link.

"Look," he said. "I'm not at liberty to talk about an old case—"

"The reason you're not with the Bureau anymore."

He shrugged. "The Bureau's not with me. Give it a rest, Lauren."

"When this just got a lot more interesting? I don't think so."

He ran a hand through his hair. "Off the record, because if you print one word about my…failure, I will make you pay. Four years ago, yeah, I was the lead investigator on a kidnapping. Long story short, we finally found the kid—a three-year-old girl—and I lost my temper with the perp. Seriously lost it, but what that guy had done…" He glanced beyond Lauren to the far wall. Travis shook his head. "A couple days later I was officially out of a job."

"Did you…was she…"

"Rescued? No, and I will never forget the look in her parents' eyes when they were told. I had nightmares for months afterward, always running, bursting into that place, searching… She was never there. I couldn't find her. But in the real world, sad to say, I did, and she was not…alive."

Lauren's throat had closed. "I'm sorry, Travis."

"Yeah, well, but in the process, I'd made the Bureau look bad. Unprofessional. I turned in my gun, my badge, the usual routine. My superior all but told me not to let the door hit me on my way out." He spread his arms. "And here I am."

So, now she knew. Lauren had no aspirations to become a mother herself, but her hardened reporter's heart went out to that little girl's family. And to Travis. No wonder he'd been slow to engage about Lucie McCafferty's disappearance. He was okay patrolling the town, talking to citizens as he passed by, writing a few tickets for speeding or running Barren's sole red light, but this came too close to the case that had ended his FBI career and, above all, broken him.

"I'm sorry," she said again, a word she normally choked on, and reached out a hand to briefly cover his.

"Forget it. You're right. I'm still in law enforcement."

"And the difference is, Lucie's alive. Her case gives you a second chance."

Travis drew back, then squared his shoulders. "Then let's focus on her, whoever she is now. I'd really like to crack this—for Max. And Averill."

Lauren wondered for the first time if, in fact, she'd overstepped her own boundaries. Maybe they weren't as limitless as she'd thought.

THE NEXT MORNING Rachel went about her duties, taking care of Zoey, doing laundry—an endless task—and thinking, worrying, about Chad. She'd dreaded his arrival in Barren, but yesterday at the Bon Appetit he'd been utterly charming. He'd even apologized for trying to grab her arm and for his treatment of Max.

Rachel had driven them in her own car to the restaurant, but when they'd arrived back at Cattle Track Lane, she'd begun to regret that Chad had left his rental sedan in Max's driveway. After they ate, she could have sent him on his way from the restaurant to the nearest motel.

Instead, at the house, he'd walked her to the porch and up the stairs, leaned against a post by the top, snowy step as if in no hurry to leave. "Rach, I have to say Jack Hancock's a wizard in the kitchen. That may have been the best meal I've eaten in a long time."

She agreed. "He never misses. Barren is lucky to have him."

Chad leaned closer. "Remember when you, me and Jason tried that fancy Michelin-starred place in Indianapolis?" They'd been celebrating something, and the reminder made her heart ache.

Rachel eased back from him. "We didn't like one thing about it—the atmosphere, the snooty service, the food."

He didn't seem to notice her growing discomfort. Chad laughed and said, "Jason left the guy a five percent tip."

"Those were the days," she replied lightly, edging toward the front door.

Chad pushed off the post and followed her. "You were always part of them. We were like the three musketeers." He paused. "Now we're only two."

Rachel's heart sank. She could see what Chad had done. Again. Bringing up the closeness they'd all shared, dragging her back into that other, happier time when life had seemed filled with possibility and an endless future, when she'd loved Jason and hadn't known she would lose him so soon.

"Chad, please. Don't ask me to...come home again." If that's all he wanted.

"Why not? Because I stepped out of line once?"

"No," she murmured, "because I did, too, and I won't betray Jason's memory again." She hadn't told Max that part. Rachel had a hard time admitting it to herself.

He bent closer again. "Maybe he'd like to know that you're happy now, moving on—why not with his brother? Jason and I were pals. I still don't see anything wrong with that."

"You know I do, though."

The reminder of their last argument before she left Indiana was all too clear. So was the license she'd given Chad before that to persist. If she'd refused to eat with him, shown him the ring, would he have gone away, as she'd hoped? But as they'd walked into the restaurant, Rachel had removed her gloves, tugged off Max's ring and slipped it in her purse. Because their engagement wasn't real? Or because she didn't want to hurt Chad? Had she unwittingly given him permission again to assume the wrong thing about their relationship?

Rachel needed to pick the right moment, try to redirect her relationship with Chad first. She didn't want him taking tales to Kathy. "I do treasure the memories of us all together, but that was years ago."

"He's gone," he insisted. "We're not. We're here, and alive. I've missed you."

When he tried to kiss her, Rachel held up both hands like a traffic cop. "Don't," she said. "It's wrong." To her relief, he'd stared at her for a few seconds, then backed down the porch steps, hands raised too, and without another word gotten into his car. And left.

Rachel had no doubt he'd be back. How could she protect Max and Zoey?

CHAPTER SIXTEEN

Travis took a badly needed to-go mug of coffee with him and headed over to Max's clinic the next morning. He was astonished to find Clara at the front desk. "Glad to see you looking better, G."

"Not you, too?" she said. "Max gave me that nickname." She sniffed. "Gorgeous. Now it's all over town."

"Can we help it if you're Barren's favorite girl? But, really, should you be here two days after getting out of the hospital?"

"I spent enough time in bed there, doing some rehab and walking those halls. I'm only working for an hour or so. Answering phones, taking payments, making appointments. How hard is that?"

Travis thought those few hours could easily stretch into the whole day, but that was between Clara, Max and her doctor. He stifled a yawn. "The vet in?"

"He's with a patient. I can squeeze you in after that."

"I'll wait." For a few more minutes they chatted, and Travis learned that Clara and Sam Hunter were planning to attend some winter festival together next month halfway across the state. He smiled.

"Clara McMann has a boyfriend," he said in a singsong tone as if they were kids in a schoolyard.

She blushed. "I shouldn't have told you. Sheriff, if you spread that around, too—"

Clara didn't get to finish, but she was obviously pleased by Sam's attention and Travis felt glad for them. Max had stepped out of a nearby exam room with a woman holding a large cat. "Call me if that medication doesn't help and we'll try another. Urinary tract infections can be stubborn, especially in males, but I think he'll be fine." He added, "Just keep him away from Mrs. Higley's cat."

"You think he could be the father of those kittens?"

"Well, you're neighbors—and both cats roam. Or did."

Travis couldn't hold back a yawn. New life was something special, including in the feline world. But at 3:00 a.m., after hours spent tossing and turning, thinking about the birthday party picture Lauren had shown him, he'd been rousted from bed by a phone call. He was always a light sleeper, and he'd dressed while trying to talk Finn Donovan down off an emotional ledge. His wife, Annabelle, was in labor, which Finn claimed was a few weeks too early, and they'd needed a police escort to Farrier General. A short time later, baby Donovan entered the world, squalling and red as a Valentine's Day rose. Travis had stuck around to admire the infant through the nursery room glass, clap Finn on the shoulder and accept a cigar from the new father, before he hightailed it back to Main Street.

Travis had even teared up a little at the hospital, which he'd never admit to, but Finn's face had been a study in awe. Ever since, Travis had been asking himself why he'd never married or had a family of his own. Well, he knew—Barren's star reporter had dug up his past—but this morning the idea held a certain vague appeal. The swift image of Lauren that shot through his head did not.

No sleep last night must have made him punchy to even consider the notion.

"Hey, Max." Travis watched the cat woman leave the clinic and walk to her car. "Wanted to give you a heads-up. First," he told Max and Clara, "the Donovans are proud new parents."

Clara put a hand to her chest. "Oh, that's splendid news. Everyone all right?"

"Doing fine. They have a baby boy." He turned to Max. "Got a minute?"

"Hold my ten o'clock, G." They went into Max's office, where Travis quickly recapped his conversation with Lauren about Lucie McCafferty, or whoever she might be now. "Living somewhere, maybe near Denver, it appears. Palling around with kids like Maura Aiken, whose father owns half a dozen companies, several in the *Fortune* top fifty—" Travis had done some research of his own last night "—and earns millions each year." He wasn't ready to accept everything Lauren had suggested, but as a cop his brain was busy. If true, who had taken Lucie from the mall in Farrier ten years ago?

Travis had seen the look of compassion in Lauren's eyes when he'd spilled his own story. Shocking in itself, but she had a past of her own. Could he trust her not to write an article on *him*? He hoped so.

Max sank back in his desk chair. "Wow. That is news."

"Nothing solid yet, but I thought you'd like to know."

"You think if we find Lucie, Averill could turn up, too?"

"Anything's possible. In the meantime, keep this to yourself, Max."

"That would sure help straighten out Zoey's situation for me."

"I'll keep you posted."

With a bounce in his step, and wide awake now, Travis went out into the hall, then started for the main door. He had that jazzed-up feeling he always used to get on a case. Maybe he'd ask Lauren to meet him for lunch or dinner, discuss his new findings.

"Don't work too hard, G." He winked at Clara on his way by. "And give my best to Sam."

She threw a paper wad at him.

IN THE PAST few weeks, Rachel was often in the nursery when Max got home, doing her best to soothe Zoey's latest crying jag. Tonight was no different. He called out from the entryway below. "Upstairs," she said, then "help."

In the nursery he took the baby from her,

rocking Zoey in his arms. She gazed up at him through teary eyes. "Did you call Sawyer?"

"Of course. He had to admit it's colic and sent his sympathy."

"Some doctor," Max said, although he must be joking too. As if he and Rachel were both Zoey's parents, bonded by a common problem.

Rachel sighed. "We're going to try that different formula. Zoey will see Sawyer in a few days. He assumes we can hold on until then."

Max brushed a strand of hair off Rachel's cheek. "You've had a hard day, but here's something to lift your spirits. Have you heard, G—I mean, Clara—and Sam Hunter are actually seeing each other?"

"We guessed as much at the hospital. How nice." She said, "Did you have a better day than I did?"

As if they were truly a couple and shared each other's daily events, the good and the not-so-good. He grinned. "This morning, as soon as I reached the clinic, Clara practically jumped into my arms. She'd already heard about our engagement, I'm thinking maybe from Sophie." His sister had been over the moon at the announcement. "Clara said she couldn't be happier to get the news, but I managed to stop her from making a sign for the front desk. *Congratulations, Max and Rachel.*" His gaze shifted. "I had to practically kick her out of the office at noon so she'd go home to rest. Chad leave town yet?"

"No."

"Did you talk to him?"

She felt a flash of guilt. She hadn't wanted to fill Max in yesterday, pleading time to process the event, and as usual he had left home early that morning. He'd posted a note on the refrigerator telling Rachel he had a call at Wilson Cattle before eight o'clock. Zoey had still been asleep, and so was Rachel who had never alerted Max to take his shift the previous night.

"It was fine. Chad liked the Bon Appetit. He didn't broach any awkward topics until we got to the house afterward. Then he tried to…kiss me, but that didn't happen."

"I see you're not wearing the ring." Which would discourage Chad. She'd forgotten to put it back on today. "Rachel, our engagement gives you the perfect way out." Zoey's eyelids had drooped, and Max gestured for

Rachel to turn down the blanket in the crib. "Maybe you've changed your mind," he said.

"No. I haven't." She remembered their kiss when Max got the DNA results and, more recently, his clumsy, quasi-proposal to benefit them both. Why hadn't she used their sham engagement to protect herself from Chad? To quiet town gossip? For Zoey's sake. To protect her and Max. Another visit from CPS was also never far from Rachel's mind. She said weakly, "But Chad is still part of the family that means a lot to me. I don't want to hurt him."

"So, you'd give him the chance to hurt you again instead."

"Max, I told you. I know him. When the time is right, I need to let Chad down gently, urge him to go back to Indiana. Without me. But I would like to preserve whatever relationship I have left with his mother and dad, which I can't do if I make him angry, just send him packing."

"I don't trust him," Max muttered.

"You're afraid he'll do something rash?"

"I'm afraid you'll let him. I'm worried that, yes, you're doing this to protect me, Zoey, even his parents, when really you're not strong enough to just say no."

Rachel felt the blood fade from her cheeks. "What?" he said. "What haven't you told me?"

She fussed with the crib blanket, smoothed Zoey's sheet, which had a design of suns and stars. "When I was still at the Whittakers' house, staying there after Jason died, at first Chad never pushed, as I told you, never said anything remotely too personal, never told me how he felt. He was just…there for me, for all of us." She lifted Zoey from his embrace, then laid her gently in the crib. She turned back to Max. "But then, as if he'd waited for *his* moment, he caught me at a bad time. It was my wedding anniversary—or would have been—with Jason. That one time, after Chad brushed away my tears, we kissed. I did let him, and everything changed. At least for him," she said. "I felt awful, it was way too soon for me to even think of another man, and guilty for demeaning my own memories of Jason. It was wrong to lead Chad on even when I never meant to."

"Rachel, you were grieving. He took advantage of that. He'd probably been waiting for the opportunity. It's as clear as glass to me. He'll manipulate you in any way he can to get what he wants. You need to stop that now. I'm here to help," he said.

Help him down the front steps, Rachel imagined him saying.

But Max just said, "Whatever you need."

"I have to do this myself. In my own way. In my own time."

"Okay, I hear you. I don't have any right to tell you what to do." Then, as if he couldn't help himself, and this was the worst idea he'd ever had, Max drew Rachel into his arms, holding her close. "But do whatever you need to do soon. Before Chad hears about us from someone else." The first news of their engagement had begun to pop up in town. Sophie knew. So did Willow, Cody and Clara. Who else? "It doesn't look good for him to be hanging around, taking you out, only that once, I hope…when we're supposed to be getting married."

"I don't want to make anything harder for you, Max."

"Then don't," he said, his tone shaken. "I don't want anything to be harder for you, either." He tilted Rachel's face up, then lowered his mouth to hers and kissed her. Again. As if he had every right to do that at least. Her heart was beating loud enough that he must hear it. Feel it. Max slowly eased back but held her gaze with his, as if to transmit his deepest feelings for her.

Maybe she recognized the look because it mirrored her own emotions.

He caught Rachel's hand, running his thumb over her bare ring finger. He assured her that he'd be here if she needed him, then went downstairs to eat the dinner Rachel had left in the warm oven.

He'd seemed hurt that she had taken off his ring. And he'd left her wondering. Did Max truly care about her beyond their sham engagement that was about to light up the town? After betraying Jason's memory with Chad, had she done the same with Max?

"I CAN TELL YOU, I was pea-green jealous," Logan Hunter told Max the next day.

"I'm not jealous."

Logan ignored that. "Remember, Blossom had this guy before me, she was on the run from him when we met, and I wanted badly to save her from him. That is, after I stopped fighting myself not to care about her too much. Why don't you let Rachel know how you feel? It's obvious."

"After Averill? I might not be any better for Rachel than Chad is." In fact, she was seeing him again today. And Max felt irritated, which he could admit to himself. Should he tell Rachel about his feelings for her? He hadn't done so the night before when he had the chance. And what if she didn't share them?

Was the ring about his own wishful thinking? Max had been hard-pressed not to stop her, or try to, from going to Jack's the other day. He'd thought about them the whole time. What they were doing, talking about, and if Chad had charmed her into thinking of him as more than her brother-in-law. His own talk with Rachel last night hadn't reassured him. What if he told her how he felt? And she rejected him?

He bent down to examine the abscessed hoof on Logan's horse. "This doesn't look much better than the last time I was here."

Which wasn't good news.

Logan patted the gelding's neck, his tone sad. "No hoof, no horse."

The old saying didn't ease Max's mind, either. He straightened. "Sundance has had a good life." It might be time to let him go.

Logan took off his Stetson, then resettled it, clearly unwilling to make that decision yet. "What about trying a different antibiotic?"

"Might do the trick," Max agreed, knowing how much Logan cared for the horse. He always considered his clients' feelings, and as long as Sundance seemed comfortable enough… "I'll follow up then in a few days."

Logan looked relieved. "While you're here now, come see Nick's pony. I'm thinking we need to sell him if you know of any buyers. Nick can't ride him anymore. He's too big and has his horse now as well. We can't keep the pony if he's not working."

Having heard the reluctant note again in Logan's voice, Max trailed him down the aisle to another stall. Both of Logan's observations were true. No ranch could afford to let an old horse or pony linger, and right now finances were tight on many of the spreads Max visited in his practice. As they watched the pony pick through his hay in the stall, Max said, "How are you and Blossom doing?"

Logan must have guessed what he meant. "We've sure had our moments about bringing another baby into the family, but it was Daisy who helped us decide. Remember when I told you she wanted a sister to play with? And then realized it would be years before the baby was old enough?" Logan did the hat thing again, smoothing his hair before he put it back on his head. "Blossom and I had a long talk—and instead of having our own baby, we hope to adopt an older kid. It'll be good for everyone, I think."

"I bet Daisy's happy now," Max said with a twinge of unexpected envy. He almost lost the gist of Logan's next words.

"We haven't told Daisy yet. We want to apply at an agency first, see what may be possible, but I don't doubt she'll be picking out paint and curtains for the room connected to hers through that Jack and Jill bathroom. Kind of like a girls' dormitory." Logan was smiling. "Everybody wins, you know. Can't quite believe I'll have three kids then, but it's the right decision. I'm happy with it." He studied Max. "What about you? Any wedding plans yet?"

Max rolled his eyes. "You heard about the engagement?" The news was indeed spreading fast.

Logan clapped Max on the shoulder. "I hope you realize this whole town will turn out to see you and Rachel get married. You'll have to step on people like Jean Bodine pronto or they'll take over the planning." The WB's matriarch had "managed" several weddings and now considered herself to be an expert.

He hesitated, suddenly envisioning that ring back on Rachel's finger, their engagement becoming real instead of fake. A commitment from her that he'd never imagined giving in return.

"We haven't started making plans."

"Everything okay, Max? You don't sound that excited."

"I, uh, sure I am. Guess that's just the usual pre-wedding jitters. I don't even want to think about a guest list for the invitations or where we'd go on our honeymoon." The one that wouldn't happen. Rachel might run off with Chad, leaving Max to explain why she'd broken their supposed engagement. "Rachel's got some personal issues to resolve first."

And true to form in Barren, Logan already knew about Chad, too. "I don't mean to become one of the gossips around here, but

Blossom heard Rachel was with some guy the other day, headed into Jack's place."

"Chad Whittaker. He's her brother-in-law, visiting from Indiana."

"Ah," Logan said, giving the pony a pat before they left the stall and went out into the barn aisle.

"Logan, that pony appears sound. I may be able to find you a buyer." Several of his clients had kids the right age. Max added, "Or if you and Blossom intend to adopt, wouldn't you need the pony for your new little girl?"

"I may," Logan agreed. "Depends on how old, how big she'll be. Guess I should wait, then. And about Sundance—"

"That hoof may yet heal. He's likely got some living left to do." Like Sophie's dog Remi, which she'd rescued from doom. Max had even gotten used to Sky, accepted her as part of his household. As Rachel had said, she was a sweet dog. Lately she'd taken to lying at his feet, her head across his shoes, and when he walked in the house, she greeted him, tail wagging. It kind of gave him a kick, really.

Outside the barn he and Logan shook hands. "Thanks for coming by."

"Anytime. Let me know what you decide

about the pony. I'll be back to check on Sundance." But Logan's queries about Rachel had unsettled Max again.

A short time ago, he'd thought he and Averill were headed for marriage and look what had happened. Max had promised to avoid another relationship, yet he'd entered into this faux engagement to Rachel. And there was Chad's role in her life. Plus, the surprising news about Lucie McCafferty. If she were found after all this time, that could change things again. Sworn to secrecy by Travis, Max hadn't even told Rachel about the sheriff and Lauren's discovery yet. A news report about Lucie might bring Averill out of hiding. What would happen then with Zoey?

Max drove back into town, feeling glad for Logan and Blossom and their family, which might soon include another child, but half fearing he could still lose his own little girl, the baby he had never expected to have. To love with all his heart. And then, of course, there was Rachel. Was he falling in love with her when he'd vowed never to do so again with anyone? Could he let her know how he felt? Would he be enough for her? Or would he lose Rachel, too?

CHAPTER SEVENTEEN

TRAVIS HAD GIVEN Max the heads-up yesterday about Lucie McCafferty, and today he met Lauren for coffee and another strategy session. They had to connect Maura Aiken now with Averill's missing sister. The photos of her and Lucie at five years old or so were interesting, even intriguing, but Lauren had been right. The amount of personal information kids posted online invited every evildoer in the world to prey upon them.

"Considering the other girls and Maura at the party, I assume our Lucie also has a well-to-do family. Such people tend to congregate, and I've been able to link some of the others whose pictures were captioned in the newspaper with equally prominent backgrounds."

Lauren agreed. "Maura's personal page too has more pics from that party. Not everyone was tagged—identified—but unless they're her Facebook friends, they wouldn't be. I'll keep looking." She leaned forward, elbows on the table. "Quite a few of them attend the same school. I could call—"

"Don't. That place is probably exclusive, protective of its students' privacy—rightly so—and no one will enlighten us. We need another way."

She smiled. "My, aren't you the dedicated sheriff this morning? Can't you throw your weight around?"

"Lauren, the original case—a missing child here—would have been my jurisdiction at first, if I were sheriff then, but kidnapping, if that's what happened, made that a federal matter. A cold case now." And Travis didn't have access to that file. Those local newspaper stories had given them little useful information.

"Then what if I put a few inches of copy in the paper, hinting that we're close to solving that mystery from ten years ago? Someone might know something."

"The *Journal*? We talked about that—about Averill then. Absolutely not."

"I'm a reporter. That's what I do. Break stories."

"Not this one. Not yet." He thought a moment. "I'm wondering, though. I get that the people she's with now would want to safeguard her privacy as well—but maybe not just because they're important in their own way or because she's a kid. What if her current parents were the ones who snatched Lucie at that mall? Crossed state lines into Colorado? I'm guessing that was a private adoption there, and those records are sealed."

Lauren's sharp gaze had brightened. "You mean that desperate person—couple—we talked about who wanted a child they couldn't have themselves."

Travis pointed his coffee stirrer at her. "Or someone they hired. You leak the story prematurely and everyone involved goes underground. We might never find Lucie, then."

"I get you, Travis," she said, smiling, although he didn't trust the look in her eyes. "But you're just so adorable when you get all fired up."

Travis ignored her. The situation was way too serious for flirting. He'd already thought of contacting the FBI, using his old contacts, asking them to reopen the case, but that seemed too soon as well. He wasn't exactly their favorite ex-agent. And to be honest, he didn't relish giving up control just yet. Once the feds had the case again, Travis would be back writing tickets and giving Breathalyzer tests on Saturday nights.

He hated to admit this, but he liked working with Lauren. Assuming he could keep her behind virtual bars while trading theories and information, and he did the actual detective work.

The question was: Where to look next?

And how to avoid surrendering himself to Lauren's flirty eyes.

"Thanks, Sophie, for saving me this morning." Rachel juggled Zoey's carrier with the baby tucked inside into the great room at Gabe and Sophie's ranch. She set it down beside the sofa and Zoey's legs kicked free of the blanket as if she were anticipating a wonderful time with her aunt and uncle. "I'm sorry to impose."

"Don't be silly. I'm always glad to see this little munchkin." Sophie lifted the baby, settling her against the slight swell of her stomach. "Now that my morning sickness has ended—most of the time—I'm all yours. At least today." Sophie had taken the morning off from work to help Rachel, who was meeting Chad at the café soon. She hadn't wanted him to come to the house again. "What's the occasion?"

Rachel didn't relish telling Sophie exactly why she needed a babysitter, and the awkward talk with Max last night was fresh in her mind. But Sophie deserved the truth.

"My brother-in-law's here. Surprise," she added. "We're having brunch."

She would let Chad down gently, then see him on his way. Briefly, she told Sophie about the situation.

"That's a tough one," Sophie said. "I understand that you'd like to maintain a relationship with your in-laws, but this guy…from what you've said, he seems weird. Are you sure you should do this, Rachel?"

"If I don't, he'll stay or come back, call and text me all the time."

"I'd appeal to his sense of fair play, assuming he has one."

"That's the thing. It's not as if he's some monster, though Max and I had a difference of opinion last night about Chad. This morning I have two problems. Both are stubborn."

Sophie half smiled. "At least Max isn't being his usual clueless self. In fact," she said,

"I like his gradual change, and if he saw something in Chad to be wary of, you should pay attention." She glanced at the landline phone on a nearby table. "Let me call Gabe at the barn. I'm sure he'd be happy to go with you, not as a threesome while you talk, but staying close in case you need him."

"Sophie, I'll be okay. We're meeting in public."

"You couldn't just text him, cancel this brunch or whatever, tell him plainly to leave town? That you've decided not to see him again?"

"I would, but he'd paint me to his parents as some cold, ungrateful woman who doesn't deserve their loyalty or their love. His mother's already halfway there."

"Why are they so important to you now?"

"I love them. I care about them." And if she were being honest with herself, Jason's parents, even Chad, were her last connection to her late husband. Maybe Max was right about her, and she wasn't strong enough.

Sophie's gaze held hers. "Rachel, we worked together. I know how you value always doing the right thing. But you're walking a tightrope here and Chad must know how you feel about his parents. He's using you." She paused. "Does he know about you and Max?" Sophie's eyes had gone to Rachel's bare ring finger. "Or is everything there not good, either?" Sophie had squealed with delight when Max told her he and Rachel were engaged. She'd been the first person he called. Sophie had made a beeline to Cattle Track Lane to hug and kiss them and tell Rachel she intended to be her matron of honor.

"Max has been my rock," she said. "We're still…engaged."

"Hmm." Sophie put Zoey against her shoulder and the baby laid her head against Sophie's neck. "My brother and I aren't always in agreement, but I love Max with every part of my being. We once had just each other—our parents gone, their loss a deep wound inside—and he took over to raise me when he would rather have done something else with his life then. I'll always be in his debt."

Rachel wanted to tell Sophie everything, but she and Max had agreed to keep the fake part of their engagement secret for now, even from his sister and Gabe.

When she didn't speak, Sophie nodded. "All right, I see. Not my place here. But Averill did a number on Max. I won't stand by and see him hurt like that again."

"I value our friendship, Sophie." And she started to say *I love him.* Which startled Rachel. Instead, she said, "I value Max, too, more than I can say."

"You've been good for him. Please keep it that way, for Zoey, too."

With her warning in mind, Rachel unpacked Zoey's things for the day, then hurried off to meet Chad, her heart already in her throat. Did she love Max? How could she explain her true relationship to him or to Sophie when Rachel couldn't explain it to herself?

WITH SOPHIE'S WORDS still on her mind, Rachel slid into the chair across from Chad at the café. He'd already ordered coffee for them though she doubted she could eat.

"Thank you." She took a sip. "And thanks for meeting me." But Rachel wished she'd chosen a different place. The casual restaurant had been lavishly decorated for Valentine's Day, like every other spot in town, with hearts everywhere and bowls of candy in the center of each table with the usual sayings: Be my Valentine, Honeybunch and Luv U

Forever. Rachel had forgotten about the up-coming holiday and glanced around the room, hoping not to see any of the usual town gos-sips here. She needed to make this quick, tell Chad she and Max were engaged, even though it was a sham. At least, in midmorn-ing, the café was half-empty.

He smiled. "You were right. The other night, your place of business was not ap-propriate, and I apologize. I hope your 'em-ployer' wasn't too peeved that I kept you so long. But then, we had a lot to talk about. We still do," he added.

This was the opportunity she'd wanted. But *how* to tell him about the engagement? She should have worn the ring rather than leave it at home not to shock Chad. Several people at other tables kept looking at them, and even Clara McMann, who'd apparently stopped in to get a take-out order, gave her a curious glance before she left. Yet where else could Rachel have met with Chad? She didn't want to be alone with him. The hard-est part of all this was knowing she was just as guilty as he was.

He toyed with his spoon. "So, let's talk… Rachel, you don't need that job with the vet.

Caring for a baby. Isn't that a constant reminder of the child you lost?"

"At first it was, yes."

"You can find something else in Woodville, close to Mom and Dad. To me," he said, his gaze wandering over Rachel. "I realize you're still hung up on Jason—"

"Chad, he was my *husband*. I'll never forget him, and what did I do? I tarnished our relationship, our marriage, our love for each other. With you. I can't forgive myself—and I certainly won't forgive you."

He looked taken aback, then suddenly smiled. "You always were a bit…rigid. I know, because of your parents, and no wonder you took to mine as if you'd been born to them instead. That's understandable. But time passes, Rach. Jason's been gone now for years."

"I don't need the reminder," she said.

"You could have what you want again. Mom and Dad will welcome you back without question. So will I."

"Really? That sounds easy, but it's not. I stayed in Woodville after he died until your behavior forced me to move away, to leave people I care about. Don't *you* feel the least bit guilty for how you acted with your own brother's grieving widow?"

His tone hardened. "No, because you *let* me hold you, care about *you*. I always have. Did you never see that? I didn't try to get closer to you then because I had some foolish, one-sided fantasy. I could tell you felt the same way about me."

"Chad, please." She should have known she wouldn't be able to reach him. His voice had risen, and the barista at the counter was looking at them now, perhaps wondering if she should call the manager. Two women at the next table were talking behind their hands in low voices, their gazes flicking toward Rachel. If she'd wanted to avoid gossip in Barren, she'd picked the worst spot.

Rachel glanced toward the exit door, wondering if she should leave. Making a scene wouldn't help.

Chad leaned back in his chair as if he were trying to calm himself, arms crossed. "Don't think you can play Goody Two-shoes any longer. Admit it, Rachel. You feel guilty and now you're telling yourself that you made a mistake so you can get off the hook—"

"You told *me* you admitted *your* mistake—"

"My only mistake was letting Jason marry you instead of me."

"Oh, Chad." How wrong could he be? Rachel didn't know how to defuse the situation before it truly got out of hand. She felt glued to her chair. This was playing out even worse than she'd feared.

"My parents may not see the truth about us yet," he said, "but why keep fooling yourself? You and I, we'd be good together. Happy. Jason would want that. For both of us."

Rachel's blood seemed to chill. She'd put herself on full display here in front of people who, within the hour, might spread the news about her tense meeting with Chad. Already, a couple in the corner were clearing their table, their eyes on Rachel.

As they left, the door remained open, and to Rachel's dismay Max walked in. He paused for a moment, then went to the counter and ordered a breakfast sandwich. He nodded at her, then Chad, probably seeing the tension between them.

"Ah, nice," Chad murmured. "Did you plan this rescue attempt?"

"Max is here for something to eat, not to confront you." She prayed.

"I wouldn't be that sure." When Max strolled over to the table, Chad didn't rise. "Hey, Doc. I guess Rachel thought she might need reinforcements."

Max's steady gaze held Chad's. "Rachel can take care of herself, but it seems I was right about you. I don't like your tone."

"Max," she said. "Everything's fine. I'll be home soon—"

He glanced around. "Where's Zoey?"

"With Sophie. I won't be much longer."

Chad stood up. "We'll take as long as we need. We haven't finished here."

"Yes, you have," Max said.

Rachel rose from her seat, too. "Chad, sit down. Please."

"No," he said and reached for Rachel's arm as if knowing she wanted to bolt.

"Take your hands off me," she said.

Every head in the place had turned, people's mouths agape. Chad, his shoulders squared in that military posture, went toe to toe with Max, who broadened his stance, his hands forming fists at his sides. "I told you once. Don't touch her again."

Chad lightened his grasp but loomed over Max. "Back off, *Doc*. Why don't you go fix somebody's cat? Huh? Or do you think you have some personal claim here?"

Max looked at her, one eyebrow arched. "Rachel?"

She swallowed, hard. She could see the challenge in his eyes.

The manager emerged from the kitchen. "Not in my shop. Take this outside, you guys—"

"I said let her go," Max growled.

Rachel finally tugged her arm free. There was only one way to stop this. The manager had turned away, then disappeared again, probably to call the sheriff. "Chad, please don't let this turn into a fight—I should have told you sooner. Max and I are… We're engaged."

"What?"

"I didn't know how to tell you—"

She didn't get to finish. This, too, would be partly her fault, just as that one kiss from Chad had been. He moved to grab her arm again, his eyes blazing. But this time he didn't get that close before—

Max raised his fist and punched Chad in the face.

Rachel could already hear sirens in the distance.

CHAPTER EIGHTEEN

"I COULDN'T BELIEVE what you did," Rachel told Max the next morning. She'd been too angry with him, with Chad, to say much yesterday. Last evening had been spent in stony silence. "What were you thinking?"

"You sound like my lawyer."

His brown eyes looked sad, and she knew he must regret what he'd done. But to hit Chad? Travis Blake had arrived at the restaurant as Chad was gingerly touching his jaw, and the next hour had been even more stressful. The good news? To Rachel's relief, and probably Max's, Chad had refused to press charges. He'd rushed out of the restaurant to go back to his motel between Barren and Farrier, nursing his wounds both physical and emotional. Travis had released Max with a warning to keep away from Chad. Obviously, since then Max had talked to his attorney.

"I've never even thought of doing something like that before. Because of Averill, hoping she'd turn up, I haven't petitioned the court yet to change Zoey's name on her birth certificate or settle the matter of my paternity in front of a judge, but that's been scheduled now. I'm told this doesn't look good."

"You think?"

Max had not only jeopardized his position regarding the baby, but he'd made their engagement look to be more than it was. Played the jealous boyfriend. "Well," she admitted, "you're not alone. I imagine Chad's on the phone right now, telling his parents what a piece of work I turned out to be—and I expect, as they usually do, they'll take his side."

"Rachel. You have a place here, you're accepted in Barren—never mind the gossip. If your in-laws always side with Chad and won't understand why you left, maybe they aren't as accepting of you as you think."

He had a point, but Rachel wasn't ready to examine that. "What a mess, Max. When I told Chad you and I were engaged, the shocked look on his face turned the few heads that weren't already swiveled our way. Thank goodness Lauren Anderson wasn't having brunch there at the time or this would be all over the *Journal*'s next edition."

"Well, she wasn't there," Max said, his mouth turning mulish. "What was I supposed to do, Rachel? Stand there and let him hassle you? You just said it yourself. We're supposed to be engaged." He glanced at her still-bare ring finger. "Or am I the one not getting the message?"

"What does that mean?"

He shifted his weight from one foot to the other. Through the baby monitor, they both heard Zoey snuffling in her crib upstairs, making the sweet noises she always did when she first wakened. Soon, she'd need a bottle, and Rachel wanted nothing more than to cuddle her close in the rocking chair in the nursery with its freshly painted walls and white furniture. The room Rachel would have decorated in the same style for her own baby.

"If you'd worn that ring when Chad came to town—"

"Why does *that* matter so much to you? We're playacting," she said.

"Rachel, all you would have had to do then was wave my grandmother's ring in his face—he'd have given up. What other choice would he have? I tried to send you that message at the café, at the house before. I realize you have a lot of emotional issues to consider about him, his parents, even your own loyalty to Jason's memory. I was trying to protect you."

"And I was trying to do the same for you."

Rachel could see by the stiff set of his shoulders, the look in his eyes, that he might feel dangerously close to the same emotions she felt for him. How would she have reacted if Averill had met him at the café yesterday? Did he fear that she might choose Chad over him? If, indeed, he did care that much. "Max, what are we doing when above all you have Zoey to think of—"

"Not only her now. Don't tell anyone, but Travis gave me a heads-up yesterday." He ran a hand through his hair, making his cowlick stand up, but the endearing gesture didn't make Rachel smile now. "Lauren saw a picture of what she thinks is Lucie McCafferty. Same age approximately as she was in the photo Averill took the day she vanished. They think this one was snapped shortly after that, likely by her abductor or the people who have her now. Travis hopes to find out who they are, where she may be living."

"You mean she was taken then adopted by another family?"

"Who may or may not know that 'adoption' wasn't legal. He and Lauren are working on that."

"Together?"

"Yeah. It seems like a long shot, but maybe then they can find Averill, too."

For Zoey's sake, and Max's, she hoped they would succeed. But if Averill did come back, and Lucie was found, what would happen then? Would Averill and Max reconcile, as she'd imagined, even when he'd claimed they were through? For the sake of their baby, they might well make a different decision, and where would that leave Rachel besides out of a job? Not that she was the most important person in this equation. *You always do the right thing,* Max had said, but it was her mother's voice she heard.

Without thinking, she reached out to take Max's hand. "I'm sorry I made things worse yesterday."

He squeezed her hand. "We'll get through this—I hope without harming Zoey."

Or Max's standing with the court, his legal rights to his child. CPS had been here once, and the agency's positive report about Zoey's care had settled the matter temporarily, but Rachel living with Max did not, and yesterday, in front of other witnesses, he'd punched Chad.

What could Rachel do now that could possibly help?

AFTER HE SPOKE with Rachel, Max left for work. They weren't going to settle anything today, but he also didn't believe things would end well. The fact that it was Valentine's Day tomorrow couldn't lift his mood. He was worried about Lucie McCafferty, about Averill. He'd tried to leave her another voice mail begging her to call him again, but her inbox was still full, and he couldn't leave a message, which worried him even more. Where was she and for this long? If Travis and Lauren had found some lead on Lucie, maybe Averill had too, as he'd first thought. But, then why hadn't she either succeeded or come back by now, disappointed all over again? What did her one phone call mean? *I'm sorry, Max. I'll explain soon. How's the baby?*

He swept into the clinic past the huge red heart hanging on the door, then under an overhead banner that read Love Is in the Air, written in glittery silver letters, to the front desk festooned with its chain of, yes, more hearts.

"Good morning, Max." Clara's cheeks looked becomingly pink, which pleased him. Her sickly pallor was gone, and she had a new glow about her—was that because day by day she was feeling better or because of the large spray of flowers that nearly blocked her from his view?

Max gestured at the elaborate bouquet. "Let me guess," he said, teasing. "Mrs. Higley is grateful for our help with Beauty's latest health crisis." Perhaps a case of feline sniffles that she'd insisted meant another overnight stay at the clinic.

"Not Mrs. Higley." Clara rearranged one of the blooms on the desk. "I hear you're Barren's new superhero."

"Don't start," he said with a groan.

"I do wish I could have seen the excitement."

"Sawyer would be glad you didn't. The last thing you need is another cardiac episode."

"I'm healthier than you are," Clara said.

"He has me on that Mediterranean diet, and my numbers will be better than they've been in twenty years. I'll outlive you."

"I'm sure you will." Max pulled a small red box from behind his back. "Don't tell Sawyer, then, but this is for you. Since you've already gotten a gift from an admirer, happy Valentine's Day a bit early. From me. I would have picked the biggest chocolate medley I could find, but again, your health."

She flushed even deeper. "Why, thank you, Max. You're a dear. I wish I'd started working for you ages ago."

He watched her open the box, then select a truffle. "I do love you, G. I mean, Clara."

"And what about Rachel? You owe her a treat after that business at the café. Did you buy her candy for Valentine's Day?"

"No." Max had chosen a more personal gift for Rachel. After their conversation earlier, he wasn't sure he should give it to her. Committing to a real relationship would be daunting, even when the very sight of her walking into a room was enough to light up his world. And after risking her reputation yesterday, she probably had her doubts about a relationship with him. Even Zoey's welfare was in question if the system decided he wasn't a fit parent for her.

"Well." Clara shifted the flower vase so she could see him better. She assessed Max's expression. "I wonder if my advice about Rachel not long ago failed to reach its target. That was not your problem at the café." Her eyes glinted. "Are your knuckles sore?"

Max flexed his hand. "Yes, they are. I'd appreciate it if we don't discuss this any further. Who's my first patient?"

"As a matter of fact, your sister's dog. Remi's due for his yearly shots and wellness exam. Sophie will bring him in at ten o'clock," she said, then added, "I do hope you're not going to let Rachel get away. With me running interference—I'll handle those tongues that started wagging yesterday—how can you not live happily ever after?"

"Don't start planning the wedding," Max said, then the words, bottled up inside him for days, burst out. "Clara. We're not really engaged." Too late, the damage already done, Max clamped his jaw shut.

"My word." Clara's shocked tone shouldn't come as a surprise. He and Rachel had lied to everyone in Barren, but somehow Clara's opinion mattered the most. Max avoided her gaze to look at the floor as he tried to explain, leaving out Chad.

"To safeguard Rachel's standing in town, to protect Zoey from those wagging tongues, and to keep the county happy, meaning CPS or a judge, we decided to, um, fake an engagement."

"With your *grandmother's* ring," Clara said, shaking her head. "She must be turning in her grave. Fake? Do you believe what you're saying? Maxwell Crane, it was plain to me from the first day I saw Rachel with you that this is a match for the ages."

"It's not," he insisted, unwilling to examine his own turbulent feelings, which he had yet to share with Rachel.

"At the hospital, you couldn't take your eyes off her. And I thought you were a smart man."

Max felt like a little boy being scolded by his mother. "Whatever is between me and Rachel is for us to work out. Not that we're headed where you think we are, Clara." Where he might wish they could be, assuming he could ever tell Rachel how he felt. For now, Zoey, Averill, even Lucie McCafferty came first. His face hot, he headed for the break room and more coffee. "If I were you, I'd water those flowers from Sam Hunter before they die."

Clara gasped. "How did you know—"

"This whole town knows you've been seeing him." He paused. "I think—we all think— it's great. Maybe the wedding bells you've been hearing are for the two of you, not Rachel and me."

THE GIRLS' NIGHT OUT group normally met in the evenings, which was more convenient for those women who worked outside the home and didn't get off before five o'clock and those who had young children to bathe and put to bed—at which point they all needed the camaraderie and, of course, a glass of wine. No one wanted to miss Valentine's Day tomorrow night with their spouse or significant other. Thus, a lunch at Jack's restaurant had seemed called for. As always, the food was delicious.

Blossom sat back in her chair with a sigh. "I'm going to start my diet, or rather restart it, as soon as I get home. This meal must have added ten pounds."

"Ah," said Nell, "but isn't the Bon Appetit worth it?"

Today's special was a rich cassoulet that many people ordered. Rachel had barely tasted the dish; her mind started to wander, reliving—rehashing—her earlier argument with Max. Of course, someone noticed.

Shadow bent her head to catch Rachel's eye. "Hello. Where has our blushing bride-to-be gone?"

"Please. No more teasing." Her friends—only Annabelle, as a new mother, was missing today—had been relentless since the night Rachel and Max had become engaged, not that the others knew it was only pretend. They offered suggestions for the wedding, its timing, how many guests should be invited, the venues for the ceremony and reception until her head ached.

Rachel was again wearing the ring, in part to convince her friends that the engagement was real. They'd seemed to doubt her at first, and she'd decided it was necessary to show them its symbol, which they'd each examined with enthusiasm, a few with tears in their eyes.

"This ring belonged to Max's grandmother,"

she'd explained, and more tears had appeared. They were a sentimental bunch.

Now Rachel saw half a dozen phones being whipped from bags, and thumbs started flying. "Oh, no, not more planning." Max had complained that Clara was in full wedding mode at the clinic, but she couldn't hold a candle to this group. And then there was yesterday's melee at the café. Rachel had suspected that would be on everybody's lips today, but so far it hadn't been mentioned. Rachel said, "It's way too early."

"You need to book a reception hall at least a year ahead—longer if it's somewhere really popular and fancy."

"We're keeping the wedding simple."

Several women hooted. "In Barren, there's no such thing."

"I mean it," Rachel said, flushing.

But already Cass Bodine and her mother-in-law Jean were all in too with the planning.

Nell held up her phone. "Look at this gown. Have you ever seen anything as splendid?"

There were murmurs of agreement as she passed the phone around the table. Even Rachel liked the gown, but she'd worn white before for Jason, and besides, this wedding would never happen. She hated to maintain the lie. Together, she and Max would have to reveal the truth.

The next half hour during dessert, and more calories, opinions flew. Jack was voted the best caterer to handle the food and drink, the florist in Farrier was judged to be better than the smaller shop off Main Street here, and some thought Sky should walk Rachel down the aisle. By the time the luncheon group broke up, she was exhausted. On the way out the door, Nell sidled up to her.

"Everything still okay? I heard about the dustup at the café."

"Who hasn't?" Rachel said with an eye roll. "I'm glad no one brought it up." She hugged Nell, then started off without letting Barren's best cowgirl get in another word. "I'm blissfully happy—and so is Max."

THE CONTINUING WINTRY weather didn't seem right for Valentine's Day tomorrow. But then, Lauren didn't plan to celebrate the romantic holiday. Her fingers itched to break the story about Lucie McCafferty, but she'd decided, after Travis's most recent caution, to hold off until she spoke to him again. If her excitement over her latest finding ignited his, too, which she thought it would, they were close to solving the mystery. Fortunately, she didn't have to track him down. On her way back from lunch, she ran into him outside Earl's Hardware.

"Why the Cheshire cat grin?" he asked, pulling her aside so other people could get past on the narrowed sidewalk. All winter the snow had been piled on either side of the street too, and in mid-February the gray mounds blocked many of the angled parking spaces.

"Travis. I know who Lucie is. I found more photos on Maura Aiken's page—her timeline. I had to go back a way, but—you'll love this—the girl I believe to be Lucie is tagged there. Lily Elizabeth Shaefer. There's another picture from the party in which the girls are all matched with their baby photos. Bingo. I'm sure she's Lucie. Her father's a high-powered attorney in Denver."

"Lily, Lucie, I can see that," Travis said, looking over her head at someone across the street. "The two names are similar enough that at her age Lucie might have made the change without too much trouble." He turned back to Lauren. "You're shivering. It's cold. Let's go somewhere else to talk. Too many eyes and ears here on the street."

Under the leaden sky, they picked their way down the block to Travis's SUV. Inside, after starting the engine, he fiddled with the dashboard controls until heat rushed from the vents. Lauren leaned against the passenger door.

"Where do we go next?" she asked, then answered her own question. "We need a current home address. For Lily. That shouldn't be hard. Then what if I pay a visit to her family? Just sniffing around a bit, testing the waters. Nothing too nosy."

Travis blinked. "Are you out of your mind? They'd probably slam the door on you. Remember, tipping people off tends to send them into hiding. I realize you reporters can't resist poking a notebook or microphone into someone's face—"

"What would you suggest?"

"The Feds probably won't reopen the case from what we have now. Or they might, but the FBI likely won't listen to me. Unless we can identify the agency that handled her adoption and that leads us to her abductor, we're still in a blind alley."

Lauren made a clucking noise like a chicken. "Your 'I'm just a country sheriff' side is showing. What happened to that gleam in your eye last time we talked?"

"It's county, not country. That gleam was me trying not to succumb to your many charms."

His tone had been deadpan, but Lauren batted her eyes. "You wouldn't be able to handle me," she murmured, as if she were throwing down a gauntlet.

Travis scoffed. "On my worst day, I can deal with you, Lois Lane."

Lauren doubted that. "Then stay the course here, Sheriff. But you have a point. What's our plan? To get Lucie home to her sister? We don't even know where Averill is. Yet. Or who took Lucie. And what did that person tell her? She was five years old then, not a baby. She'd remember Averill, her family, even possibly her own address at the time. Why didn't she tell someone she'd been kidnapped?"

"I don't know. To all of that."

"Then let's start asking questions, finding

answers. My end goal is much bigger than Lucie McCafferty."

Travis played with the steering wheel. "Aw, Lauren, and here I thought you had a heart."

She sent him her best smile. "There's another side to this, remember—for you. This could be your chance to redeem yourself with the FBI."

"Not to mention absolving yourself after that fact-checking business with your ex. He might even take you back at the paper."

"That's just mean, Travis." Her former editor and would-be husband at the time would never do that. "I don't want him to," but she would love to scoop him. Big-time. Lauren hadn't realized just how much until now. She could almost taste victory.

"Sorry," he said, as if he meant it.

She straightened, then eased open the passenger door. "I have to go. Work to do. I'm going to see what I can find—from a distance—about Mr. Shaefer, Esquire."

Lauren almost felt sorry for Travis. She shouldn't have reminded him of his own failure.

Yet she didn't like his telling her what not to do. So... She hurried back to her office through the snow and ice, booted up her computer, then wrote a brief bit after all for the *Journal*'s digital edition tomorrow. With a faint twinge because she was inviting Travis's wrath, Lauren hit Publish. *Averill, come home. Info about Lucie.*

CHAPTER NINETEEN

RACHEL HADN'T HEARD from Chad since the episode at the café two days ago. She'd assumed he'd left town, left behind the star-crossed romance he'd imagined with her. Saved Rachel from another confrontation. She'd felt tempted to phone Kathy, see if he'd gotten home safely, but her assumption was wrong. When Max's doorbell rang, she saw Chad standing on the porch, his tall frame blurred by the frosted glass in the front door, his face obscured by some large object.

Zoey was taking a nap, and Max was at the clinic this morning. She prayed he didn't come home while Chad was here. Virtually alone in the house except for Sky, so deep in a doggy dream that she'd only twitched an ear, Rachel girded herself for battle, then opened the door.

Chad touched his bruised jaw. "Thought I looked more presentable this morning without an ice bag on my face—" which explained his absence yesterday—"and I wanted to bring you this." He thrust a huge bouquet of flowers at her. "Happy Valentine's Day."

Rachel had no choice but to take them or watch the beautiful arrangement fall to the floor. "Chad, you shouldn't have."

"I remember Jason always bought you roses."

"He did," she said, blinking. "He never missed an occasion, birthdays, our anniversary, the day I'd told him we were pregnant."

But why did Chad always lead Rachel down the road of memory? Make her miss Jason all over again? Did Chad really think that would make her turn to him for comfort, as she had once? Max had been right that Chad manipulated her.

"May I come in?" He wore his puppy dog look.

"I'd rather you didn't." They were still standing in the half-open doorway, the cold air rushing inside. "Chad—"

"I need to apologize. I must have provoked your *fiancé*, but you do realize he's got a nasty temper? I was shocked to learn you're engaged, but you should rethink that." He stepped into the house, and she had to move back out of the doorway. "Rachel, I'm concerned. I do want only the best for you—and that's not the good doctor."

Rachel cocked an ear for any sound from the baby monitor. She wished Zoey would wake up, start crying so she'd have an excuse to leave the room. "I need to get these in water," she said instead, then went toward the kitchen.

Chad followed close on her heels. "Rach, I should have ducked. I didn't intend to make a scene the other day—I was forced into it."

She bent down to choose a vase from a lower cabinet. "Don't make this about Max."

"You'd really be wise, after the embarrassment you must have felt at the restaurant, to reconsider." He glanced at her hand. "Give that ring back. I hate to keep saying the same thing but come with me to Indiana. Mom and Dad will be so glad to have you home. At last. We can start over, take things slow."

Rachel straightened, holding the crystal vase. She pushed past Chad to the sink, ran water, put the flowers in, then did her best with shaking hands to tidy the bouquet. She shouldn't accept his gift. She should give it back, usher him to the front door, shut and lock it behind him. She would do anything to protect Max and Zoey, yet she knew she'd also hurt Chad. She didn't want to set him off again.

She put the flowers on the table in the kitchen that had become as familiar to Rachel as her home with Jason. She tried to keep her voice firm. "Chad, this is my home now." At least until Max didn't need her anymore for Zoey.

"Seriously?" Chad played right to her own doubts, her fears. "You're this guy's *employee*, not the grand love of his life. You may think he's the right one for you, but to him you're just a convenience. Know why he really took that punch at me? Because, sure, he doesn't want to lose you. As his baby nurse. That's all. I bet he's not even paying you what you're worth, and when you're no longer of any use to him, he'll toss you out." Chad hesitated, then added, "He doesn't love you. I do."

Rachel knew what he said might well be true. Max might have feelings for her—he'd admitted he enjoyed the kisses they'd shared—but his focus had to remain on Zoey, on finding Averill—and now, possibly, Lucie.

When that happened, Rachel would no longer be "engaged" or have a job. Which didn't mean she should follow Chad to Indiana like the good girl she'd been raised to be, never making a fuss, always doing the right thing. Pleasing Chad when she knew he was all wrong for her.

Rachel tried for a gentler tone. "I love your parents. I love you, too—but not in the way you want me to. You'll always be Jason's brother, my brother-in-law, but no matter how much you may wish things were otherwise, I can't be with you, Chad."

He looked stunned. "You don't know what you're saying."

"Please, go home. Without me." She held his wounded gaze, watching as her words sank in. His broad shoulders slumped before he gave her a smile, his eyebrows lifting.

"Well. Guess the flowers didn't work."

"They will," she said, "for someone else. But you can't make someone love you, especially not forever." The same might be said about her and Max. As if...

"So. You're actually going through with this? Marrying the doc?"

She didn't want to answer that question. She didn't want to lie to him. Or herself.

Her gaze slid away from his. "Forget me. I want you to find the true love of your life, Chad."

He took her hand, and Rachel let him. "You're making a mistake."

"If I am, it's mine to make." Years ago, her upbringing would have prevented her from holding her ground with Chad, even with Jason if it had come to that. Caring for Zoey, managing Max's house, had given her a new belief in herself. Rachel had to do the right thing now, not to please her mother or win her dad's approval. For herself. She wasn't sure yet what that might be, except to say, "Please be happy. Jason would want that for you— and, as you once told me, for me as well."

"He'd be happy to see us together."

Rachel carefully withdrew her hand from his. "That's not his decision. I'm sorry," she murmured. "Let this fantasy of us go. It's impossible, Chad."

He gazed at the flowers on the table, then shook his head. "You know, when I was in the military, like Jason, we had the slogan, 'Failure is not an option.' I guess we were wrong."

"This is not a failure. It's just not meant to be."

She saw the exact moment when he accepted the truth, when his formidable confidence, his arrogance and the certainty that he'd get his own way deserted him. He looked at Rachel. "Well," he said. "I'd better hit the road, huh? This isn't the way I planned to spend Valentine's Day, but okay, I'll tell the folks—"

"I send my love. I'll call soon." And hope Chad's mother didn't hang up on her. Kathy would see how brokenhearted her son felt as soon as he walked in the door. But then, Rachel realized something else. As with her own parents, she'd let her concern for Kathy and her husband, her desire for her in-laws approval, go too far.

She followed Chad to the front entry. From upstairs, she heard Zoey begin to stir. Chad bent to kiss her cheek, and when she looked up, he was gone, striding toward his car at the curb. Leaving his last words behind him. "You can keep the roses."

THAT AFTERNOON TRAVIS marched down Main Street to the *Journal*. Considering the wary looks he got from various passersby, carrying gift bags and bouquets of flowers, he must have fire in his eyes. Every shop in town had romantic displays in their windows. Hearts and flowers. But Valentine's Day was far from his mind. After he'd learned about the short plea in the newspaper's digital edition, which bore no byline, he'd ordered himself to cool down because his first instinct was to destroy her keyboard. He was sure that had come from Lauren.

In the newspaper's reception area, he knocked snow off his boots, then, with a brief nod at the woman at the desk, said, "Official business." He strode into Lauren's office, where her busy hands were clicking away again at her keyboard. "Anderson. What do you think you're doing?"

She glanced up from her computer. "I suppose you mean that digital piece."

"When my dispatcher, who has plenty of time on her hands between 911 calls at the department, pointed that out, I thought she was joking."

"You didn't want me to talk to the Shaefers. So, I tried another tack. Our original one."

"Yours." Travis leaned against the doorframe. "Are you deliberately trying to sabotage this case? To hurt Averill and Max? Why? I doubt she'll see that bit about Lucie, but if she does—"

"I will have flushed her out when no one else has been able to find her. What if she already knows something that could help us? Even if she doesn't realize it. As a cop, ex-FBI, you might be able to pick up on that. You're welcome."

"Averill McCafferty has spent the past ten years searching for her kid sister. We have little to tell her yet. It's too soon, Lauren. You'd be breaking her heart all over again."

"She also abandoned her own child. Don't you wonder why?"

"If we could settle that matter for Max, which is why I got involved in the first place, yes, I'd be happy but—"

"You're making my point. I seem to be trying—harder than you are—to put all the pieces together." She swiveled in her chair to reach for a paper. "I've printed out some interesting stuff, too, from Shaefer's law firm. From a distance, as you told me to."

He snatched the single sheet from her and scanned it. "They handle adoptions."

"Discreetly," she agreed. "Private to the max."

Travis took the chair in front of Lauren's desk. "Shaefer wouldn't handle that child's adoption himself."

"No, but one of his partners could. I think we're closer than we thought. Somebody knows who brought Lucie to Shaefer." She batted her eyelashes, a disturbing habit that Travis tried to ignore. "Then I'm forgiven?"

"Only if you scrub that piece from the internet like it was never there."

"That's censorship," she said.

Travis felt a quick stab of guilt. "Call it whatever you like. Just fix your mistake." He tapped his knuckles on the top of her desk, then stood. "Thanks for the good work you did. Better let me 'try harder' to do my part now. Take things from here."

Steam practically came from her ears. "Right after you've agreed that it's good?"

"And your work is done."

Her mouth had set, but Travis detected a faint quiver. "You cops are always trying to shut out the press."

He glanced toward the door. "I mean it,

Lauren. As soon as possible, I'll try to turn this over to the Bureau."

"And see where that gets you."

She had a point, but he would have to use his old contacts in the hope they'd reopen the case. They didn't mess around with kidnappings. Besides, the FBI had all the resources of the federal government.

Lauren made a sound of utter frustration.

"Someday," she said, "you'll have to find a backbone, Sheriff."

He kept his tone mild, though her words stung. "Today is not that day."

She tossed a pen down on her desk. "You know what? I wish I'd never had dinner with you that first night to strategize. You're not going to handle me," she said.

"I already did." Travis stalked into the hallway and out to the reception area, where the woman at the desk gave him a searching look he refused to acknowledge. As his long strides covered the icy sidewalk between Lauren's office and the sheriff's department, a part of him felt guilty for laying down the law to her. He realized he also missed the sense of satisfaction in closing a case. Someone else—he prayed—would have to do that now. If the Bureau agreed to reopen at all.

Without Lauren to spice up his day, Travis would be back writing tickets and busting up the occasional fight at Rowdy's bar—or, most recently, the café. Spending his nights alone.

Oddly, he already missed her.

THE FIRST THING Max would do when he got home that night—later than he'd planned because at six o'clock he was still seeing patients at the clinic—was to work up his nerve to give Rachel the gift he'd stashed in his pocket. By now, Valentine's Day was almost over, and she probably doubted they would mark the occasion at all. But should they? He hoped she hadn't prepared a special dinner that might dry out before he got there. Most of all, he hoped she'd forgiven him by now because they'd been walking on eggs around each other since he'd popped Chad at the café.

He also hadn't forgotten his run-in here with Clara yesterday. Max was glad she was working half days and had gone home.

"All right," he said to the woman standing on the other side of the stainless-steel exam table. "Looks like this guy is good to go."

She'd come in on her way back from California with Cuddles, the little ferret, for a follow-up appointment, and Max had worked her into the day's schedule.

"I was lucky—he was—that I happened to call your clinic that day. I don't know what I would have done without you or the other vet you referred me to. I believe you had a medical emergency with a friend?"

"Clara," he said. "My receptionist. But she's okay."

"And I'm wishing I lived here instead of Arkansas."

"Always glad to help. Animals are my business," he said with a smile. And they'd been the complete focus of his life until he'd hired Rachel. No, when he'd met Averill. Obviously, he needed the reminder that, no matter how Clara felt, he shouldn't take his pseudo-engagement to Rachel any further, at least before Averill returned, if she did, or until he'd worked out custody for Zoey. Until then, he could not move forward to a possible future with Rachel. Clara's words dug at him anyway.

It was plain to me from the first day I saw Rachel with you that this is a match for the ages. Had Clara been right, and Max wasn't seeing the truth? Or wouldn't let himself? Despite his own promise, had he already fallen in love with Rachel? Yet how could he take such a risk again when he hadn't been enough for Averill? He hadn't helped her. Was he brave enough to tell Rachel how he felt? And what made him—or Clara—think Rachel would welcome that commitment? Max wasn't about to go through what he had with Averill.

Yet he'd almost given up any hope of seeing her again. He'd be wiser to concentrate on his upcoming court date to change Zoey's birth certificate and officially confirm his paternity, which his lawyer had advised him to do after Max's temper got the best of him with Chad. The attorney had managed to schedule a private hearing with the judge for tomorrow.

He walked his little patient and her owner to the door through the now-empty waiting room, turning off lights as they went. "Before you go, I forgot to ask—email me a picture of Cuddles?" Max maintained a bulletin board with photos of his clients in the main room and wanted to add the ferret.

"I'd be happy to." To his surprise, she pecked him on the cheek. "Thanks again. I'm sure you saved his life. I don't know what I'd do without him."

"Take care." Max loved the satisfaction of knowing he'd helped, but the other vet in Farrier deserved the thanks.

Leaning in his doorway, Max watched her slip the ferret's crate into her car, then buckle the seat belt around it. Not all his patients were given such a personal touch. As the car pulled out of the lot, he waved goodbye, and the woman waved back. He probably wouldn't see them again, but he'd have the reminder of a job well done in that picture of sweet Cuddles on his bulletin board. Maybe he wasn't as anti-pet personally as he'd thought because Sky, too, had won his heart. He'd just turned back into the clinic to lock up, intending to be home before seven, when another vehicle rolled into the lot.

Whoever it might be, cat or dog or ferret, he would treat it, which was no hardship.

The clinic was, again, his life—or should be. Had to be. He'd worked hard enough since last March when he and Averill broke up, not quite a year ago, to make sure of that. Another image of Rachel flashed through his mind, which Max did his best to ignore, as a woman got out of the car. Something about her made his blood rush faster. He'd never seen that sedan before, but as she raced toward him, empty-handed without a pet in sight, she looked all too familiar.

For another instant, he couldn't seem to comprehend what he was seeing. Just when he'd given up all hope, was finally putting his life back together… She was here in his parking lot.

Averill McCafferty.

CHAPTER TWENTY

"WHERE IS LUCIE?"

Unable to answer, Max stood in the doorway, staring at Averill, who wore a panicked expression. She'd left her car's engine running, jumped out and run across the lot. He'd assumed another emergency, another sick or injured pet to treat. Instead, his unhappy past was standing in front of him.

"I don't know. Travis Blake—the sheriff—told me he'd had a lead in tracking her, but when I spoke to him last, he didn't have any specifics. How did you—"

She waved a paper at him. "You mean you didn't have anything to do with this?"

"I can't see what you're holding in my face. Go shut off your car, Averill." When they were both indoors again, Max switched on the lights he'd turned off on his way out with the ferret. In the waiting room, he read the two-line printout. His hands were shaking. Lauren Anderson's work?

"From the *Journal*'s online edition," Averill said. "When I saw this, I was so shocked I couldn't think straight. Someone has found Lucie?"

"I really don't know." Max wanted to kick himself for not using Lauren's skills himself weeks ago. He hadn't thought of that. But then, perhaps no one else had, either, or feared they'd hurt Averill. How had she even seen this? "I'll give Travis a call." Then he paused. "First, you have some real explaining to do. Where have you been, Averill?"

"On the other side of the state. I had to go, Max."

"Keep talking." He couldn't decide whether he was angry, even furious, with her or whether he felt relieved that, after all, she seemed to be safe. And well. Probably both emotions applied. Max took a long look at her. Averill wore dark leather gloves, a nice navy coat and a white wool beret. Her auburn hair was longer now, the ends curled to frame her face, and her blue eyes looked suspiciously moist, but Max didn't feel sympathetic. "You can begin with why you left our baby on my front porch, then ran!"

Guilt flashed across her face. "I'm sorry. I had no other choice then."

"*Sorry* doesn't cut it. And all you could do was leave me a short note? *I can't take care of her. There's too much going on right now. She's yours.* Really?" Although that note, even unsigned, was further proof in a way of his paternity and would be part of the hearing tomorrow.

"It was an emergency. I was on my way out of town to help someone."

"Help someone," he repeated. "What about your own child? What if I hadn't been home then? The weather was freezing. She was only weeks old—"

"Two," Averill said. "She was born on Christmas Eve."

He took a bracing breath. "What did that note even mean? For a weekend, a couple of days, a year? Forever? You abandoned her, left me to cope after blindsiding me that I have a daughter. I've been hamstrung ever since not knowing what to do legally. I looked for you everywhere. So has the sheriff. And why didn't you tell me you were pregnant? I would have—"

"We weren't together anymore, and I was frightened. But I had nowhere else to turn."

"I understand about your mother. I talked to her myself, and no wonder you have problems, I get that, but you could have come to me long before the baby was born. What is wrong with you?"

She lifted one eyebrow. "Many things. You knew that, and I've been in therapy ever since we broke up. I've made a lot of progress. But, Max, that's not why I'm here now."

"Where. Exactly. Have. You. Been?" he asked again, raking a hand through his hair. "Because I can't imagine any reason why a mother would give up her newborn baby without any other explanation than 'I can't take care of her.' I'm guessing you had no new lead on Lucie, which was my first thought."

"It's not as if I left the baby at the sheriff's department or a fire station under the Safe Haven law…and I'd met someone, Max. He understands me, we…were starting to think about marriage when he got sick. I'd been running back and forth to Kansas City, taking the baby with me, when the hospital called the day I left her. He'd had appendicitis, which should have been a simple fix with surgery, but he'd developed an infection. He was in the ICU then, in danger of not surviving."

"I see. You prioritized your boyfriend over your own baby."

"Yes."

Max had sounded harsh and softened his tone. "So, you took off to be with him."

"Yes," she said.

"What did he think of the baby?"

"He was supportive. John was with me when she was born."

Max's stomach sank. *John somebody, not me.*

Averill said, "I know how this all sounds... but he's had a long, difficult recovery. I've been in KC with him since then. He was just released from the rehab facility they sent him to after the hospital. I couldn't leave him."

"You couldn't leave him." Max kept repeating what she said, trying to get his brain to accept her story. "Did you—do you—care about *our* baby at all?"

She winced. "Of course I care. I knew she'd be safe with you. I left you a voice mail not long ago asking about her. I trusted you, Max, to care for her when I couldn't."

"But I couldn't trust you. I tried my best to make us work, Averill. And that was the result? Not that we broke up because now I realize that was bound to happen, but I never thought you would do something as heartless as to walk away from the innocent, vulnerable, helpless baby who needed you—even for a good reason."

Averill buried her face in her hands. "You can't know how hard that was for me, leaving her and so soon, while feeling frantic for the man I love, and after losing Lucie so long ago. Please understand. I don't blame you for being mad—I deserve that—but I'm here now."

As if she were coming back from the grocery store. "Worried about Lucie."

"I'm not heartless, Max. I couldn't handle trying to care for—"

"You didn't care enough, apparently, to give the baby a name."

Averill looked away. "When she was born, I couldn't decide. I was told I could file an amended certificate once I'd chosen a name. But then John got sick."

"A birth certificate without acknowledging my paternity. I had to get proof of that, even when I had no doubts myself that she's mine, and once I see the judge tomorrow, her name will be Zoey Crane." He'd been a fool to wait this long.

"Zoey. That's nice." Yet Averill looked crestfallen, as if he'd betrayed her rather than the other way around. "You're going to court?"

"I should have done so before, but I kept hoping you might come back. That we'd straighten things out. Together, for Zoey's sake."

"And we can. She's my daughter, too, Max. I still have rights."

"That's for the court to decide." Max couldn't believe he'd once hoped to spend the rest of his life with Averill, and he couldn't hold back his angry words. "In case you're wondering, I haven't been nursing my broken heart while you were gone. I've met someone, too. We're engaged—and she takes excellent care of Zoey. As far as I'm concerned, you forfeited any right to that baby when you dropped her on my doorstep."

"Max, I always intended to come back when John got better. I'm her mother."

"Then you'd better hope the judge agrees." He hadn't made this part of the decision until now. "Because I'm not going to stop with the birth certificate. After that, I'll sue for full custody." He turned away. "But before I call my lawyer again, I will call Travis for you."

BY THE TIME Max got home, Rachel had begun to wonder where he was. Usually, he called if he was going to be late or if some emergency had come up. From the look on his face when he opened the door, she guessed a tragedy had occurred. Which proved to be partly true.

"Averill's back."

Rachel had expected to hear those words at some point, but they still shocked her. "When?"

"Just as I was ready to leave the clinic. I thought I was seeing a ghost." He explained about the piece in the paper's online edition. "Why didn't I think of that? Maybe I could have wound up the search for her much sooner instead of bringing Travis into it—"

"Has he talked to her?"

"I called him, sent Averill to him at the sheriff's department. I have no idea what new information he or the *Journal* might have on

Lucie." Max looked pale, and Rachel imagined she must, too.

She'd always known this would happen, at least some version of it. Just as she'd known she would need to deal with Chad. Weird that both had happened on the same day. Ever since she'd taken the job here, she'd imagined Averill walking in, throwing herself in Max's arms, hoping to reconcile. Reclaim her child. He'd said that wouldn't happen, but she'd always feared he could change his mind.

While Rachel's thoughts spun, Max told her about their conversation at the clinic. "Averill and I wrangled like two cowboys wrestling a steer. Even if her story about the new boyfriend is true, that doesn't give her the right to turn up out of the blue, make demands about Zoey. As if she never just left the baby on my porch."

Rachel rubbed at a spot of tension between her eyes. "I can't blame you for being upset—"

"I'm more than 'upset.' I'm going to try for full custody of Zoey. How could I turn her over to Averill—even for a day—when she might up and leave town again at any moment? What if this boyfriend of hers has a relapse? Averill still has issues. She's one of those people who seem to live in crisis."

"That's not quite fair," Rachel said, playing devil's advocate.

"Why would you take her side?"

"I'm not, but I can understand how she must feel, at least about Lucie." Rachel thought about the twin losses of her baby and Jason. "And I can stop worrying about Chad. He came by but he's finally gone," she said. "I was afraid—at first—that he'd make everything worse today than it was at the café—" she gave Max a pointed look "—but I think I delivered the message. I feel terrible that I hurt him, but he no longer has any illusions about me."

"None of that was your fault, Rachel. I'm proud of you." And relieved, she guessed, from his expression. "You didn't betray Jason's memory with Chad. He was the one who betrayed his brother." Max's eyes cleared, and he gazed at the bouquet Chad had left. "His parting gift?"

You can keep the roses. "I don't think he saw it that way, but yes."

Max stared down at his boots, caked with mud from a visit to a local rancher, she supposed. Normally, he would have taken them off at the door. "And about our engagement—"

"Clara knows it's fake." Rachel had cut Max off, unable to keep quiet any longer.

He blinked. "Yeah, that is *my* fault. She's tried matchmaking several times, which I've always tried to deflect, and yesterday I blurted out the truth. I should have told you, but we'd quarreled about what happened at the restaurant, and I couldn't think how to bring it up. How did you know?"

"Apparently, Clara went to the café today for coffee."

"Every day," he said.

"She ran into Sophie there and told your sister. Clara said she's very disappointed in you—" Rachel broke off, then "It seems several people overheard. Sophie called here right after that, looking for you, but talked to me instead. I assume the news will be everywhere by now."

Max groaned. "I'm sorry, Rachel. I never meant to put you on the spot. I know you had even more at stake than I did, that you still do."

"We're both on the spot," she said, "but I'm

the only one who can fix that." Their lie wasn't
the worst part. She looked down at the ring
on her finger, having made her painful decision but not wanting to say the next words.
"Max, this engagement was never a good idea.
I should leave you now to straighten things
out with Averill."

"Rachel."

"You're both Zoey's parents, and the court
would likely prefer the baby to have an intact
home—"

"Averill hasn't been here. Which is why
you were in the first place. Why would you
think of leaving just when there's a good
chance to bring this whole thing to a close?"
He paused. "Or were you only waiting for
Chad to go away?"

"No, I need to leave because having me
as an overnight 'guest' in your home with a
young child here doesn't look good—"

"Rachel, never mind the gossips or Averill.
What is this?" He stuck a hand in his pocket,
then withdrew it. "I thought we were doing
okay."

"—and because a pretend engagement,"
she said as if he hadn't spoken, "a lie can't
possibly help Zoey's case. Your case," she

added as the baby monitor on the end table emitted a soft, shushing sound that meant Zoey was stirring.

"I was always the temporary caregiver," she insisted. Living a sham version of her own broken dreams. A solid relationship with Max, a sweet baby to cherish as she'd never been able to with her own, a permanent place in this house, which she had come to love. "I will not be the person to jeopardize your chance to maintain custody."

"Whatever damage you believe there's been, it's already done. The first court hearing isn't even about custody. I'll speak with the judge, tell him or her—"

"What, Max? I don't care as much that I look bad, which is a change, isn't it, or even that people talk, but I do care about Zoey. I want the very best for her future—and that can't include me now."

"No? Or are you just stuck emotionally in Indiana? Blaming yourself for what Chad did."

"I'm *trying* to protect you—"

"How? By leaving without even…letting me in? Rachel, I…" He couldn't go on.

What had he been about to say? "I know

Averill broke your heart. I know how you feel about making a real commitment to someone else—even this pretend engagement. Tell me, Max. What other solution can there be?" She could feel his gaze follow her to the stairs. She'd be leaving him in the lurch, but likely Sophie…even Averill would step in. At least temporarily. Sadly, Rachel had already made that first decision. "I need to pack."

From upstairs, Zoey began to cry, as if she'd overheard them and didn't want Rachel to leave. Rachel felt the same way, but at the bottom of the steps, she stopped—and tugged off the ring that had belonged to Max's grandmother.

"Rachel."

She shook her head, not looking at him. "I'm going. Because what I had to learn, to be able to tell Chad to leave, is that I have to live my life for myself." The baby's cries from above grew louder. "But before I go, Zoey needs me." One last time she'd soothe her, feed her, rock her to sleep again. Rachel would be gone before morning along with any chance she might have had for a life with Max. For happiness again. She would try to find that somewhere else.

"Rachel," he said again. "You may think you're doing the right thing, but you're not. Don't let your parents, your upbringing, determine what that is now."

"You're saying I'm being rigid."

He looked as if he wanted to smile. "You can't help yourself."

Sophie had thought so, too, at one time. Rachel wished she and Max had never told the lie about their engagement, but at least she would leave with her dignity intact. If only she'd stayed an employee at arm's length instead of growing close to Max. Now, Averill was home. Thank goodness, Rachel hadn't told Max she loved him.

"And you're not seeing the truth," she insisted, handing him the ring. "Your head must still be in the clouds, Max. This isn't some play on a stage. It's real. If you can't see that, I can."

As he took the ring, their fingers brushed. Rachel stepped back, and Max dropped the ring, which jingled against something, into his pocket.

Rachel could feel her heart breaking. She remembered the day they'd gone riding. He'd looked deeply into her eyes afterward and seemed about to say something that might have taken their relationship to another level. And yet, as if she'd needed proof he couldn't commit, he hadn't said another word now, either.

She turned, then went up the stairs.

As she hit the top step, Rachel was already crying as hard as Zoey.

"There, there, baby," she murmured as she entered the nursery. The room she had painted, decorated, as she would have for her own child. Yet she'd done it for Zoey. She was losing her now, too.

From below, she heard Max all but whisper, his tone ironic, "Happy Valentine's Day."

CHAPTER TWENTY-ONE

"THE FBI HAS agreed to reopen Lucie's case." Travis leaned against Lauren's office door-frame the next morning, but she kept typing without looking up. "Good news, huh?"

"Not if it means somebody else gets my story first."

"I doubt that will happen anytime soon," he said. "Takes time to build a good case, fig-ure out who took Lucie to Shaefer—and if he knew or didn't know the adoption was illegal."

"Fascinating." Lauren reread the copy she'd been writing for her next "Who's Who in Barren" feature about Finn Donovan. She'd included paragraphs on his and Annabelle's new baby, the former sheriff's happy home life now, and a brief recap of his tragic past. Still smarting from Travis's putdown when last she saw him, she refused to meet his eyes. Clickety-clack went the keys. "Go ahead, apologize again if you want."

"Huh?" he repeated.

"Never mind. I'd know you weren't sincere anyway."

"What did I say?" he asked when he must know exactly what he'd said two days before. "I'm not trying to shut you out. We've just gone as far as we can with this. Okay, all right. I'm sorry if I messed with your head. That good enough?"

"You accused me of thinking only about the next big story."

"That's not true? Tell me another."

"Because of me—and, I admit, your work, too—we came close enough to interest the Bureau. Yes, I should feel satisfied."

"But you don't. Your 'big story' isn't about Lucie, just as it wasn't about Averill—is it? Don't go poking your nose any deeper into my past, Lauren."

She stopped typing. "Don't tell me what to do," she said, her tone sounding weak even to herself. "Travis, getting stuck in this town has been a nightmare, and while I shouldn't care what people think, I've realized I sometimes do. Things might be different if I had won Citizen of the Year two summers ago—"

"But you didn't."

The silence in the office felt awkward and Lauren hit the keyboard again. "Stop correcting me. If you want to gloat, I didn't win last summer's award either. Lizzie Maguire did." Then Lauren changed topics. "By the way, did you hear?" She did have a scoop of sorts for Travis. "This morning at the coffee place Claudia Monroe was spreading gossip like butter on a croissant." She looked up, still typing at a hundred words per minute, a bit slower than her usual speed. "Averill McCafferty's back in town."

Her triumphant tone didn't seem to impress Travis. "I already talked to her."

"And you didn't call me?" Now, he'd scooped her instead. "What else do you know?"

He sighed. "Averill has an explanation for why she left Zoey with Max. She has a new boyfriend, apparently, who has been at death's door, which is why she dropped the baby off. I'm not convinced of *her* sincerity, but things have gotten worse. Max is going to sue for full custody, and there'll be a fight."

"Wow. Thank you very much." Her mind had started whirring like the old CPU under her desk. "Let's see. What's the angle to use

here? Human interest. Who's the most sympathetic figure?"

"Do you ever quit? I didn't tell you so you
could try to ruin Max or Averill. The lives
of people I happen to care about are at stake
here, and all you can think about is breaking
that story." He shook his head in apparent dis-
gust. "You're no better than Claudia Monroe."

Her gaze fell. "I'm more appealing,
though," she said.

"Cut it out, Lauren. Try, for once, to have
some genuine emotion. You wonder why Sophie won Citizen of the Year instead of you?
Then Lizzie? Why folks in this town don't
care to kiss your ring? That's why," he said.
"Anyway. Thought you should know. The FBI
is in charge now—and I'd advise you to keep
a lid on the whole thing, which you failed to
do with that little bit in the digital edition of
the paper."

"I deleted that. But it brought Averill to
town, didn't it?"

"Brilliant. She thought Max placed it
through you." He pushed off the doorframe.
"I'm going back to my office now to play solitaire on the computer."

"That is pathetic. Or maybe you're just depressed after that other case of yours, losing your job—the job you really wanted."

He shook his head again. "You may be right, but I really don't know how you manage to look at yourself in the mirror."

His words stung, but so had hers. She hadn't meant to remind him of the reason he, too, was here in Kansas, working a job for which, like Lauren, he was overqualified. Yet, just as he kept pushing her buttons, so did she with him. Sometimes her mouth got away from her, her typing hands, too, and the look he gave her caused a small frisson of guilt to arc across her nerve ends. Had she taken out her ruined love life, her lost career, her unhappiness at the *Journal* on Travis? More than once, she had to admit. And why? She did like him, those green eyes and that half smile that hid his pain. He had a point. Her mean-spiritedness didn't make her happier.

"Travis." She couldn't keep from pleading. "Don't go, please."

"Huh?" he said yet again, which almost made her smile. He was so cute.

He was also correct about her. She thought of Lucie McCafferty/Lily Shaefer, an unsuspecting teenager whose life might soon be turned inside out. The heartache, the guilt her adoptive parents, complicit or not, would feel. And Averill. She had the feeling that if she let Travis walk out the door, he'd never come back. On the street he, too, would ignore her when she'd enjoyed their sparring, the work they'd done together, the few meals they'd shared. The occasional light in his eyes, as if he did like her when few other people even tried. Lauren had to admit she had given them no reason to.

"I don't mean to be a witch," she murmured. "Travis, I'm sorry for everything I've said that hurt you. My ego got burned, badly, in Chicago." Like his in Wichita, and here she'd only added to that sorrow. "So did my…heart."

For an instant she thought he'd say *what heart*? And he'd be right. It wasn't the towns-folk of Barren who were the problem. Why should they try to befriend her? It was Lauren who needed to make the attempt, to fit into this little town she'd often thought too quiet, even boring, and she'd been wrong. She would start with Travis. After a short silence, he sighed again.

"Apology accepted." Apparently, he wasn't one to hold a grudge. "I'm sorry I said what

I did about your ex taking you back before. Want to grab a bite to eat? My stomach's growling and I forgot to have breakfast. I was on the phone with my old boss. About Lucie."

"You mean do more strategizing?"

"No," he said, letting his smile out, "I mean give folks something to talk about."

Lauren's chest seemed to fill with a warmth she'd rarely felt before.

"You and me," he added as if he thought she was worth saving from herself.

Travis straightened from the doorframe, then pulled her up from her chair, and they left the office without Lauren bothering to shut down her computer. It would be there later, and so would the unfinished feature on Finn, but Travis Blake might just be the biggest story of her life.

More important than any huge scoop—well, almost—than Lauren could imagine.

RACHEL'S PLAN TO leave hadn't quite worked out. As she rocked Zoey to sleep for her morning nap and listened to Sky's soft snores at her feet, she heard Max's truck back out of the driveway. She struggled with an empty, helpless feeling that seemed to carve her up inside. Last night after she'd given back his grandmother's ring, she'd thought she couldn't feel any worse. But as she'd packed once Zoey finally fell asleep, she'd continued to weep.

Ever since Jason's death, she'd mourned his loss and that of their baby. Later, with Chad, she'd felt guilty for betraying her husband. Yet this new sorrow was fresh and seemed to pierce her very soul again. So much that last night Rachel had gone to Max and offered to stay while he attended his hearing. After that…silence. They'd barely spoken this morning. But when he got home, how could she leave this house, this tiny human being? How could she simply carry her bags downstairs as soon as he got back from the courthouse and not feel her own heart breaking again? Another silent question made her cry harder, the tears soaking into Zoey's blanket. How could she leave Max, too?

If at first they'd been wary of each other, bonded only by their mutual concern for Zoey, Rachel had come to appreciate the kindness that often underlay his still sometimes clueless nature, his gentle manner with his veterinary patients and their pet parents for whom he always had such compassion. She liked not only helping him with Zoey but also cleaning his house and making dinner for Max after he'd spent a hard day at the clinic, the simple things they'd shared like popcorn and a movie in the living room at night while they both listened for Zoey on the monitor. His love for his baby showed so clearly in his warm brown eyes, and she liked his way with her, too. She even liked that boyish cowlick in his dark hair. She'd definitely liked their kisses. Rachel *loved* all of that. She didn't just love Zoey… She loved *him*.

She couldn't leave. In a way, Max had saved her. If not for him, she could have been without a job, homeless without a place for Sky, and forced to leave Barren when she loved the town, too. He could have refused to accept her dog, and yet he hadn't. Max had walked the floor with Zoey when, instead, he might have slept every night, leaving Rachel to the task for which he'd hired her. He'd defended her with Chad, protected her when she didn't want him to just as she had tried to protect him. She'd needed him. Their faux engagement might be over now, his grandmother's ring back in some drawer today, but what if right now Max still needed *her*? Maybe there was a way to help, to repay him, after all.

Rachel wiped her eyes, carried Zoey to her crib and covered her with a fresh blanket. Then she went downstairs with Sky padding after her to call Sophie. With luck she'd be able to leave the baby at the library with Max's sister for an hour.

Hadn't Rachel opted to make her own decisions? For herself? And what she really wanted, what would also make her happiest now, was her own place here in Barren with Max and Zoey. Which meant fighting for them. She might just have time. The court hearing probably wouldn't last long, and she needed to hurry, but the judge needed to hear her message. And so did Max.

MAX STEPPED OUT into the hall at the courthouse. During his talk with Rachel last night, he hadn't missed the sense of irony. If the town had its way, they would have married in the spring or early summer. The plans had already started flying. There would have been a huge party afterward, a gauntlet of well-wishers throwing rice or birdseed, as he and

Rachel ran to a waiting rented limousine. The start of a new life together.

Instead, torn between keeping Rachel with him and doing right for Zoey, distracted by the thought of today's hearing, he hadn't fought hard enough for Rachel. On Valentine's Day he'd kept his gift for her in his pocket with the ring she'd returned. He'd chosen his daughter over Rachel. If she hadn't offered to stay while he was at the hearing, she'd be gone by now.

"I won't mention you—our arrangement—unless I'm pressed," he'd assured her. "This should be a simple matter of the judge granting a new birth certificate for Zoey and my submitting the DNA proof of paternity." To supplement that, he had brought Averill's first note about the baby, which was evidence of Averill's abandonment. The actual custody fight would happen later.

In the hallway now several people milled about, waiting their turn in front of the judge, but Max and his lawyer had already seen him in chambers. Their meeting had been brief, even friendly.

Feeling a bit washed out from the emotional ordeal, though, and as if his minor victory was hollow, Max was lost in thought when he suddenly spied Averill, walking through security near the main doors. Why had she come? She was with a dark-haired man he assumed to be her current boyfriend who was leaning on a cane, hunched over as if his stomach hurt. Max supposed it did, considering the infection that had nearly killed him. As they approached, he looked thin and pale. "Averill," Max said with a nod at the other guy.

"This is John." She turned. "Meet Max."

The two men shook hands. Max said, "You're too late, Averill, to block my name on the new birth certificate. The hearing's over."

"I would not have blocked you." Averill looked at the floor. "John and I have talked. We came to hear the outcome of the hearing. The baby... If I'd known how you feel about her, I would have used your name in the hospital, Max. You still would have needed the amended certificate, though, with her first name as well."

As Zoey's mother, Averill had the right to put any name she wanted on that certificate. Yet instead of starting a battle today, she'd shown up—late and why now, he wondered. When her gaze lifted, Max saw tears in her eyes. His hadn't felt dry in the judge's chambers, either.

"It's an emotional thing," he said, "going into court, even for a relatively routine matter like this, witnessing firsthand the power of the law, hoping to come out on the right side." The next hearing would be more contentious.

"Is there a right side?" Averill looked as if she might begin to cry.

Max shoved both hands in his pockets. He glanced at John. "Listen, Averill. I, uh…"

John leaned more heavily on his cane. "I'll let you two talk. Sweetheart, I'll be over there. I see an empty seat."

Max watched him make his way to a bench near the windows. "Is he okay? Considering how he must feel after his illness, he still came with you today."

"I told you. John's always there for me. I'm there for him. We're going to look at rings this afternoon." She half smiled, but all Max could think was that Rachel had returned his grandmother's ring. "Max, I don't want to hurt you, but I'm in love with John. I know you and I were done before I realized I was pregnant with… Zoey, but I'm glad you have someone in your life now too."

I did, he thought. Averill's new relationship had come as a surprise, but he hadn't realized how much he needed, wanted Rachel until she'd gone upstairs last night to pack. By now, her suitcases were probably standing in the hall and Rachel was just waiting for him to get home from the courthouse so she could leave. Then there'd be awkward goodbyes, his thanks for all she'd done for Zoey—for him. The front door would close behind her, and her car would pull out of his driveway for the last time. If he saw her again, assuming she stayed in town, it would be when he bumped into her at the café or Jack's or in the grocery store. Tonight, he and Zoey would be alone, the house feeling empty even when the two of them were there.

"So. What comes next?" Averill's gaze stayed on John, chatting with another man who'd sat on the same bench.

"The custody hearing." Max consulted the schedule on his phone. "My lawyer set it up for late next week—which is equally fast, according to him, but I'll be glad to get this settled or at least started." He showed the screen to Averill. "Is this date okay with you? Do you have representation?"

"John recommended someone. I haven't called her yet."

They stood, facing each other, her eyes as sad as Max's must look. Perhaps she was wondering how the next hearing, even a series of them, would turn out. If Max would get full custody, as he'd told her he would try for yesterday, if Averill would, or if they'd have to share custody. *Is there a right side? she'd said.* "Ah, Averill, why are we doing this?"

"I only wanted to see my baby. It was you who brought up custody."

Max didn't feel good about that. At the clinic, he'd let his temper get the best of him, which he rarely did. Except with Chad. "I came down on you too hard yesterday. No wonder John must have felt he had to come with you this morning."

"He wanted to come." Averill didn't need to attend, either, yet she'd been here, concerned about Zoey, needing to know the hearing's result. She'd never been the most stable person he knew, for good reason, but she'd always had a good heart. She'd spent the past decade searching for her sister, feeling guilty for her part in Lucie's disappearance, and that search had become her obsession. Panicked more recently because of John's illness, she'd left Zoey with Max, knowing he would care for her.

He cleared his throat. "I'm happy for you, Averill." And he wasn't just saying that.

She did smile. "John knows all my short-comings, my hang-ups—and still loves me anyway. So did you, but maybe it was having Zoey that showed me a different path to take."

"I understand why you did what you had to do—for him. Not that I'd expected to become an instant dad that morning when I found Zoey on my porch. She has changed my life, and I hope I'm helping her to become a happy, healthy little girl. I love her, just as I loved you." He paused, knowing that on one level he still did because of Zoey. He saw John glance their way with a trace of anxiety in his eyes. "We did okay, didn't we? With Zoey. So." He drew out the word. How could he de-prive Averill of contact with her own child? Their child. "For now, what do you say we forget this custody thing?"

Averill nodded, fresh tears in her eyes. "I'd love that, Max. Today I was going to save us both the drama of another hearing anyway, give up my rights to Zoey. That's also why I'm here, but then we couldn't find a parking space and by the time we walked in your appointment with the judge was already over. I admit, I'm in no position right now to take Zoey from you, even if I could. John and I are in kind of a transition period while he recovers from the infection. He's unable to work right now, and I'm still looking for a job." She glanced at Max. "Not that any job could replace my position at the desk in your clinic. In fact, I'm trying to find a spot in another vet practice. We're moving soon to Farrier, looking for a place there. I'd like two bedrooms," she said. "Or, possibly, three if we can get a rental house because I hope I'll have Lucie to think of as well. I've talked to Travis. Max, I can hardly believe that after all this time, I may see her again—and she's safe."

Max touched her arm. "I'm glad about Lucie. That situation isn't—won't be— easy. But Averill, it was never your fault that she was taken at the mall. Maybe in the short term we can work out some sort of visitation schedule with Zoey. You can get to know her a little at a time."

"And Lucie, too," she agreed.

Max smiled. "Lucie, too," he said. "Later on, we can decide on Zoey's custody. Together. How does that sound?"

"Perfect," she said, blinking. "Max, I really do want to be part of her life."

"Would you like to at least 'meet' her now? Again?" Averill hadn't seen Zoey since she was two weeks old. "She's growing every day. You could come to the house."

Averill gave Max an astonished glance, then looked again at John, who shifted on the bench as if he felt uncomfortable. "Not today, but thanks. I need to get John back to our hotel." Her face brightened. "If it's all right, maybe we'll drive over in a few days. I'll call first."

"Sounds good." Max knew he hadn't handled things well with Averill yesterday. No wonder she couldn't quite believe this shift in his stance. As she was turning away, Max glanced toward the exit and, again to his surprise, saw Rachel walking toward him with Zoey, wrapped in the same pink blanket she'd had the day he'd found her in the basket. What was she doing here?

A bit breathless, she rushed over to him, then stopped when she saw Averill. "I couldn't stay away. I've come to speak on your behalf, Max, in front of the judge. Maybe I can help to convince him—"

"The hearing's over, Rachel. It's okay." He touched Averill's shoulder. "I think there's someone here who'd like to see Zoey, though."

Max nodded at Rachel, who hesitated, then held out the baby for Averill to hold. Inside her cozy blanket, the baby cooed softly, and Max watched Averill's face crumple. "Oh, look at her," she said. "Isn't she beautiful, Max? Hi there, Zoey."

He couldn't seem to speak. He couldn't look at the tender expression Averill wore as she talked to Zoey, all but shutting him and Rachel out. He saw John rise slowly from the bench to approach. He put his arm around Averill's waist, and she leaned against him, burying her face against his shoulder.

And Max felt more alone than he ever had in his life. He glanced at Rachel, who stood there, frozen in place. The decision to bring Zoey to the courthouse must have been hard for her. But what would Rachel have said in court? About him.

Something niggled at the back of his mind, but he couldn't grasp what that was. He jingled some change in his pocket and the coins clinked against the present he hadn't given Rachel on Valentine's Day. He was no longer in love with Averill, as she wasn't with him, but when she handed Zoey back to Rachel and the two women exchanged misty smiles, all at once Max knew. He'd tried not to fall in love again, thought that after Averill he wouldn't be enough for Rachel or any other woman. But being enough also meant letting someone else make their own decisions. Rachel had overcome her losses to be here for him, which took courage. Did *he* have the bravery to tell her now that, yes, he did love her?

He hoped that testifying about Zoey had given him that courage.

He slipped his arm around Rachel's waist. There'd been a moment when he'd feared that their last minutes together would be awkward, fraught with regret. Final. And wouldn't that be a lot worse than putting his feelings on the line? Because he couldn't protect his own heart forever. If he didn't tell her how he felt, he'd lose her. For good.

"This is my... Rachel," was all he could

say because his throat had closed. What if she rejected him?

Averill looked between them. "We've met. I'm glad to see you again, Rachel."

A moment later, Averill and John were gone, walking slowly toward the main doors of the courthouse, their hands entwined. John leaned on her a little. And Max was left with the two people he loved with all his heart. How to convince Rachel to stay? Longer than forever.

RACHEL WALKED BESIDE MAX, who carried Zoey, from the courthouse toward their cars in the parking lot. Her heart was still hammering. "Max, I know I shouldn't have come." But she hadn't been able to keep from putting Zoey in the car, racing through town, fearing every minute that she'd get there only to learn Max had somehow lost in court. "But tell me. How did this first hearing go?"

"Far better than I expected." Max told her Zoey's name, his name, would now be on her birth certificate. His paternity was now established with the court. He explained about his talk with Averill, the agreement they'd come to instead of fighting over custody. "There may not be another hearing. That will depend on how things work out over time, but I'm impressed with the changes she's already made in her life."

"And did you see her face when she held Zoey?"

"Yeah. It's enough to make a tough guy weep."

"You're not so tough," she said. "Averill must be happy to know about Lucie, too, even when that's a sticky situation."

"True, and she and John still have rough days ahead with his recovery. They need— we all need—to take things slow." He cleared his throat. "What would you have said to the judge?"

She felt a flush rise in her cheeks. "Um, that there has been nothing between us for people to talk about, that I know what a good father you are, how much you love Zoey, that I never meant to make things worse for you with Chad—"

"That part never came up. Rachel, this hearing was only about her birth certificate and the DNA."

"—but most of all, I..." Then she couldn't go on.

Rachel had never expected to love again when she'd moved to Barren, made a new, if lonely, life for herself. Yet with Zoey she'd become like a mama tiger, and as for Max… She studied him as they walked across the lot, dodging piles of snow here and there. His dark hair gleamed in the sun, and because Zoey had reached up, his cowlick was mussed again, as it most always was.

She tried again. "Max, I can't leave yet," she said at the same time he said, "Rachel, we need to talk."

She was already shivering, not from the cold. The mid-February sun had almost warmed the winter day and the temperature was actually above freezing. But what would Max say? With Zoey in one arm, he paused to fold Rachel's scarf more tightly around her neck, then tucked Zoey more deeply into her blanket, which should have reassured Rachel. He'd thought of them first. Sheltered them.

So much feeling, she thought as they began walking again, when for too long she'd tried not to feel. Ever since Jason's death, she'd been frozen inside and later riddled with guilt over Chad. Now, the hood of Zoey's white snowsuit peeked out of the pink blanket, its bunny ears making Rachel want to laugh rather than cry.

Tears gathered on her lashes anyway. She wished she'd never given back Max's grand-mother's ring, wished it could grace her fin-ger for the rest of her life. *Happy Valentine's Day, Rachel.* Last night with Zoey in her arms, she'd cried herself dry. What if she failed now to let him know how much she cared for them both? What if then she *had* to leave?

As they reached her car, she struggled to find the right words. "Max, I'm not always the best judge of my emotions. But last night…" She told him about her crying jag in the nurs-ery and again this morning. "I did grow up needing to do the right thing to the nth de-gree, and when we talked last night, I really thought I was doing that—for myself, for you and Zoey."

"You weren't," he said, "but then, neither was I. For me. I'm sorry I accused you of being stuck in your old life." He drew a breath. "Rachel, I said once that I don't want to lose you—I don't. Look, I know I'm not the most aware guy in the world, but what I do know is that I…" He finished weakly, "I wouldn't want anyone else to care for Zoey." He reached into his pocket and drew out a small box wrapped in paper with hearts on it. "I didn't give this to you last night when things went a bit south. Maybe now is a better time."

Inside the package, which she tore open, Rachel found a silver charm bracelet that flashed in the sun. She turned it in her hands. One charm was a baby carriage, the next a replica of his house on Cattle Track Lane, another had Zoey's name in a pretty script… and her heart sank. What was this gift trying to tell her when Max seemed to have run out of words? Or lost his nerve. And so had she. "Oh. A memento of the time I've spent with you." Employer and employee until he found someone else to share his life and Zoey. A goodbye present. "Thanks, Max."

"Look closer," he said. "There's another charm."

Rachel examined the two figures she hadn't seen, close together near the clasp, looking like…her and Max together, and her heart skipped several beats. "You mean—I can stay in my job?"

"Sure." He smiled. "That is, if you don't mind keeping me along with it." And she realized that the two were a couple, like on a wedding cake. Rachel with Max. He drew her close, wrapping his arms around her and Zoey as if they could be—as if they already were—a family. He seemed to take a bracing breath. "Rachel. When Averill and I broke up, I felt hollowed out, no longer myself. The last thing I wanted then was someone else because it hurt too much."

"I felt the same way when I lost Jason."

"But then, there was you. There *is* you," he said, "and I have no idea how I could ever get along without you. I don't want to even try. The house would be empty without you, and it's not just my home, it's yours, too." He kept Zoey between them as if she were in a cocoon, warm and safe. A single tear rolled down Rachel's cheek and he caught it on one finger. Max looked deeply into her eyes, more focused than she had ever known him to be, as if he could see into her wounded soul. "I love you, Rachel," he murmured. Then with only a slight hesitation, he lowered his mouth to hers. She kissed him back until Zoey started to wriggle, and Rachel heard her soft, sucking sound that meant she needed to be fed.

And she thought, *things are different now*. Jason was truly gone. So was the baby Rachel had carried for too short a time then lost. With a small sigh, she laid her past to rest, just as Max had for her. If Rachel had ever wanted to do the right thing, this was it, her own way to be happy once more, and at last she said the words. "I love you, too, Max. More than I ever thought I could love again."

"Me, too," he admitted. "We've had our bad times. Let's focus now on the good."

Rachel couldn't have agreed more. Max touched his forehead to hers, his mouth curved in a smile. "About that engagement…"

"I think we should…"

"Make it real," they both said at once.

Max laughed, and for the first time in years without any shadow of the losses she had suffered, so did Rachel. Her memories could be locked away in a corner of her heart. This man she loved now loved her, too, and together they had a place to belong, a daughter to share.

"Let's go," Max said, releasing her so he could slip Zoey into her car seat. "Meet you at home."

Always, Rachel thought.

EPILOGUE

The next summer

"Hurry, Max, we'll be late." Rachel had been trying to nudge him about leaving the house for the past half hour, but he'd been buried in some veterinary textbook, trying to nail down a tricky diagnosis for one of his patients. Every now and then she'd heard a "hmm" or an "aha" through the closed door of his home office. When she appeared in the doorway now, he finally looked up and blinked, twice.

"Hey, when's this shindig?"

"You're due at the fairgrounds in fifteen minutes." Max would be the vet for the town rodeo that was becoming an annual event. "I've got Zoey ready—"

He rose from the desk chair and slung an arm around her shoulders, planted a kiss on top of her head. "Then what are we waiting for?"

Rachel fought an urge to groan, but she'd

learned in the past five months, since those moments outside the courthouse, that Max, being Max, would never completely overcome his tendency to zero in on the topic that interested him most at the time and be completely oblivious to everyone else around him. Rachel supposed she just needed to accept the reality that her husband's mind worked a bit differently than hers. She found the trait endearing—because often that focus meant Zoey and Rachel—except for today when they had to dash to the fairgrounds.

Rachel's mother would have had a fit because they were tardy, as she would have called it. But then, she wasn't here, and Rachel no longer marched to the drumbeat of her parents' expectations. Jason's family's either. Or anyone else's. With Max, she'd had to learn to be looser, more casual about doing the "right thing." She'd even initiated contact with her parents again, shored up whenever things got tough by Max's steady support.

At the fairgrounds, Rachel saw many of the people she knew well by now, talking, laughing, kids running around everywhere. In her car seat, Zoey wriggled to get free. At seven months, she could sit up without support and delighted Max and Rachel with her cooing, burbling sounds as if she thought she was speaking English.

"Hold your horses," Max told her, getting out of Rachel's car, but he was grinning. Zoey had him wrapped around her little finger. He was never going to be the family disciplinarian. The only person who spoiled her more was Averill.

As they crossed the grounds, Rachel spied Blossom Hunter and stopped to give her a hug. After a brief hi, Max kept going with Zoey, presumably so he could check in at the nearby chutes. "Congratulations, you," Rachel said, and Blossom beamed. She'd told Rachel yesterday that the adoption of their new little girl, a seven-year-old, had just been finalized.

"Happy day, that's for sure." Blossom gestured toward Logan, who still wore chaps after competing in the calf roping. His horse had survived its hoof infection last winter and Sundance stood ground-tied nearby. Logan was showing Daisy and her new sister how to lasso a fence post. "We've all been getting acquainted for months," Blossom said, "and Logan's the one they both run to. Angel adored him at first sight."

"She looks like him, don't you think? She even has Logan's dark hair."

"No kidding. She might have been his daughter from birth. It's as if we've been a family all along. Nick, who's more interested in video games these days, has been slower to accept her, but we're working on that."

"He'll come around." She hugged Blossom again. They chatted until Rachel noticed Max with Zoey in his arms, bending over to examine the side of a very large horse. "Oops, rescue mission," she told Blossom, then hurried off, promising they'd get together soon for a picnic with the girls and Zoey.

After claiming the baby, she ran into Sophie, who looked ready to pop as she watched Gabe on a horse that bucked its way around the arena ring. Sophie turned to kiss Zoey's cheek. "My favorite niece's first rodeo, huh? I should have stayed home instead of waddling around like this," Sophie said with an eye roll, "but I wanted to be nearby in case Gabe breaks his neck." The crowd in the stands cheered him on as the buzzer sounded and relief washed over Sophie's face.

"Were you really worried?"

She fanned herself as Gabe safely slid to the ground, then tossed his hat in the air. "I worry about everything these days—hormones, I suppose." She was due to deliver within the next month. "Did you hear? We caved during the last sonogram. We're having a—"

"Boy," Rachel said, smiling. "Max told me. That's wonderful."

"I almost feel eclipsed," Sophie said. "I mean, it seems everyone in town is either expecting or just had a baby." Rachel had to agree, adoption included. Besides Blossom's new daughter, Kate and Noah Bodine were pregnant with a brother for their son Teddie, the Donovans' baby girl was already five months old, and Cody and Willow Jones had a very active little boy in Harper. Sophie looked at Rachel. "You two planning another yet?"

As if Zoey really was her child with Max, which pleased Rachel. After all, she'd cared for Zoey since she was a newborn. Plus, she and Sophie were close now, sisters by marriage since Rachel's May wedding to Max, their old tensions resolved like her past. She

gave Sophie, her matron of honor then, a be-
atific smile but said nothing.

In the silence, Sophie's eyes widened, as
if she already knew her secret. In fact, Rachel had taken a pregnancy test that morning while Max hunkered over his textbooks,
but she hadn't told him yet. She wanted to
pick the exactly *right* time. "Looks like we're
about to 'adopt,'" she said instead, keeping
Sophie in the dark.

Max had finished examining that big horse
and was talking to Cody, the two men in deep
conversation. "He's been trying to talk Cody
out of the horse I've been riding. Buck," she
added, "and he has a nice gelding Max wants
to buy." She had to admit, their weekend rides
were not only becoming a habit. Rachel truly
enjoyed the time she spent with Max on their
"dates," as he called them, and, despite his
name, Buck was a sweetheart. "We could
board them with Cody and Willow at the WB
for now."

"Max had better watch out. The cowboys
in this town will have my brother running
cattle before he can blink. Even Gabe has offered him a piece of our land."

"Good luck if they can get his attention long

enough to write a check." The prospect didn't trouble Rachel. She wouldn't mind moving from town, having open space for Zoey to grow up in, a small ranch with a house bigger than the one on Cattle Track Lane that would be new and theirs from the start.

As if Rachel had summoned him, Max strolled over and took Zoey from her. "You're not going to have that baby right here, are you?" he asked Sophie.

She laid a hand on the mound of her stomach. "Sawyer says this little one seems comfortable right where he is, and the baby may come after my due date." She paused. "What do you hear from Averill?"

In the months since the court hearing, Max had received the new birth certificate, and he and Averill had gradually developed a workable relationship.

"She and John are buying a place between Farrier and here. They're okay, Sophie. He's back to work—graphic design—and Averill's working at that big vet practice nearby. I believe she's been promoted to office manager. In fact, they're coming for dinner tomorrow."

"Averill's spending time with Zoey—supervised for now," Rachel put in.

"You don't think she'll eventually sue for custody?"

"No," he said. "Averill claims she's a better 'aunt' than she was a mother." He glanced at Rachel. "She feels Rachel is the wiser choice. Later, when she's older we can tell Zoey the truth."

Rachel envied Sophie and Max's closeness as siblings. Rachel had been an only child, and her relationship with her brother-in-law, Chad, was still a shaky one. Fortunately, his parents hadn't shut her out. They were talking about coming to spend Thanksgiving with Rachel and Max. The plan pleased her. And Chad would be busy that weekend moving into an apartment, which he'd share with his new girlfriend. He'd also gotten a job.

Max hailed Clara, who was walking toward them hand in hand with Sam Hunter. "Hey, G." She gave him a stony look and he said, "Clara, where's our invitation to the wedding?"

Sam flushed and Clara swatted Max on the arm. "Just because you're a happily married man now, which gives me some satisfaction that you aren't as thickheaded as I thought, doesn't mean—"

"I haven't proposed," Sam cut in. "I'm working up to it."

Now it was Clara whose face turned red. "Well, I'll be."

"Stop teasing, Max," Rachel murmured, "or you'll end up without help at the clinic."

"I can't get rid of her," he insisted, grinning. "But you should set your matchmaking sights on other people, Clara." He pointed at Travis Blake who was angling toward the food stands with Lauren Anderson. Travis lifted a hand. Through his help with Averill and Lucie, he and Max had become close friends, but the town had nearly lost its sheriff. The FBI had been so impressed with his work on the case they'd offered to reinstate him. Travis—perhaps in part because of his growing relationship with Lauren—had refused. "You should work your magic on Barren's newest couple."

Clara said, "I guess Lauren decided there are other things in life besides chasing after a big story." As her relationship with Travis progressed, the *Journal*'s star reporter had begun to soften her edges and was no longer the social pariah she'd once been in Barren.

To the contrary, she seemed to like it here. "I think this town has grown on Travis, too."

"Maybe he had enough excitement about Lucie," Rachel said. "Or rather, Lily Shaefer." The girl who'd been abducted years ago was still with her adoptive family, who had known nothing about the adoption being illegal. They had agreed to let her get to know Averill again before they told Lily the two of them were sisters. No one involved with the case had thought it a good idea to take Lily from the people who'd given her many advantages and with whom she'd spent two-thirds of her life thus far. Sadly, though, Averill's mother hadn't asked to see her.

As for Lucie's abductor, according to Travis, the Feds had tracked him down but were still building their case. Lucie hadn't been his only victim. He'd profited from a scheme to find kids for other childless couples.

A sudden roar went up from the crowd in the nearby grandstand. Today's rodeo had just ended with the bull riding, which Dallas Maguire won. Again. The events had been his idea several years ago, but like Sam, who always took first place in the chili cook-off, Dallas had yet to be beaten. In both cases, no one seemed to care. Winning wasn't the intent of the competitions; community and friendship were.

Rachel leaned against Max with Zoey between them. "This is a good town," she said, "full of good people." She was married to one of the best. "I wonder who Barren's Citizen of the Year will be this time." The award would be given out soon today, but Rachel noticed Clara looking pointedly at her.

"Oh, no," she murmured, "not me."

"You were nominated. Ask Max." Clara kept staring. "Go on," she prompted him. "I know you're guilty. Twice over."

Sophie spun around as fast as she could. Her center of gravity had shifted with pregnancy. "*You* were the one who nominated me two years ago? And now Rachel?"

She had to smile. Max may have kept his part in the nominations from her and Sophie, but now Rachel had a secret of her own, at least until they got home. She could hardly wait to tell him.

Max studied his boots then looked up. "Well, you are my favorite sister, Sophie. My wife deserves the same recognition. The in-between-year award went to Lizzie Maguire and I had nothing to do with that."

He lightly kissed Rachel who savored the moment, knowing that after so much loss she now had everything she could ever want in Max, Zoey and the new baby she was carrying. She gazed around at the dust still rising from the arena, the mix of horses, cattle, dogs, including Sky, of course, romping in the grass with Remi, the sunlight slanting across the fairgrounds. The people she knew and loved here. Her eyes settled on Max. "I love you," she murmured.

"Same goes." As Sophie walked away to meet Gabe, he kissed Rachel again, this time more soundly, then planted one in Zoey's silken hair. Rachel nestled against his side, more content than she'd been in a long time. Looking forward to all the years ahead.

Blossom had said it was a happy day. And it was, but even more.

"This," Rachel said, "is what I call a happy ending."

* * * * *

Get 4 FREE REWARDS!

We'll send you 2 FREE Books plus 2 FREE Mystery Gifts.

FREE Value Over **$20**

Both the **Love Inspired®** and **Love Inspired® Suspense** series feature compelling novels filled with inspirational romance, faith, forgiveness and hope.

Get 4 FREE REWARDS!

We'll send you 2 FREE Books plus 2 FREE Mystery Gifts.

FREE
Value Over
$20

Both the **Harlequin® Special Edition** and **Harlequin® Heartwarming™** series feature compelling novels filled with stories of love and strength where the bonds of friendship, family and community unite.

YES! Please send me 2 FREE novels from the Harlequin Special Edition or Harlequin Heartwarming series and my 2 FREE gifts (gifts are worth about $10 retail). After receiving them, if I don't wish to receive any more books, I can return the shipping statement marked "cancel." If I don't cancel, I will receive 6 brand-new Harlequin Special Edition books every month and be billed just $5.49 each in the U.S. or $6.24 each in Canada, a savings of at least 12% off the cover price, or 4 brand-new Harlequin Heartwarming Larger-Print books every month and be billed just $6.24 each in the U.S. or $6.74 each in Canada, a savings of at least 19% off the cover price. It's quite a bargain! Shipping and handling is just 50¢ per book in the U.S. and $1.25 per book in Canada.* I understand that accepting the 2 free books and gifts places me under no obligation to buy anything. I can always return a shipment and cancel at any time by calling the number below. The free books and gifts are mine to keep no matter what I decide.

Choose one: ☐ **Harlequin Special Edition**   ☐ **Harlequin Heartwarming**
                     (235/335 HDN GRJV)   **Larger-Print**
                                                                          (161/361 HDN GRJV)

Name (please print)

Address   Apt. #

City   State/Province   Zip/Postal Code

Email: Please check this box ☐ if you would like to receive newsletters and promotional emails from Harlequin Enterprises ULC and its affiliates. You can unsubscribe anytime.

> Mail to the **Harlequin Reader Service:**
> **IN U.S.A.:** P.O. Box 1341, Buffalo, NY 14240-8531
> **IN CANADA:** P.O. Box 603, Fort Erie, Ontario L2A 5X3
>
> **Want to try 2 free books from another series!** Call 1-800-873-8635 or visit www.ReaderService.com.

---

*Terms and prices subject to change without notice. Prices do not include sales taxes, which will be charged (if applicable) based on your state or country of residence. Canadian residents will be charged applicable taxes. Offer not valid in Quebec. This offer is limited to one order per household. Books received may not be as shown. Not valid for current subscribers to the Harlequin Special Edition or Harlequin Heartwarming series. All orders subject to approval. Credit or debit balances in a customer's account(s) may be offset by any other outstanding balance owed by or to the customer. Please allow 4 to 6 weeks for delivery. Offer available while quantities last.

Your Privacy—Your information is being collected by Harlequin Enterprises ULC, operating as Harlequin Reader Service. For a complete summary of the information we collect, how we use this information and to whom it is disclosed, please visit our privacy notice located at corporate.harlequin.com/privacy-notice. From time to time we may also exchange your personal information with reputable third parties. If you wish to opt out of this sharing of your personal information, please visit readerservice.com/consumerschoice or call 1-800-873-8635. **Notice to California Residents**—Under California law, you have specific rights to control and access your data. For more information on these rights and how to exercise them, visit corporate.harlequin.com/california-privacy.

HSEHW22R3

COUNTRY LEGACY COLLECTION

19 FREE BOOKS IN ALL!

EMMETT
Diana Palmer

COURTED BY THE COWBOY

THE RANCHER AND THE BABY
Marie Ferrarella

Cowboys, adventure and romance await you in this new collection! Enjoy superb reading all year long with books by bestselling authors like Diana Palmer, Sasha Summers and Marie Ferrarella!

YES! Please send me the **Country Legacy Collection!** This collection begins with 3 FREE books and 2 FREE gifts in the first shipment. Along with my 3 free books, I'll also get 3 more books from the **Country Legacy Collection**, which I may either return and owe nothing or keep for the low price of $24.60 U.S./$28.12 CDN each plus $2.99 U.S./$7.49 CDN for shipping and handling per shipment*. If I decide to continue, about once a month for 8 months, I will get 6 or 7 more books but will only pay for 4. That means 2 or 3 books in every shipment will be FREE! If I decide to keep the entire collection, I'll have paid for only 32 books because 19 are FREE! I understand that accepting the 3 free books and gifts places me under no obligation to buy anything. I can always return a shipment and cancel at any time. My free books and gifts are mine to keep no matter what I decide.

☐ 275 HCK 1939   ☐ 475 HCK 1939

Name (please print)

Address   Apt. #

City   State/Province   Zip/Postal Code

Mail to the Harlequin Reader Service:
IN U.S.A.: P.O. Box 1341, Buffalo, NY 14240-8571
IN CANADA: P.O. Box 603, Fort Erie, Ontario L2A 5X3

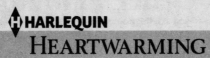

HARLEQUIN
PLUS

Try the best multimedia
subscription service for romance
readers like you!

Read, Watch and Play.

Experience the easiest way to get
the romance content you crave.

Start your **FREE TRIAL** at
www.harlequinplus.com/freetrial.

HEARTWARMING

A Baby on His Doorstep

—

Leigh Riker

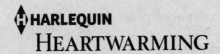

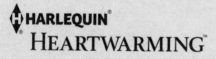

HARLEQUIN®
HEARTWARMING™

ISBN-13: 978-1-335-58493-9

A Baby on His Doorstep

Recycling programs for this product may not exist in your area.

For questions and comments about the quality of this book, please contact us at CustomerService@Harlequin.com.

Harlequin Enterprises ULC
22 Adelaide St. West, 41st Floor
Toronto, Ontario M5H 4E3, Canada
www.Harlequin.com

Printed in U.S.A.

Rachel's gaze followed Max...

The shop owner, Sherry, was leading him toward the rear of the store. "Clara emailed me your list for the baby. You need a car seat? Instead, let me show you our newest all-in-one stroller."

In Barren, someone always seemed to be getting engaged, married or having a baby, which must keep Sherry in business. But having a baby left on the porch was certainly new. Rachel inspected the racks of hanging clothes. *Adorable.* The merchandise, not Max, she told herself.

She couldn't deny he was an attractive man. Warm, trustworthy, straightforward. Single. Her awareness of Max surprised her when, because of her losses and the guilt she bore, she still felt mostly frozen inside.

"Actually," she heard Max say, "I just need the car seat."

Sherry clucked her tongue. "Don't be hasty. I sell a lot of these convertible strollers—it's a car seat and a baby carrier too. You can even go jogging."

"If I had time," he said, tilting his head. As he straightened, his eyes met Rachel's across the room. Almost as if he were similarly aware of her as she was of him...

Dear Reader,

I love newborn babies! I've never found one on my doorstep. If I did, after mothering the two boys I love with all my heart, it would have to be the girl I never had. But while writing this latest book in my Kansas Cowboys series, I liked imagining how that unexpected, blessed surprise might feel.

In this story, after a painful breakup with his one and only girlfriend, veterinarian Max Crane isn't about to get involved again. He has enough to worry about, caring for his busy practice and the baby he never knew he had. Hiring attractive widow Rachel Whittaker isn't a good idea...yet he desperately needs help. And thus, two hearts risk getting hurt again.

I loved helping these two work their way through a bunch of obstacles and their past heartaches. What do you think their chances are for happily-ever-after and a family together? No fair, peeking at the last page! I hope you enjoy Max and Rachel's story as much as I liked writing it. I'll miss them—as I do every past character in this series.

I'm off now to daydream about finding a sweet baby on my doorstep. While I'm at it, I think I'll imagine a full-time nurse to go with her. No more sleepless nights for me!

Happy reading,

Leigh

Leigh Riker, like so many dedicated readers, grew up with her nose in a book, and weekly trips to the local library for a new stack of stories were a favorite thing to do. This award-winning *USA TODAY* bestselling author still can't imagine a better way to spend her time than to curl up with a good romance novel—unless it is to write one! She is a member of the Authors Guild, Novelists, Inc., and Romance Writers of America. When not at the computer, she's out on the patio tending flowers, watching hummingbirds, spending time with family and friends, or, perhaps, traveling (for research purposes, of course). She loves to hear from readers. You can find Leigh on her website, leighriker.com, and on Facebook at leighrikerauthor.

Books by Leigh Riker

Harlequin Heartwarming

Kansas Cowboys

The Reluctant Rancher
Last Chance Cowboy
Cowboy on Call
Her Cowboy Sheriff
The Rancher's Second Chance
Twins Under the Tree
The Cowboy's Secret Baby
Mistletoe Cowboy
A Cowboy's Homecoming
The Runaway Rancher

Visit the Author Profile page
at Harlequin.com for more titles.

To Adrienne Macintosh, editor extraordinaire,
who always makes each book better